SOUL of the CROW

JESSACA WILLIS

To Kieran.
This book was only possible because of you.

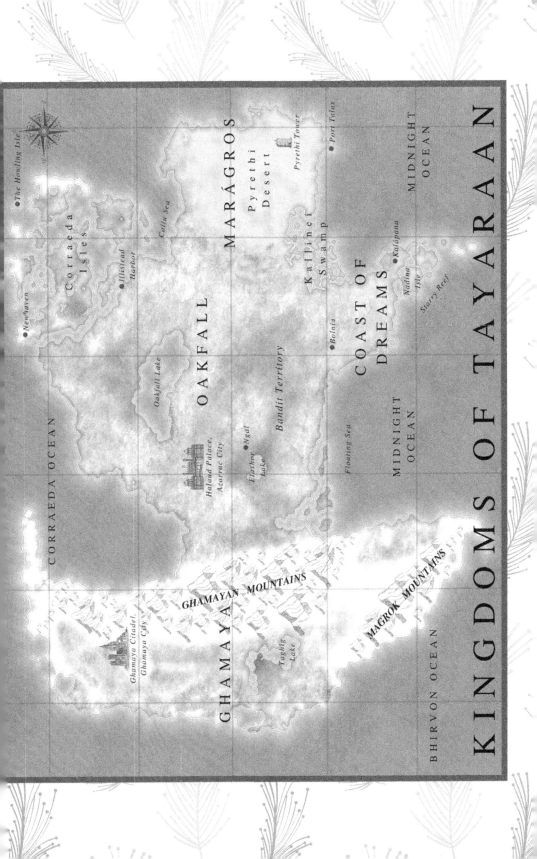

BOOKS IN SERIES

1

TAKEN BY SHADOWS

SINISA

When the shadows reach for me through the floorboards, blood is still warm on my fingers, and terror pierces my heart. I flick my wrists, desperate to shake away the proof of my crime. After all, that is why the shadows have come.

But not even a thorough bath could save me now. The blood stains my soul for the underrealm, a marking that I cannot escape.

The darkness shifts, growing into talons large enough to wrap around an entire boar. They latch around my ankles instead, squeezing tightly enough to puncture my skin. The yelp that escapes me is as much from pain as fear. I know what is to come. I know what happens when someone commits murder, and I know it is inevitable.

I just thought I'd have more time.

I can hear the other orphan children screaming and pattering down the stairs, afraid of the shadows. Afraid of me.

Some instinctual swell of desperation has me struggling against the black fortress-like grip, but the claws only dig deeper into their prey. I am about to cry out when I see the lifeless body again out of the corner of my eye. Blood pools beneath him, around him. It covers him so thoroughly that I can't even see where I stabbed him.

I didn't mean to—*yes, you did.*

I wish I hadn't—*don't lie to yourself.*

Each excuse I make is muted by some inner darkness I never knew existed. But the truth doesn't ease the rampant heaving of my chest. I thought I was supposed to feel safer now, maybe even victorious.

Caw.

I twist to the wall behind me, my feet anchored to the ground and preventing me from getting a better look, but I can hear the rustling of feathers filling the dormitory. I see the flutter of darkness surrounding me.

The gulp of air I swallow feels more like rocks.

I'm not ready. I'm not ready. I'm not ready.

My breathing hastens to a point so close to hyperventilation that for a second I convince myself that the darkness closing in is just me losing consciousness. Maybe this is all just a hallucination, a dream, a nightmare.

But I know that's not the truth.

A beak appears from one of the walls. More follow, beaks and feathers and wings, until hundreds of crows are swirling in the room with me, iridescent in the light of the moon. They close in around me until all I can see is black. All I can feel is the greasiness of their feathers flapping against my skin. All I can smell is death.

In one motion, I become weightless. I can feel myself flying— floating—but I don't see where. I *know* where, though, and that knowledge alone makes my heart thrash.

There's only one place they would take a murderer like me: Veltuur, the underrealm.

I am to become a Reaper.

Tears sting my eyes. I'm not ready to say goodbye to my life. I didn't even get a chance to say goodbye to my friends. I don't want to become a Reaper. I don't want to have to kill anyone else.

Seconds as long as eons pass. I am suspended in darkness, like I am dangling over a bottomless chasm.

Finally the frantic fluttering dwindles as, one by one, the murder of crows leaves me utterly alone. I'm left with nothing but the chill of the air. I didn't even notice my eyes were closed until the birds were gone, but now I'm too frightened to open them. I don't want to see where they've taken me. Part of me thinks that if I just keep my eyes closed, this nightmare might end. But I've had this thought before, hundreds of times, and it has never once been true. The nightmare never ends.

The air is dense and still. The longer my eyes remain shut, the longer I feel like death is pressing in on me. That thought is all it takes for me to finally open them wide.

I am not dangling above a chasm.

Instead, I find myself standing before a vast forest. It's obscured by such a heavy and ominous fog that, at first, I mistake the dark branches for silhouettes of monsters, mangled and twisted. Each tree is crooked, like the black trail of smoke that rises from a pyre. My chest continues to rise and fall in a jerky rhythm, the shallow breaths through my nose the only audible sound in the eerily silent forest.

Above the gnarled black trunks is a canopy of spider-leg branches, highlighted throughout by round, glowing red leaves.

It is immeasurably quiet, the kind of quiet that makes my ears hum. As I'm admiring the contrast of the vibrant leaves against the gloom on the ground, one of them blinks. Then another, and another, until I realize the source of the hum—or rather, the rustling. These leaves *aren't* leaves; they're eyes. Thousands of crows are perched in the branches above, creating a dark void of feathers to black out the sky, each bird only discernable from the next by its radiant, hateful eyes.

If I was frightened before my arrival, I am petrified now. Being alone in a strange, horrifying forest heightens every sense in my body to a level of alertness only known to those confronting the face of death.

"Sinisa," the very air whispers, and I whip around searching for the source of the voice.

A pale, sickly man—little more than wrinkled, decaying skin on spindly legs—steps out from the shadows. His hands, tucked against his hollowed belly, are covered almost entirely by billowing red robes.

The fabric drapes over his face, casting each crevice into shadow, falling all the way to the ground and pooling like blood at his feet.

This reminds me of something—the pooling of blood—but the memory comes and goes so quickly I can't latch on to it. My mind is just as foggy as the land around me. I know I had a past before I arrived, but the harder I try to squint at it, to search for the memories that made me *me*, the less of it I can find.

"Welcome," the man says in his hoarse rasp, though I barely see his lips move. It's like the night itself speaks. "You know what is to come?"

I start to shake my head, but thoughts that aren't mine invade me. They're not tangible, and there are no words, but they soothe me with the sense that I *do* know, even if I shouldn't. It's not like I've ever been to Veltuur before.

"Yes, Councilspirit," I say, feeling my apprehension dissipate, settling to the ground like the fog at my feet.

The longer we stand here, the more those emotions dwindle. All the dread, the guilt, the regret, gone, until all I feel is...nothing. I don't even remember what had me so worried before. A calm settles over me, making me feel at peace. No, not at peace—that's not the right word.

Blank. Erased.

More bodies of shadow and decay, adorned in crimson robes, step from behind the trees, until I am surrounded by a half dozen creatures. Though as a group they are reminiscent of the first—their velvet robes identical—individually they are vastly different. Some with spindly appendages, others covered in grotesque ripples of melted flesh. However the one thing they all have in common is an air of death. These are the husks of mankind, what is left of the people who found themselves in a position not too dissimilar from mine at one point in time.

This should scare me too, but for some reason it doesn't. It's like the oxygen here stifles fear, smothering my every thought and will. Who I was is suffocated until all that is left is who I am about to become, who they want me to be.

"Then go," the first man says, a thin finger extending. "Walk among the trees and select your crow."

A nearly mindless puppet, I do as I am instructed, and though I'm not sure how I will do what he's asking, there is no doubt in my mind that I will do it with ease. It's like there is a hand at the small of my back, like Veltuur itself is guiding me. Everything that needs to happen will.

I turn back around, facing the opening I'd first laid eyes on. This forest is expansive, forever growing, stretching farther than the eye can see, and yet, there is a patch that calls to me. Like it is mine and mine alone. Like I belong to it.

As I walk down the staggered openings between the foliage, shadows scurry along the forest floor with each step. I know their names, though I don't know how. I've never seen a Wraith before, but the longer I am in Veltuur, the more I start to understand it, the more I become part of it.

The Wraiths move too fast to truly glimpse them, but I see the talons and enough to know they are the same misshapen monsters that... I can no longer recall. The harder I think, the foggier my memories become until everything up until this moment is one small blur, ready to blink out of existence.

But the man's robes pooling on the ground like blood, that image remains. It's the only one I can keep hold of, and so I do. I cling to it like it's my only lifeline, my only sense of self, like it's the story of my birth and therefore it's the most important piece of my entire existence.

There is a particularly knotted tree, one whose bark bulges in patches as long as my hand, that summons me. I am careful not to trip over its roots, which creep out from the dirt much farther than I would expect, as I traverse the underbrush to get closer. It must be old, ancient even.

As I draw nearer, the ruffling of thousands of wings ceases until I hear only one bird. I take a deep breath, letting the scent of moss and slugs slide its way into my lungs, before looking up. One crow sits, glaring down at me with immortal eyes.

I hold out my arm.

Caw, it says, cocking its head away from me.

If I could feel anything in this place, I might've blushed when it didn't come.

My pleading gaze travels back to the Councilspirits to see if I've completed the task. Perhaps all that was needed of me was to *find* a crow, and here I am having found one. But none of the six figures behind me have stopped staring at me in that expectant way. Truth be told, many of them seem to be growing impatient.

I snap back to the crow.

"Come here," I command, stomping my foot.

The bird squawks again.

Before either of us do anything more, the ground begins to quake beneath my feet. A low rumble disturbs the realm. The birds in the other trees begin cawing frantically. I sense the danger too, the warning in the tone of the air, and I'm not sure if it's directed at me or the crow.

"Get over here!" I say, more sternly yet, and make my arm even more rigid.

This time, the crow listens. It dives from its branch like a spear aimed directly at my heart. Before the point of its beak can penetrate my chest, it curves upward and lands on my shoulder with an unbalanced thud.

Caw, it croaks in my ear.

I turn back to the looming figures.

"She has chosen," one of the seven says, his voice crackling like fire. "The Councilspirits pronounce Sinisa Strigidae, the newest member of the Reapers. May she serve Veltuur well."

2

CONTRACT TO KILL

SINISA

I awaken beneath my scarred tree to the familiar sound of crows. The rumpling of feathers, the squawking, the blinking that should be almost imperceptible is orchestrated into an ominous and delightful symphony. Their song is a moonlit night. It is the comfort of home, but perhaps that's because for these past few years it is all I've known.

I spot Crow with ease among the birds above me. The bluish-black glint of its wings is similar to that of any of the others, but there's something about the way it carries itself that always stands out to me. It's hunched a little more, like its back has given up on it. I've tried examining it, to see if it's an injury or something—although I'm almost positive that the crows of Veltuur can't be injured—but it won't let me get a good look at it. All crows are obstinate, hateful things like that. It's just embedded in the Reaper-crow relationship. If we didn't need them to pass in and out of Veltuur, I doubt any Reaper would willingly work with the winged creatures.

"Crow," I call, and all of the birds fall silent. Mine turns to me with an odious glare. "Don't look at me like that. You know the drill."

Crow doesn't budge.

I'm in no mood for another obstinate day from it. Some days,

Crow seems more obedient than others; I'm not sure why. It'll come and go at my bidding without so much as a squawk.

I was hoping today would be one of those days.

Today is special, after all. Today I claim my five thousandth soul, allowing me to petition for the role of Shade, a promotion of sorts, although nowhere near as prestigious as becoming a member of the Council. Honestly, I think those roles have been set for the rest of eternity.

I take a second to pin the front section of my hair up to keep it out of my eyes during the day's events, before stretching from the sodden earth. It's a short distance to the hollow on the other side of my tree, but I take my time trailing my fingers along its knotted bark. When I reach the black hole, I plunge my hand inside the shallow cavern and pull free a dry piece of splintered wood. All of the trees in Veltuur have a hollow, where a Reaper's daily assignments appear. It's as if the trees themselves are delivering our orders, but I know better.

The chunk of wood ignites at my touch, red embers burning without heat in my palm. The red fades to black, coals turning to ashes, and the remnants crumble between my fingers as I let them sift to the ground, though they don't make it. They never do. Wraiths scuttle across the woodland beneath the haze and devour the ashes just before they reach the earth. Grotesque creatures, they are, surviving solely off death order remnants and the Reapers they're permitted to torture.

I turn back to the leftover dust in my palms just as a mental blast of power, something more vibrant than memory, bursts in my mind.

The first force hits me like the power of the moon high overhead, and I am overcome by something akin to a vivid dream. I catch a flash of pink hocks and sharp hooks as I intrude on the crowded streets. Inside the breezeless city, I am sweating. It's more than just mere images though. The vision attacks all of my senses, and before I know it, I recognize the bustling sounds and rank smells of the market as well. Everything is so realistic, it's like I'm already there even though I am merely an observer. For now.

As soon as the image forms, it fades.

There's a pause. A long one. The dwindling seconds make my throat dry, and I start to worry that I might only have the one assignment for the day. That wouldn't normally be a problem, but today, with only one kill, that would mean I won't actually meet my goal.

My heart plummets the longer I wait until finally there's no hope. With only one life to claim, I'll have to wait one more day to petition to become a Shade. Considering I've already waited this long, I know that one more day won't *kill* me—as if I could die anyway, not as long as my servitude is active—but I can't help but let the reality deplete me.

Just as I'm accepting defeat though, another blast of images burrows into my thoughts, ripping me away from my self-pity. I see a crown, gold and dazzling with jewels. I feel the softness of green velvet against my skin, a fabric I don't think I've ever felt before and one I don't want to stop touching. But I drop the fabric when I see who's wearing it: a small girl with a joyful smile, despite her lips being damaged by a jagged crack that trails up to her nostril.

Once again, just as the vision begins, it too dissipates. This time, no more come and Veltuur reappears around me.

Although there are never any words spoken or written, I understand my assignments. Today there are only two lives to be claimed, and thank Veltuur, it is just enough to reach my goal.

"Wretched day, Reaper Sinisa," rasps a familiar voice from behind me in the fog.

Turning, I bow deeply. "Very much so, Councilspirit Leumas. The best kind."

The red robes drag along the damp earth as the Councilspirit limps toward me. He reaches out his bony, frail fingers to cup my chin, raising me with little effort. As my gaze befalls him, I smile. It's the kind of smile only a mentor of great respect and love could ever earn. If it weren't for Leumas, this day might not have come for another dozen years. He took me under his wing when I first came to Veltuur, taught me the ways of the Reapers, and inspired me to be more. At his instruction, I met each of my orders with eager efficiency. I showed Veltuur that I could handle multiple contracts a day, and in doing so, I've climbed through mountains of deaths far faster than any other Reaper among us.

Leumas grins sweetly, sickly, in return. "I see you've received your orders for the day. Is it enough?"

The question bubbles in my stomach, an excitement I've never felt before. Leumas knows of my intentions of applying for my ascension. Actually, he's been instrumental in encouraging me to do so. On numerous occasions he's told me he thinks I'll make a fine Shade, so when he asks now, I do not want to disappoint.

I nod eagerly. "I was just going. Don't want to leave death waiting."

His eyebrows quirk with amusement. "No, we wouldn't want that."

"Come, Crow," I say, looking over my shoulder and finally wiping the ashes from my hands onto my red tunic. "Take us to the meat merchant."

Caw, it protests, but it's an empty objection. The crow flies to my shoulder, and within seconds, I am feathers, I am shadow, I am dust, I am nothing, as Crow fazes us into Tayaraan, the realm of the living.

We appear in a blaze of smoke. People gasp as it dissipates, and though I can't see them yet, I know they're scrambling to get as far away from us as they can. Reapers are common enough, but still mostly feared, despite the contribution we bring to society. Without us, where else would their souls go?

As the haze clears, I find myself standing beneath an awning, an array of brightly colored fabrics with embroidered designs and tassels hanging all around me. I recognize the marketplace of Oakfall instantly, for it is the only place I've ever visited to have the Oakfall king's banners at every street crossing.

One step after another, I move from one stall to the next, maneuvering my way through the bustling marketplace until I recognize a particular shop of handwoven bracelets and beads. Our destination is just a few streets away.

I don't know if Crow does it on purpose, but we are never exactly where we should be, only close. It never simply fazes us to the life I'm meant to claim. Instead, it makes me work for it, like the recalcitrant creature it is.

Before I can smack Crow over the head, I'm drawn instead to the singsong chanting of children:

Reaper, Reaper,
Death's little keeper;
Not a believer?
I wasn't neither;
But one touch: bleeder,
A crow's approaching, eager;
Reaper, Reaper,
Vile, wicked creature.

When I finally come across the little urchins, I stomp a single step toward them, and they scurry beneath the hem of a woman's skirt. I hate these people. I have no memory of my life before becoming a Reaper, but considering that life ended with a pool of blood, I'm fairly certain that these mortals did nothing for me then, and they want nothing to do with me now.

As I walk down the cobblestone road, a path opens with every step I take. Even the donkey with a cart full of date-palm clambers out of my way, like it, too, knows who I am. I am not easy to miss. If my crow isn't a *dead* giveaway, I am easily recognizable by the flawless skin of my face. Unlike the mortals, I bear no runes on my forehead. I lost mine the day I was initiated, not that I even remember having any. I don't even know what color they were or which of the runes I had earned.

With Crow in the sky, I make my way through the streets with my head held high, the masses continuing to part like the wind broken by an arrow flying by. The scent of warmed wheat guides Crow and I down the crowded streets. As abruptly as we turn every corner, the aromas shift. One stretch of the market is sweet with the scent of candied peaches and pears, while another is heavy with clove and cardamom. But when we finally reach the familiar block, all of the previous scents bleed into the stench of raw flesh.

Halfway down the path, I nod at another Reaper as he strides by in the opposite direction. The life he is here to claim must be nearby, otherwise he and the crow gliding behind him would've fazed, but that's not why my attention lingers on him. There's something unsettling about this Reaper. Most of our kind are poised, unperturbed by emotions, and focused only on our kill orders. It's just the way of things: every living thing must die, and we aid them in their journey to the afterlife in Veltuur.

But this Reaper's eyes dart from one dark corner to another, distracted, maybe even afraid. It's so uncharacteristic that it causes me to search the area myself for any signs of the danger he seems to think is lurking.

Not too far behind him, I find what I'm looking for. A male figure cloaked in black ambles through the crowd in the Reaper's wake. His robes are unmistakable. Whereas the Councilspirits wear red cloaks and the Reapers, red tunics, black cloaks belong to the members of Veltuur who reside between the Councilspirits and the Reapers, the title I desire.

This Reaper is being tailed by a Shade.

Subconsciously, I straighten, not too dissimilar to how I've seen mortals straighten in the presence of guards. The Shades are our watchers, the enforcers of the rules and ways of the realm of the dead. Despite being exactly where I should be, following my orders without a fault, finding myself in the presence of a Shade puts me on edge on any day, but especially today. Today I can't afford for anything to go wrong.

I put myself in the Shade's path, preparing to bow deeply as he passes to express my gratitude for his work, and desperate to be seen and deemed worthy by one of my future colleagues.

Where the sun hits his flesh, I see the blue veins beneath nearly translucent skin. He tilts his head up at me as he walks by, revealing two black eyes framed by hair as golden as the bread baking just a few roads back. But once his eyes catch the light, I see the red that dazzles deep within them like deep chasms of blood.

Many of the Shades are unknown to me because they work separate from the Reapers, but this one I recognize. His name is Nerul, and not too long ago, he was also a Reaper.

Until his ascension as a Shade a few moons ago.

Before I can move out of his path, Nerul knocks a firm shoulder into mine. "Watch it, Reaper," he snarls, looking at me with such vehemence that it's hard to believe we once knew each other at all, let alone that we belong on the same side, serving Veltuur.

The force sends me stumbling back into the carcass of some animal—likely a hog, judging by the size—and I watch speechless as Nerul continues to follow the other Reaper.

I stare at the back of their bobbing heads until they disappear around a corner. Sure, somewhere in the back of my mind there might be an ounce of sympathy for the Reaper and the fate he might be facing soon—having the Council send a Shade after him is *not* a good thing—and I can even admit that part of me churns at Nerul's dismissal of me, as if I was no more than a pesky gnat hovering near his food. But mostly, as I watch them vanish from sight, I find myself daydreaming about my own ascension. Soon, Nerul won't be the only one with prestige. After today, we will be equals once more.

The reminder that today is my last day as a Reaper is like a burst of warmth in my cold veins.

I steady the swaying carcass and signal overhead. "C'mon, Crow. No more wasting time."

Crow swoops down from the sky to soar beside me as we enter the front door of the meat market together.

If the stench of flesh was pungent from the outside, it's even more rancid baking beneath the tin roof of this stifling stall. The stacked displays of meat cuts leave little room for anything other than standing in the center of the small enclosure, while we wait to be greeted.

The woman inside stops fidgeting with one of the few slabs of raw meat and stands to face us with a smile that falls the instant she sees my rune-less forehead and the crow sitting like a scavenger on the counter before her.

Her plump cheeks, already pink from exertion and heat, falsely brighten further at our entrance.

"Well, hello, f-friend," she says, the word sticking to her lips like a horse rearing away from the edge of a cliff. "Glad you could come."

Her grin widens, likely hoping I don't notice how it's edged with fear and disdain. I do though. I always do. No matter how hard some of the mortals try to conceal their true feelings about us, there are others that wear their abhorrence like armor, and it speaks loudly enough for the whole.

"Th-this way," she stammers again. "We got them out back."

Before she turns around, I see the markings on her forehead: the star of birth; the teardrops of fear that frame it; the three dots forming a path beneath it that signify her proficiency in speech; and lastly, the symmetrical lines above either eye that mark her experience with heartbreak. Her runes are as light as peaches, almost seeming to glow from her mahogany skin.

Crow stretches its wings and launches off the counter, only with no room to fly, it lands shortly after on my shoulder and together we follow the woman.

She leads us outside, through a simple wooden door that opens into a small pasture—if that's what you can call it. There's a trough, a bale of hay, and a corral barely big enough to fit two cows. Instead of bovine though, its crammed with four hogs and a single crate that's so stuffed with chickens that their wings jut from every opening in the twisted wire.

Seeing all of her livestock makes me realize that when she guided us out here, she had said *them* not just *it*.

"The contract is for *one* pig," I say flatly, making my way to the fence.

The pigs squeal at my presence, but the space is too confining for them to put more distance between us, sending each of them into a greater frenzy. I inspect them briefly, letting my gaze fall over the rear, the belly, and the shoulder of each one. One of them squirms more than the others, rearing and thrashing with every step I take. I feel the pull between us and recognize instantly that it is the one I've been sent to kill.

"B-but we need more meat. I'll hardly have enough loin and ham from just one sow. My customers will want chicken too—"

"You could always just kill one yourself," I say with a wicked grin.

The woman blanches, her bottom lip bobbing. "I can't—I couldn't... I'd become a—"

"Relax, it was just a joke," I say, rolling my eyes. These mortals have no sense of humor when it comes to matters of Reapers. They're so terrified of ever becoming one that even the mere suggestion sends them quaking. "Look, I don't make the rules, I just follow them. I have one contract for one pig, so that's all you're getting from me. If you want more, then write another request and bury it like you did all the others. I'm sure it wouldn't take *that* long for the scripture worms to collect and deliver it."

"It'll take a day at least, and the Festival of Wings starts tomorrow. The people need the meat today. They need to start preparing it—"

I extend my fingers and drown her out by reaching between the wooden rails to touch the plumpest hog between the eyes.

Death itself billows in plumes from my fingertips. I channel it into the pig's skin, and its eyes go wide with fright. Since becoming a Reaper, I've learned that every living creature seems to know when death has finally come for it, like an inherent sense that's only triggered the once. This swine is no different. It sees my hand and knows its end has come. Luckily, it doesn't have to be afraid for long. All it takes is one gentle caress of my toxin and the pig collapses with one final breath, mud splashing up on my black, knee-high boots.

My job complete, I step aside to give Crow space. It spreads its wings, smacking me in the eye, before launching forward. Crow swoops to the pig's dying flesh and rests upon the sow's limp shoulder.

Crow's beak opens wide. I see its thin tongue sliding hungrily in its mouth before it lets out a ravenous, *Caw!*

Only in Veltuur do crows' eyes burn red. In the realm of the living they are usually black as ink.

Except for when they feed.

As Crow unhinges its mouth, its eyes dazzle like that of rubies against the moonlight.

To the mortal eye, nothing happens. All that the mortal woman can see is the crow's mouth opened in a gurgling cry.

But as I am not a mere human, I bear witness to what it is really doing.

A colorless, shapeless miasma lifts from the pig, hovering toward Crow's widening maw. It's like the swine's very essence is being pulled from its lifeless body. As I've seen thousands of times, the vague form resists at first, seeming to cling to its host with sticky hands. But the resistance never lasts long, especially not in beasts.

Crow snaps its head back, and as the hazy thing reaches its beak, it guzzles the cloud in one-two-three quick gulps.

There. Death fulfilled; contract complete. Four thousand nine hundred and ninety-nine lives under my belt. Only one more to go.

Emotion has no place in my expression as I address the merchant. "The pig is ready. If you'd like the other creatures taken care of, you'll have to request another contract."

Part of me wishes otherwise. I'd much rather fulfill my Shade requirements here in one stop, but that's not the way things work. I go where I'm told. I claim those ready to be claimed.

I'm already halfway in the doorway when her jaw starts bobbing. She wants to insist I do more but is too afraid to suggest it.

I stretch my arm out to Crow, but let it fall to my side before it has the chance to stubbornly decline. "Take us to the palace," I command.

Crow stretches, and for half a second, I think it's not going to obey me. I assume the day will come when one day it won't. But today is not that day. Today, Crow hops off the pig, squawks at the woman as it bounces past her, and jumps onto my shoulder.

The world disappears behind murky gas, and we're off to our next assignment.

3

THE NEXT HEIR

ACARI

"Y ou're doing it again," my handmaiden teases, dipping the comb into a basin of spring water.

"I'm not doing anything—doing what? I'm just sitting here, completely void of all doing-of-things. Except for blinking...and probably breathing."

A soft giggle, one that I see from the reflection of the mirror before me, makes her eyes crease. "You're worrying about becoming king, my prince," she says, running the comb through my dark hair.

I shudder. There's that word again: *king.* I am no more a king than I am a merchant or a craftsman. I have no ornate skill or extensive training in ruling the kingdom of Oakfall, and yet, despite what would be considered best judgment, I will ascend into the role regardless. Who decided that the only necessary requisite for the crown should be heredity? It seems a little less than sufficient. Just because of my bloodline, I will sit on a throne that I've never wanted, nor was it intended to be mine before a few weeks ago.

But here I am, the new rightful heir, the new future king. *King.* What does that word even mean? I wonder if it came before the word *kingdom*, or if it was the other way around—which begs the question, what of the kingdoms ruled by queens? Why aren't they called *queen-*

doms? Struck by the intellect of the Divine Macawna! Does the Queen of Ghamaya refer to the kingdoms as *queen*doms. She probably does —why wouldn't she? Which begs a further question: when I'm king, do I refer to them as queendoms in her presence as well?

"Acari?" a distant voice calls.

Probably because I was thinking about the Queen of Ghamaya, my first thought is that it's *her* calling my name, and a scene plays out of our hypothetical first formal greeting, where I accidentally tell her that her *king*dom—instead of *queen*dom—is fortunate to have her, and the entire room uproars with unrelenting laughter at my utter incompetence and ignorance.

But once the nightmarish daydream clears, I realize the inflection of the voice isn't harsh like most of the people of the Ghamayan Mountains. This voice is soft and lilting, less like a deadly roar and more like the purr of a kitten.

A lady with sun-kissed skin as golden as baked baklava steps into view. A single tress of charcoal hair hangs from a torn piece of fabric tied around the top of her head, holding her hair back. The hairstyle leaves her runes completely visible, the magenta spilling from her skin like petals dancing in the wind, and I can't help but stare at the small blank sections above her eyebrows. Unlike me, she has not earned the markings of grief yet. I think I would be jealous, if I wasn't relieved that she hadn't experience that kind of pain yet.

"Hmm?" I ask, my thoughts soaring back to me like they were coming from the faraway Ghamayan Mountains themselves. "Oh, sorry. I was soaring—I mean thinking."

She clucks her tongue, a smile breaking through like the sun rising beyond the horizon. Before retrieving a comb, she turns me back around and resumes brushing the long length of my hair. "I told you that you were getting lost in that void in your mind again."

I look over my shoulder, duck my head away from her combing, and fail at restraining the goofy grin that's reckless to meet hers.

"All and sundry know my mind is anything but a void. You should hear the endless cycle of thoughts that I have to deal with; they just go on and on and on. It's, like, can't a guy get some peace and quiet from himself?"

She laughs again, a chuckle that threatens to bloom in a patch of warmth over my face and chest. "Then your mind wants what your feet do not."

"And what's that?"

"To venture," she says at last.

Our eyes meet in the mirror's reflection, but only for a fraction of a second before she casts her gaze back to the ground.

For her to have such intimate familiarity with me is the catalyst that sets fire to my cheeks, and I am grateful she's staring at the intricate tiling instead of at me. It's moments like these that make me want to reach for her, to cup her face into my hand, to raise her gaze so I can see her eyes again.

But if I've never reached for her before, I certainly don't now. Our futures are set, and pretending otherwise will only make things harder.

"No one knows me like you do, Hayliel," I say hopelessly.

She has a name that should've belonged to one of the Divine Altúyur themselves, so full of virtue and compassion.

Bowing her head, Hayliel smiles knowingly.

After a few more strokes through my hair, making sure the length of it cooperates by leaning in the right direction, she sets the comb on the table beside all of the other grooming supplies and begins working through each of them. She takes only a few seconds powdering my hair with whatever minerals and oils she usually uses to keep it smooth and in place. When we're both satisfied, she moves on to the stubble on my chin—and by stubble, I really mean something that more closely resembles the soft, nearly invisible layer of fur that covers a peach. I used to protest, but both she and my father insist a clean shave is a daily necessity.

"There," she says with a blush of her own, as one finger checks the smoothness along my jawline. "Your father will approve, I hope."

At this, I groan. "As long as I do everything that a future king is supposed to do—which I won't because I was never meant to be a king, and therefore I will surely disappoint him today, like I have all days—but yeah. I'm sure everything will go great."

"You will make a truly magnificent king, my prince," she says reassuringly.

I acquiesce with a roll of my eyes. "Did you know he has me meeting with foreign dignitaries today, reviewing matters of the state, *and* selecting our next charitable event—"

"Don't forget the costume-fitting for your blessing ceremony during the festival."

Another unavoidable noise escapes me, and I slouch deeper into my chair, wishing it would eat me like the melting sands of Marágros. Of course, how could I forget the festival. On top of the usual grooming affairs of a future monarch, we are also in the final two days of preparation for the Festival of Wings. Every person in Oakfall eagerly awaits this ten-day celebration like a giddy child every year, and under normal circumstances, it's an event I quite enjoy as well. The costumes, the food, the performances, the decorations—did I mention the food? The Festival of Wings is a time for the people of Oakfall—as well as some of the other kingdoms—to come together to honor and showcase their steadfast devotion to the Divine Altúyur, the beautiful and magnificent deities of flight—the quetzal, the macaw, the lorikeet, the peacock, the sungem, the dove, the owl, and the aracari, the bird for which I am named—who rule the realms and grant us their blessings.

But this year, I just don't feel right celebrating. Not when I'm still in mourning.

"What's the matter? I thought you'd be excited. There's nothing you look forward to more than the Festival of Wings." Almost as soon as the words come out, Hayliel's hands fly up to her mouth. "Oh, shame become me. I am being insensitive."

"It's all right," I offer quietly, and before she can apologize again, and before I let myself think more about the reasons why the festival isn't worth celebrating this year, I swing down from the chair and flash her a dubious smile. "Time to make myself presentable."

Without another word from either of us, I make my way to the carved walnut wardrobe. The simple camicia doesn't do much for warmth on its own, and I shiver when I pull back the double doors. It's normally Hayliel's job to dress me, but she makes no protest. After growing up together, we've reached an agreement: she helps minimally with the tasks that might be difficult for me—like brushing my hair and shaving—but I take care of the things I am able.

Inside, I find a doublet and robe fit for a king, and inwardly I grumble that I wish I had something less ornate, less *kingly* to wear. Easing each arm inside the crafted green velvet, embroidered with intricate designs of gold and black, I grimace again when I notice its colors match the curled toes of my slippers. Our royal insignia lines the extra fabric draping from either side of my neck to my knees, a series of flowers that only bloom in our wooded land and depictions of the birds that represent each of the Divine Altúyur.

One stands out to me above all others though, the vibrant lorikeet meant as a symbol of the Divine Lorik. As I've endured these past few weeks, I've sought more comfort from him than ever before in my life, clutching to his stories of bravery and strength as best I can. But what I've learned from the him these past weeks is that bravery also includes matters of the heart, not just physical prowess. It's fitting that, considering my brother Rikeet was named after him, I would find strength from his divinity since his death.

That, and the Forbidden Garden.

I turn to Hayliel, a mischievous grin breaking free. "Can you keep another secret today?"

From where she's standing, still behind the chair with the razor in her hand, her eyes pop wide and she checks the sunlight beaming in from the balcony window. "I am not sure you have the time, my prince."

Cringing at the title and the awkwardness it puts between us, I run a hand over my face. "Please, with you, can't I just be Acari?" I wait for a response, but when all I see is her face reddening as she smiles at the ground, I plead my case for her silence. "It won't take long. I'll be back before anyone notices I'm gone."

She starts shaking her head. "You don't yet realize how much your presence—*or* your absence—is noticed." But she doesn't press me more on it. "What should I tell them if someone comes looking for you?"

"The same thing I ask you to tell them every morning," I say, the grin I'm bearing, one that's overflowing with desperation. "That I've fled the palace to start a new life somewhere remote and boring, and, should my father pass away, that they should probably crown someone else king. I hear my uncle is partial to the throne."

She rolls her eyes at me, her smile radiating like the sun, before I leave her to tidy my corridors.

Outside my bedroom, the hallways are practically empty. I suppose the morning has only just begun, but it still surprises me since I can't remember the last time I was alone in this palace, outside of my own quarters, even before I was the *future king*. It's honestly kind of relaxing, to walk free from the judgment and expectations of those I'm meant to impress. If running away didn't *actually* require me to leave the only place I've ever known, and to barge headfirst into the unfamiliar, it might actually sound appealing after all.

Slower than I'd like, I make my way through the palace until I finally arrive at my destination.

"Blessed morning, Prince Acari," the guard says to me, slamming his spear down into the marble floor.

A long time ago, centuries before I was born, or my father was, or probably even his father, the spears the guards carried were actually sharpened. But when the Divine Altúyur decided to punish the mortals for the untold deaths they were causing, mutilating them into Reapers to do the bidding of death itself, kings and queens across all of Tayaraan blunted every weapon in their possession. No longer were guards meant to uphold the law using a force that could kill.

I'm sure it was absolute chaos in the early days; commoners storming palaces, markets, and apothecaries, taking anything and everything they wanted without the threat of death lingering over them. But, in time, at least now in my lifetime, people generally obey the laws. Why wouldn't they, when that same neighbor they robbed could summon a Reaper to have them killed. Death still motivates, it just has a different face now, one that doesn't belong to the guards.

"Blessed morning, Borgravid," I reply with a tight smile. My steps slow as I approach the glass doors framed in gold, eyeing him cautiously out of the corner of my eye, unsure whether today he'll let me inside with no fuss or—

"You know it's still called the *Forbidden* Garden, right?"

My shoulders slouch. I throw my head back, blinking up at the archway, but I'm quick to recover. "What? My father didn't change his mind about the name? I thought he'd at least consider the suggestion I gave him. Just-Another-Garden would suit this place perfectly."

Even from behind his mustache and full beard, I glimpse the amusement betraying him. Borgravid shakes away his smile just as quickly as I dispensed of my bemoaning though, staring down at me with those dark, serious eyes.

"Divine Altúyur guide you; you have to stop doing this. Torturing yourself like this is no way to honor your family's memory."

"I'm not torturing myself," I insist, but when he lowers his head, angling his eyebrows at me, I realize arguing that point is pointless. "It's not like I'm going to do it forever. I promise. There are stages of grief, and that's all this will be. A stage."

A nearly imperceptible quirk of a smile. "Self-torture is a stage? I don't remember that one."

"No...denial," I say softly, my gaze wandering to the golden floor. Although part of me is aware that what I'm doing could be considered manipulation, there's not a single bone in my body that's doing it on purpose. This is just the truth. "I just... I need to see them."

I let him make his own meaning out of the words, knowing full well that he thinks I'm talking about one thing, no idea that I'm using these visits for another.

After a brief moment of consideration, Borgravid switches the blunted spear into his other hand, the chainmail around his arm shifting over the leather encasing his chest and the golden plate in the center. With his closest hand free, he leans over and opens the door.

"Thank you," I say.

"I don't deserve your thanks, but if this is what you think you need, then I hope you find it so that you can move on to the next stage."

I nod my goodbye and step through the doors before he changes his mind.

Relief overcomes me once I'm safely inside. Though everything inside is technically forbidden, I wouldn't exactly call anything here *dangerous*, unless you consider something being so beautiful that it takes your breath away *dangerous*. White-trimmed leaves as wide as pillows hang from bushes, partially blocking the pristine paths of sand-colored pebbles. Flowers of every color of the rainbow peak from the foliage, bringing the garden to life.

I trail a hand lazily over the jagged bud of a ferocious-looking, yet baby-skin soft daminila. It is my favorite flower in the entire garden because I relate to it. As next in line, I am expected to present myself a certain way, a stern decision-maker whom people know not to cross. But I am just as soft and adorable as a baby firefur, at least judging from the sketches I've seen—of which, by the way, none of which have actually shown the fluffy rodent's fur on fire or anything, despite their misleading name. The only difference between me and the daminila is that it gets to hide in this garden all day, and I don't. That and its pollen is used as a sleeping aid, but sometimes the way my father looks at me when I'm talking, I think my words might have a sleeping effect to him too, so maybe we're more alike than I give myself credit.

I continue down the path, the small rocks muted beneath my embroidered slippers. My hand glides over the smooth skin along my jaw, and I find myself smiling at the memory of Hayliel. Here, in the Forbidden Garden, I have no doubt she'd glow beside the verdant flora, her eyes sparkling like dew atop the leaves, her soft lips parting in a smile as she took in the beauty of it all, and—

My thoughts trail when I spy the memory tree. It's not difficult to find being the largest growth in the entire enclosure and casting everything under its berth in a warm, embracing shadow. It is the last remaining memory tree and therefore off-limits to common folk. Well, it's off-limits to everyone actually, myself included, and I'm pretty sure even Borgravid doesn't know I've been violating that sacred rule...but its leaves have been the only helpful remedy to ease my grief as of late.

I duck beneath its dangling, stringy branches to make my way closer to its center. The trunk looks as strong as an ox, a thick hide of bark encasing the tree in armor. It would take a hundred ax blades to take a tree of this age down, which kind of makes you wonder how there's only one left and how all of the others were destroyed. Not to sound harsh, but it's probably for the better since the leaves of a memory tree have an addictive quality and, if used long-term, can seriously impair the mind.

And recently, I have willingly—stupidly—started learning why. Look, I'm not proud of it, but I can't help myself. No one would be able to if they were in my position. By creating a tea with just one of its leaves, I get to recall any memory of my choosing, and live out the moment vividly, as if it was really happening. In my memories, Rikeet, the rightful heir, is still alive. So is my mother.

Reaching up to a full branch of coin-size leaves, I pluck a dozen with careful fingers and place them into a pouch before securing it back on the inside of my robe. I won't be able to use them until later tonight when I am alone once more in the confines of my quarters, but having them on me, the prospect of seeing my brother and mother tonight, will be enough to get me through the day.

As I duck around the hanging branches, I catch sight of the steamy greenhouse tucked in the farthest corner of the garden, the reason Borgravid thinks I come here. It's almost entirely concealed in the overgrowth of the memory tree. Most people don't even know it's in here, but it is the main reason that the garden is *forbidden* now.

It seems impossible, but my feet are actually moving faster than my mind, carrying me to the greenhouse before I can think better of it. Going inside always only results in more feelings that I would rather not have, but every time I see it, I have to look.

"Oh," I sigh on a long breath. "What am I doing to myself?"

Despite not having a rebellious bone in my body, I enter the greenhouse.

Under the teal-tinged glass, the micro-world is tropical and thriving. The air is stifling, and I catch myself starting to wheeze. Kings aren't supposed to wheeze. They're supposed to be strong and daunting, the kind of person that makes people quake when they enter a room, but even my lungs disagree with my soon-to-be new title.

I traverse the overgrown foliage like an explorer, though I am anything but. Exploring implies adventure, adventure implies risks, and risks are terrifying.

I make my way to the back wall, where a hundred glass compartments are stacked on top of each other. My breath hitches. No matter how many times I come here, it never seems to get easier.

I force myself to take a step forward, then another, until my breath fogs the door of one of the cages.

As I peer inside, it doesn't look like much. Each small box is modestly decorated with a handful of dirt, a few twigs, and a couple of prickly rocks. To an untrained eye, it likely looks like there is nothing inside. But that is far from the truth.

The spiked rocks twitch at my nearness, and I shriek, jumping back and bumping into a table of plants when it and a dozen others charge at me. In near unison, they hit the faces of their containers with a thud and a hiss. After a few sharp breathes, I step forward again, becoming closer to an aacsi than I should be comfortable with. Its short tentacles are splayed against the glass, giving me the perfect view down its writhing throat. I expect to find the parasitic worms that I know live inside it, the ones that clogged my brother's and mother's bloodstreams in a matter of seconds, but I don't. All I see is the hollow of the death bug's esophagus.

More aacsi start hissing, disturbed by the others' sudden interest in prey. I take them all in—a hundred of the deadliest creatures on the planet. I wonder which one of them killed my mother, which killed my brother.

I'd like to blame my perspiration on the humidity of the closed quarters, the trembling of my hands because I'm doing something I'm not supposed to, but denying my fear of these tiny creatures would be pointless. Besides, there's no shame in fearing them. Even my father won't come in here. In fact, he'd rather they were all destroyed, but the Reapers wouldn't approve a request for the genocide of an entire species.

I'm not sure lifelong, isolated captivity is much different. They will never mate again, and my father has given scouts the order to search for aacsi worldwide and capture them.

By the time I leave the garden, warmth from the ever-rising sun has started to fill the ornate palace halls. Servants walk about to their varying tasks in the kitchen, the launder, and the stables. There are deliverers in some of the wings, arriving with the food, decorations, and offerings that will be used for the festival beginning tomorrow. I even recognize a few members of the royal family as they start to flood Dove Plaza, but as I make my way through my obligatory greetings, I spy my sister's wet nurse weeping on a bench where intertwining paths cross.

I rush over to her.

"What's wrong?"

I'd be lying if I didn't admit that my show of concern is primarily selfish. I'm too afraid of the possibility that she might have bad news about my sister, and after everything that happened with my mother and brother... I can't afford anything to happen to Gem.

The wet nurse startles, freeing her hands from her eyes to reveal blotchy marks on her cheeks. At the sight of me, she sniffles and dons a cracked smile. "It's nothing, your highness."

I'm so afraid to hear what happened that I can't even so much as swallow. It's like there's an aacsi lodged inside my throat, and if I make one wrong move, I'll meet my demise.

"We both know that's not true. You don't cry over *nothing*, Esabel. You once told me that you broke your arm when you were eight years old, and you didn't even shed a tear. I would've blubbered like an infant. So, I know it's not nothing. Just tell me. W-what is it?"

"It's... it's Gem. Your father—*my king* has finally made the decision."

As my eyes widen with horror, Esabel stands and dashes toward the entrance. I can hear her sobs even as she leaves, but all I can do is blink stupidly at the place where she was sitting, thinking over and over to myself, *He's finally done it.*

When I finally gather myself, there's a part of me that is compelled to chase after her. Seeing her so hurt and overwhelmed— seeing *anyone* like that just makes me want to try to make them feel better. But I know she's already gone. And to chase after her would cost me valuable time, time that I could instead spend trying to stop whatever my father has already started.

I burst into a run. On the first leap I take, my feet slide out from underneath me, landing me on my rear with one leg in front of me and the other buckled beneath me. A few of the women of the court giggle. I flush, cursing the shoes that are artful and regal in craftsmanship, but much too soft for things like running.

Head down, I scramble upright and vacate the courtyard, heading toward Quetzal Wing where I expect to find my father waiting for me. We were scheduled for a fitting before breakfast, so it's no surprise when I find him there, in the throne room, waiting.

"You're later than I'd like," he says with a sigh pausing only to take a swig from a golden, bejeweled goblet. When he pulls it away, red tints his mustache. "But you arrived before the tailor, which I suppose is of some importance. Come. Sit. Give the tailor the impression that you've been waiting longer than you have been."

There is something about my father that has always—*always*— made me feel insignificant, fragile, an ant at the mercy of his giant, regal foot. I'm not sure if it's a king-thing, a him-thing, or just an I'm-average-and-he's-mammoth-thing, but the second I walk into the room, he leeches my resolve.

I drag my feet to the empty chair, flattening my tunic under me as I sit.

"I've received another report of bandits in the Ngal woods," he begins. When he speaks, he sounds like he could command boulders into forming mountains. King Renaudin leans back in his chair, the quilted jade-green accents hanging from his shoulders almost identical to mine, except his are accented by a golden plate on either shoulder, encrusted with Oakfall's towering trees. "They've stolen another child."

For a moment, I become distracted. "Why would they do that?" But before he can answer, I shake my head, remembering why I'm here and how little time I might have. "Father, I saw Esabel in the courtbench—I mean the courtyard. Ha. *Courtbench*. That's not a thing." I clear my throat, trying to mend my fraying nerves so I can restart. "There was a bench in the courtyard and Esabel was sitting on it—"

"Get to the point, son."

I loop a finger through the collar of my tunic and clear my throat again. Taking a deep breath, I try to settle my thoughts, slowing the words that are constantly trying to spill from me. "She was crying."

"And?" he says, peering up at me from behind his tea.

It's obvious he knows what I'm trying to build the courage to ask him, but as usual with him, he's going to make me actually ask the question. To him, this is all part of my preparation. The future king needs to be able to use his words, something I struggle with daily.

I fidget with my ring, my hands in my lap. As I prepare the words behind my tongue, the pressure building in my chest, I bring my hands to the table, tracing the grooves of my own goblet. He sets his down and sits back in his chair, expectant and patient, if not annoyed. It suddenly feels like my hands are too vulnerable on the table, too idle. I run them through the length of my hair instead.

"Why did you let her go?" It's not my full question, but it's meant to be a precursor. A test of the waters that I'm surely about to drown in.

When he responds only with a raise of his brows, I force the rest out.

"Why doesn't Gem need an Esabel—a nurse anymore?"

I think I'm holding my breath. I must be. It's the only thing that explains why it feels like someone is pressing a boulder against my chest, making my head feel like it's about to pop right off and fly into the clouds before it crashes all the way back down to reality. Please-

please-please don't let my father say what I think he's going to say. Surely, he can't be that heartless and cruel.

He folds his hands over the table, pinning me into my chair with his piercing, bushy-eyed gaze. "Your mother is no longer here to protect her. The girl cannot marry. She will never live a normal life. She will never be able to support herself. She is of no use to me, and she should've been dealt with the day she was born."

"That girl is your daughter."

"She is an abomination."

"So, you hired a—a Reaper?" I say, breathless. If it weren't for the chair beneath me, I would collapse. I can't lose Gem too, not after everything.

"What else would you have me do? The Law of Mother's Love has been with us since the dawn of time. We've disobeyed it long enough."

It is a stupid, archaic law that will be abolished when I'm king. Despite my sister's deformity, she and all of the others born like her deserve to live. In the years since her birth, I've seen her experience happiness and I've witnessed the joy she has brought others. It's not true that she can't ever marry; he can't know that. She could be happy. She could live a long life and find purpose.

At least, this is the argument I would've made had I had the nerve to tell him he was wrong. But my father has a hold on me that I can't explain, and so all I manage is, "When is it happening?"

He shifts uncomfortably in his chair. "Sometime today. I am not sure when. Reapers are not known for their punctuality."

Tears sting their way to the corners of my eyes just as the royal tailor enters the room carrying a bundle of brightly colored fabrics.

"Now," my father says in a hushed voice. "Put on a smile fit for a king."

He stands and crosses the room to greet the man at the door, but I remain stuck in my chair like a pondering statue.

"Acari," my father summons, only a hint of scolding in his tone. He's good at this, at the show he has to put on every waking moment of his life and at the minute yet effective ways in which he knows how to manipulate me to do what he wants.

Under normal circumstances, his command would've worked. I would've felt chagrined enough by being chastised in front of our guest that I would've stood from my chair, donned a fake smile, and let the tailor do his job.

Only, today is anything but normal. My sister is going to die—my father has already submitted the irreversible order—and so my thoughts are everywhere but in this room.

I stand abruptly, my chair screeching against the floor.

"My apologies," I say, cutting across the room and bowing deeply from the hip. "But I am feeling unwell. I beg your pardon."

I'm out of the room before anyone can register what's happened.

4

A STORY BEFORE YOU GO
ACARI

Although I didn't know where I was going when I first left the throne room, at some point I notice I'm headed toward Gem's quarters. I say *quarters*, but it's really more like a dungeon meant to keep her imprisoned and out of sight, the place she's only rarely been allowed outside of. Will Gem die having only ever felt the sun on her skin a handful of times? Will she never know what the waves sound like as they crash along the Coast of Dreams, or see snowfall coming from the Ghamayan Mountains?

Tears pool behind my eyelids, blurring my vision and forcing me to blink. They fall freely down my cheeks.

Most of the people I pass in the halls notice my wet eyes and either avert theirs or cover their hearts with a sympathetic hand. They assume I'm still mourning my mother's and brother's deaths, a loss felt throughout the entire kingdom, and in surrounding ones too. They don't realize I'm about to mourn my sister's as well, though, because no one even knows she exists.

Using the backside of my wrist, I pat my cheeks dry and try straightening my back. I want to appear stronger than I actually am. I always have. But today especially, I want to look the role of the strong king I am meant to become, at least for Gem.

Sprouting between the sparse arjuna and banyan trees, woven into light pathway, a wooden tower is the centerpiece of Sungem Courtyard. Tucked in the back corner of the palace, most of the people who come here are here for one of three reasons: one, they're heading to the steam baths for a nice, long soak; two, they live or are staying in the guest apartments; three, they've come to visit the temple that resides in the base of the tower, never knowing Gem's prison is upstairs in the loft.

I slip my shoes off at the entrance and push through the great, wooden doors. Only one man sits inside, his eyes closed, head bowed, and I'm able to make it past him without any awkward utterance of my impending reign. Before I veer toward the stairs that are locked behind another door though, I see the golden statues of the Altúyur behind the altar and I feel their gazes beaming down on me.

Hurriedly, I approach them, press my hands to my chest, bow my head, and mutter the obligatory, "Wings give me strength," before pulling my arms back down to my sides and heading for the winding staircase.

When I reach the door of Gem's room, I retrieve the key from the ring on the wall. Between my tear-filled eyes and the darkness of this hall, it's hard to get the key in the lock, and instead I fumble it to the ground. I squat, raking my hands over the cold stone floor until I find the metal, standing to jiggle it successfully into the keyhole. The distinct sound of a stampede, an excited child charging across the tile floor, erupts from the other side of the door. By the time I get the lock to cooperate and swing the door open, Gem is lunging at me, arms wide.

An embarrassing gush of air belches its way out as she wraps me up entirely.

"Hey, Gem."

Gem releases her grip enough to examine me curiously.

"Not nurse," she says, an inquisitive smile spreading tight across her face as if it is threatening to split the tear in her lip even more. It's hard to believe that the small cleft is the source for all the secrecy and misery in her life.

"No, Esabel won't be here today," I say, guilt suddenly clogging my throat. Before it exposes me, I change the subject. "What do you have there, Gem?"

She shoves a doll into my face. Not a real doll made by some royal dollmaker—our father would never pay for such an expense, insisting it would make my sister's existence known, but I think it's really just because he doesn't believe it would be worth the rupees— but a doll that Gem's had to make herself. A series of knots hold together tattered scraps of fabric, dried maize husks, and hair. I run a finger under her neck, tilting her face up just enough to confirm that she cut some of her own hair off for the doll.

"Likes it, Cari?" she asks, beaming at me while waving the doll in my face.

Cari is the best pronunciation of my name that she has ever been able to manage, and I never correct it. It's the only nickname I've ever had, and I honestly love it.

"She's beautiful," I say, stepping around her and into the frigid room. "Just like you."

She snorts a laugh and skips uncoordinatedly along beside me. "Pla' me?"

"*Play with me*," I correct with a sheepish grin.

I'm probably the last person she should be taking advice on speaking from, considering how often I confuse and stumble over my own words, but I'm all too aware of how quickly people can judge harmless mistakes in communication, and for someone already facing so many barriers, I guess I just want her to have a leg up in this area. But I also don't want her to ever feel ashamed of her delayed speech. It's not her fault that she's been locked away for all of the few short years of her life and hasn't had much human interaction outside of Esabel, myself, and my mother when she was still alive.

Most kids Gem's age have already earned their final language rune by now, a third dot in a line separating one side of the forehead from another, but little Gem only just last month got her second.

"Of course I'll play with you. Beats pretending to be qu—*king*."

Gem unleashes the giddiest of giggles and plops on a dull mat on the stone floor. Seeing her so joyous reminds me that her light is about to be extinguished for good.

I feel so powerless. I've lost too much already to lose her too, but once a Reaper is summoned, there's no way around it. It is just a matter of time now, and I am determined to make her final hours here her most enjoyable yet. I want her to know she was loved. It's what mother would've wanted, and it's what Gem deserves.

I spend the rest of the day with her, locked away in her tower, making flower chains, playing with dolls, singing, and dancing. Despite having spent most of her young life here, hidden from the world because of a tear in her upper lip, she never seems to tire of the place or grow weary of her sheltered existence.

Father has never wanted people to know about her, and so most people do not. The townsfolk and other royal families knew when my mother was expecting, but I think most of them just assumed the baby didn't survive since few people ever saw her afterward. And by *few people*, I mostly just mean my father, mother, brother, myself, and Esabel.

With Gem being such a well-kept secret, now her execution will be much easier on my father. No one will protest—not that they would've anyways, given our archaic laws around people like her whose only crime was being born a little different.

No one will care.

No one will know she's dead.

"Save pincess!" Gem shrieks, pulling me from my thoughts.

"What?" I ask, despite hearing the words clearly. But they feel like a directive, like she somehow knows what's about to happen and is asking me to save the princess, to save *her*.

She waves the doll in her hand. "Garden saves pincess."

My brow twists. "The garden? How would the garden save you?" My eyes pop wide when I realize the slip. "*Her*. How would the garden save *her*?"

Fortunately, Gem doesn't think anything of my mistake. With a dramatic sigh, she shakes her head. "No, Garden—" She pauses, thinking so hard that her face pinches and she pops her tongue out. "Gardenen."

I have been fluent in Gem-speak since she learned her first word when she was fourteen months old: *babba*. No one could figure out what it meant. Not Mother, not Esabel, and especially not Father. But the way her eyes lit when she said it, I knew she was talking about me, her *brother*. We've always had a special connection, the outcasts of the family.

But in this I have no idea what she's trying to say.

Sensing my complete obliviousness, Gem runs over to a bookshelf and grabs one of the divine scriptures, a book bound by vellum too thick for her tiny grasp. She fumbles with it, squeezing it to her chest as she waddles over to me and plops it into my lap. I flinch, both because it is a sacred text and only a few of them exist, but also because the weight of it knocking into my ankles kind of hurts.

I pick it up and read. "*Scriptures of the Divine Altúyur: Stories of Reapers, Guardians, and Other Beings.*" My eyes narrow, searching for the answer that I'm afraid isn't there. Then it hits me. "Oh! You were talking about the *Guardians*."

Gem nods, a dimple on either side piercing her plump cheeks. "Gardenen!"

With our shared understanding, we resume playing. I deepen my voice and pretend I'm a Guardian rescuing the princess doll before she plummets off a cliff—which is really just Gem's cot. But as I whisk the princess doll to safety, I'm struck by a wiggling idea, one that won't stop burrowing in my mind, begging for my attention. My steps finally slow.

A long time has passed since there had been any talk of Guardians, after they died off centuries, maybe millennia ago. Some of them come up in folklore and history chapters, but they're never prominent in the story, so much so that even despite my rigorous education I'm not even sure I remember what the Guardians used to do or what purpose they served besides the vague memory that they were protectors of some kind.

I set the doll on Gem's bed and go back to the book.

"Store!" she gasps in anticipation of a story. She races alongside me, eager to listen.

A smile breaks my consternation. "Sure, Gem. Let's read a story. What about something about the Guardians?"

"Gardenens!" The sound of her clapping is barely audible behind her squeals.

I flip through the old text, searching for the section telling the story of the Guardians. Considering each section is separated by an illustration, I know it won't be too difficult to find.

When I reach the dark scribblings of a demon of shadows, dressed in red with a crow perched on its shoulder, my heart stops, as do my fingers. I take in every detail. The hooded cloak that covers most of the face but not the terrifying beak or ravenous eyes, its grotesque claws reaching out toward the reader, the way the creature seems fetid despite only being on a page. Reapers are prominent in many a cautionary tale, and they have always haunted my night-mares, but I suppose the sight of this one terrifies me even more today. It is like staring into my sister's future, her terrifying, abrupt, dismal end.

Desperate to erase the chilling image and thoughts from my mind, I nearly tear the next page when I turn it. I flip through the book with more fervor, blinking at each section only long enough to determine if it is what I am searching for or not.

"Gardenens!" Gem shrieks when the glowing man appears on the pages.

He's is modestly armored, draped in white robes even whiter than the beaches of the Coast of Dreams.

I turn the page and begin to read.

"As the population of Tayaraan grew, and the Altúyur's great winged reach fell short of the many needs of the people, they selected delegates to act on their behalf. They called upon the most noble and benevolent of mortals, bestowing upon them their gifts of healing and protection, and thus creating the very first Guardians.

"Among the people, the Guardians were symbols of hope and

peace. They traveled across the kingdoms curing every ailment known to humankind."

The book goes on to detail some of the most renowned Guardians in Tayaraan history, Lilliytha, the Guardian who saved Oakfall from a meteor shower that would've cost our kingdom thousands of lives, and Kiernan, a Guardian to the royal Halaud family—my ancestors— who cured them of a pandemic that swept through the city.

The more I read, the more it all comes back to me, like clouds clearing from the sky. But at every sentence's end, my memory of it starts to fade again. It's like the Divine Sungema doesn't want the story to be remembered.

Flustered by my forgetfulness, I focus even harder as I read the next story.

"Like all of the other Guardians, Tamzal had a healing touch. If someone was ill, he could leech the toxins from their body and they would be healthy once more; if they suffered a broken bone, he could reset it; if they were blinded, he could restore their sight.

"But the Guardians could not do the impossible. They could not bring back the dead, and even the most powerful among them could not stop a life-threatening wound that had already taken its hold on a mortal's life. There were limits, even to their power. But it was Tamzal who discovered that one of the limits they believed they had was wrong.

"During the War of Divinity—" the war that is said to have been the last time anyone saw the Divine Altúyur or a Guardian— "As Tamzal followed the soldiers into battle, ready to be at their side should the need for a healer arise, one of the soldiers lost their arm in combat. It was a clean cut, the blade going straight through bone before the soldier could retaliate, but it bled like a raging river.

"Fortunately, with Tamzal ready at his side, the soldier would not bleed out in the field of corpses. He would live. But as Tamzal made quick work of the soldier's arm, he discovered a way to not only stop the bleeding and mend the skin, but to regrow the limb entirely."

The book falls heavy into my lap, and I stare across the room at the cold stone walls.

I know it's foolish, but I'm filled with so much hope that I'm practically overflowing. If *one* Guardian could conjure an entire arm, I wonder if they could heal other injuries too. Maybe even the malformities that people like Gem are born with. I don't know much about Guardian power, but healing a slice in a lip seems a far easier task than growing an entire arm.

My eyes refuse the slow pace that's required to read every single word, and instead I start flipping through the pages toward the end of the Guardian section. I have to know how the war ended; I have to know if any of the Guardians survived.

Gem protests my mumbled, quickened reading, but I ignore her. This is too important; it could change everything. It could save her life.

Reaching the last page of the chapter on the War of Divinity, I slow, reading only to myself for fear of what horrors I might reveal to my younger sister.

At dusk of the final day of the War of Divinity, a darkness crept over the land. Not even the moon could protect those from its shadow. When the sun rose the next day, the battle complete, the Divine Altúyur were gone, all that remained were a few fallen feathers. And the Guardians that they had created were nowhere to be found and never seen again.

Slowly, I shake my head. This can't be how it ended. Or at least, it can't be as final as it sounds. No one actually *saw* the Divine Altúyur leave, but more importantly for my benefit, no one actually saw the Guardians leave either. Maybe they're still somewhere. Maybe they just left the battle because...well, I don't know why, but surely, I've heard of miracles occurring in different kingdoms since then. Miraculous recoveries, close encounters with death that wind up having happy endings. Maybe none of those are unexplained miracles, but instead acts of the Guardians.

I look up from the book to meet Gem's shimmering black eyes. They are the eyes of our father, only where his are ominous voids, Gem's twinkle like galaxies, like they were made of the stars themselves.

I see her life in an instant, the one our father wants to rob her of.

In one blink, I watch, clear as day, as her gleeful wonder matures into inquisitive curiosity. I see her embarking on a deep study of astronomy and philosophy, becoming one of the first noblewomen to do so. She's taking dancing lessons in a pink satin gown bulging with ruffles. I can see her becoming a proper lady of the court, even falling in love.

But mostly, for the first time in her entire life, I see her smiling, uninhibited by a break in her lip, the cleft gone.

It's just a daydream, a false imagining of one of infinite possibilities, but it's so vibrant and beautiful that I can't shake it. I don't *want* to shake it. Gem deserves that life. And if there is a Guardian out there, then she out of anyone deserves their help.

With the story already fading in my mind, I tear the final page about the war from the book, then I tear out the one about Tamzal as well.

"Where's your bag?" I ask Gem.

Her mouth is still stuck open, gaping at me defiling one of the few possessions she owns. As the tears start forming in her eyes, I remember that little Gem has had no need for a bag and therefore does not have one and so I'm waiting on a response that will never come.

"Never mind," I say, placing the book on her bed and shoving the pieces of paper into my pouch. I take her hand into mine and pull her toward the door. "We're going on an adventure."

5

A SOUL BECKONS

SINISA

The smoke dissolving around us clashes with the golden, shimmering palace walls. It's like a smudge of tree sap, tainting the once pristine room and preventing it from ever being fully clean again. It looks better this way, in my opinion. Nothing looks good *too* clean. *Too* clean is a lie.

My footsteps echo as I meander the open-air room, my eyes scanning out the archway openings, past the tall columns, and out into the bustle of people in the plaza outside.

This is the first time I've ever been inside Halaud Palace. A different Reaper usually handles the royal requests here, but I think Veltuur gave me this contract today because it knew how special today is to me, and it wanted to make sure my final collection was special too.

Inching through the room, I press against the wall farthest from the busy plaza, trying to blend in with the few shadows in the room. I walk past the hand-carved stone statue of a dancer draped in coins, paying little to no attention to her cultural attire since I've seen it many times before, but I *do* stop at the statue of an archer. Though fake, the tip of his arrow still looks sharp enough to kill, and I wonder what he might've been aiming for, if not to take a life, which most living mortals avoid at all costs.

After passing a few more ornate carvings, I finally make my way to a door that leads me into a long hallway with multiple turns at each end.

Instead of wandering aimlessly, I focus instead on the call of the soul I've been sent to claim. It's not an actual voice telling me where to go, but I feel it like a tug at my chest, a small thread meant to guide me to where I need to go.

This thread is faint though, like it's barely even there, like it is farther away than Veltuur itself.

I peer over at Crow on my shoulder, tempted to ask it if it even tried to put us near this time, but instead I just roll my eyes and resume our search. The palace can't be *that* big, and I'm sure the longer we explore, the stronger the pull will grow.

I have never been more wrong.

The palace stretches on, room after room, twisting and turning into a knot of lavishly adorned corridors and chambers and wings and courtyards. There are people in every one of them, populating every inch of the palace. Some are so busy—like the ones I find in the kitchen—that they don't even notice me, at least not until their colleagues do. Then it's the same wide-eyed looks of terror that I get wherever I go.

I back out of the kitchen before anyone can scream and turn down the opposite hallway. I recognize the columns, the trees. I see the room with the arching, open windows across the way that I arrived in, and realize that I have managed to walk myself nearly in a circle because I am in the very courtyard that I was trying to avoid.

With a growl, I march under the covered path, keeping the courtyard at a distance, but I still encounter more servants no matter what I do. Some of them knock each other over just to get as far away from me as possible, and my impatience starts to reverberate through my every step. This is taking too long. No matter how far I go, no matter which direction I turn, the call still seems just as faint as it did when we arrived.

I'm not sure what to think of it. This has never happened to me before. Reapers are bound to their mortals. We are supposed to be able to find them no matter where we go. So, it's troubling, to say the least, that I'm walking in circles unable to find the last soul I'm meant to claim as a Reaper.

But when I throw myself through the first doorway, leaving the courtyard behind me, just before I'm about to ask Crow to faze us again and hope that this time it gets us closer, there's a tug.

I follow it through another passage that leads to yet another large room decorated in curtains and gold. A tapestry hangs from every wall but one, each embroidered piece of fabric depicting one of the eight Divine Altúyur. The deeper I go into the room, the more I fall under each of their gazes. I feel their eyes pressing in on me like hot iron, and I am quick to bolt out the nearest exit.

A single guard stands across from me, an unsharpened spear at his side.

The pull in my chest grows stronger still, but I know I have not been sent for *him*, but for a girl instead. I take the last few steps forward, noticing the glass door behind him.

I stare up at the guard, his dark eyes not giving much away about him, but he *does* stare back, unwavering, and *that* is a first for any of the mortals I've dealt with.

"Have you come for me?" he asks. There is no fear in his deep voice, just a simple question, a desire to know the truth before he meets what he expects to be his demise.

It's not every day someone asks me that question. Typically, if someone knows they're about to die, they run or plea for their life. They don't meet me head-on. But he is not my intended target, so perhaps he just senses that he has nothing to fear. But then, why ask? What has he done that makes him think a Reaper has been sent for him?

The call tugs at me again, reminding me that I need to go through the glass doors behind him.

"No, not today," I answer. "You'd know if it was your time. They always know."

I move forward, intending to push past him, but to my surprise, he plants himself farther into my path. Though he's covered in armor that I'm sure would protect him, it's so rare that a mortal willingly puts themselves in front of me that it actually stops me in my tracks.

"I'm not allowed to let you enter."

My teeth grind. "You do *not* tell me where I can and cannot go. I am a Reaper. I take my orders from Veltuur, not the likes of you."

He nods slowly, glancing down the hallways like he agrees with me, but remaining where he stands. His beard almost completely conceals his frown. "And I take my orders from my king. The garden is forbidden. No one—not even a Reaper—will enter on my watch."

Crow pokes its beak out with a squawk, but the man does not flinch.

My scowl deepens, my teeth grinding against one another. "It is a Reaper's duty to claim the souls and ensure their safe journey to Veltuur. You will not prevent me from doing what I am expected to do. Not today."

"There are no *souls* inside for you to take," he says with a bark of a laugh. "The garden is forbidden to *all*. No one is inside."

The black power inside me roils. The longer I stand here arguing with this man, this *mortal*, the longer it'll be before I can return to Veltuur and finally make my ascension. I will not let an insignificant nuisance stand between me and my fate.

But, as I grit my teeth, I remind myself that Veltuur would not be pleased if I claimed a life that wasn't mine to take, and since I don't have a contract for this man, all I can do is try to reason with him.

"Someone *must* be inside because I can..." My words slow. The tug that was drawing me to this place...is gone. "That's...that's not possible."

"I promise you, it is. No one is inside," he says, mistaking my meaning.

Springing to the tips of my toes, I sneak a look through the glass. I search for any signs of life I can find—movement in the bushes, the hurried footprints in the gravel of someone who tried to hide in a hurry, a face, a whole person—but I find none.

If no one is in there, and no one has been, then what called me here?

It doesn't matter. All that matters is I have one contract left to complete and I intend on seeing it through.

"The king sent me here to bring the princess' soul to Veltuur. Where can I find her?"

The guard's thick brows furrow. "You'll find no princess here. Are you sure you have the right—"

"Yes."

"Because, you thought there was someone in the garden, but there wasn't—"

"I assure you," I say with a growl. "The request I received was from the king, and I have been sent here for his daughter, so where can I find her?"

Still frowning, the guard looks down on me with equal parts concern *and* confusion. The concern, I understand—well, not really, but I've seen it enough before to expect it. When mortals find out that someone they know is about to die, they are unanimously concerned. But it's his confusion that throws me. He could just be trying to mask his concern with it, to play up his story that there is no princess, but there's something about it that seems genuine.

"Come. I'll take you to the king," he says to me. "He should be able to clear everything up."

Before we leave, he shouts down the hall to another stationed guard. He asks the woman to cover his post in his absence. As the guard crosses the hallway to meet us, every step more cautious than the last, the first guard leaves before I can answer him.

I stand there for a moment longer, staring into the garden through the gold-trimmed doors, waiting to feel the call again, but nothing comes. *Nothing.* I can't feel the soul I'm meant to collect at all, not even the faint tug I felt when I first arrived.

Before the guard can disappear, I spin around and hustle after him.

Fortunately, we don't have far to go. The guard leads us back through the Hall of Altúyur, down the corridor I came through before taking a sharp right and entering into the throne room.

"My King," says the guard, bowing so deeply that his jade-green cape folds over the back of his calf before spilling onto the floor. "This Reaper says she has come for the princess."

The king, sitting atop a modest throne of the softest white fabric, detailed in jade leaves and gilded in gold, beckons us forward. "Yes, yes. Thank you, Captain Borgravid. I have been expecting her. Come. Come in."

The guard beside me snaps his head up, and I see his confusion turn to horror as he gapes at the king. He must be a loyal servant though, because as quickly as the expression crosses him, it falls away and he bows again before leaving us.

"Where is my usual Reaper?" the king asks, trying to sound important. I imagine that's just part of his job: to make sure everyone around him knows they are inferior.

It has no impact on me though. "I don't know anything about *your* Reaper, but the Reapers of Veltuur receive their orders and then they carry them out. I was told to come here, so here I am."

He nods, once, running thick fingers through his beard. "Your name?"

"Sinisa."

"Welcome, Reaper Sinisa, to Halaud Palace. You—" he stammers. Though I've never met him before, I can tell this kind of behavior is unusual for him. This is the kind of man who's used to being the most powerful person in any room he enters. My presence is a reminder that he's not. "You are younger than I expected."

Instead of meeting his challenging stare, I let my eyes rove over him as well, assessing the man beneath the title. He is large, I'll give him that, the bundle of embellished fabric around his shoulders making him appear even wider than he truly is. But I see through it all. I see the man who must assert his dominance to feel like he's in control. I see the man who has given me the palm to prevent me from getting too close, out of fear for what I might do to him. I see the man who is waiting on me to carry out the deeds *he* wants handled, instead of doing them himself.

After a long moment, I finally speak, my voice flat and gravelly. "Age is irrelevant in matters of life and death. Isn't that why you have no qualms killing a child?"

The king balks. "*I* am doing nothing of the sort. My part in this is to uphold the law."

I shrug, letting my eyes roll briefly to the draperies hanging from the ceiling. "I suppose. So, where can I find the deformed child?"

Surprisingly, he stands from his throne, his chest puffed out. The king approaches me, his steps assured, though I can tell from the sweat poking through his skin that he prefers me at a distance.

"Come. It's best if I take you there. The palace can be difficult to navigate for those who have not ventured here often."

6

THE FATE OF THE PRINCESS
ACARI

I trip over myself hauling out of Gem's room, dragging the patter of her small steps behind me. Circling an arm around her waist and one under her legs, I lift her against my chest and run down the winding stairs that lead into the church below.

"Excuse us! Sorry!" I yell, apologizing for my disruption of the ceremony of colors taking place, while consequently interrupting it more. But we're only there for the ten seconds it takes to finally burst out the wooden door and into Sungem Courtyard where I find my shoes awaiting me.

On any given day, this courtyard is usually less inhabited than Dove Plaza, the courtyard at the south front of the palace. But since we are just a day away from the Festival of Wings, it seems the entire palace has planned on attending church today, as dozens of lords and ladies crowd the paths. We blow through a gaggle of women sharing the latest gossip, leap over children playing Jacks on the grass, and dodge advisors and soldiers preparing for their duty like we are a gust of wind. Everyone is left disheveled by our wake.

We are quite the sight for confused bystanders: a prince scrambling through the crowds with a giggling toddler in his arms. If Gem's existence had been known, most people probably wouldn't think anything of it. Two siblings running through the halls seems a normal enough thing to do.

However, since no one knows who she is, their confusion—and, more importantly, their worry—are difficult to hide from their scrutinizing gazes.

As I race past the Forbidden Garden, I'm actually relieved, if not surprised, to find a different guard stationed there. I don't want to have to explain to Borgravid who Gem is and what I'm doing with her. Although he has always been kind to me, and although on occasion he has let me sneak into the Forbidden Garden, he has served under my father my entire life, and I have never once been so full of myself to think that he would be more loyal to me than he is to my father.

Just past the garden, I clamber into my chamber, slamming the door behind Gem and me. My chest pounds against Gem's head. She pulls back, resting her hand over it with delight as she examines its rise and fall.

"Acari? What are you doing back so soon—"

I almost drop Gem at the sound of Hayliel's voice. Instead, I only manage to half drop her, easing her the rest of the way to the ground and fixing my tunic as Hayliel steps around the corner and into view.

"Hayliel. You—you're here. Hi," I say, waving awkwardly.

"Hi," she replies, looking peculiarly from me to the child at my hip.

Gem doesn't stand still long. When she notices the magnificence of the room we've just entered, a golden, expansive contrast to the small dungeon she's called a home her whole life, Gem can't contain herself. She darts past Hayliel with the briefest of waves, vaults into the air, and plummets onto the fluffed blankets of my bed. Giggling all the while, she rolls across the mattress, taking three to four full rotations before meeting either end and then starting over.

Rather than fighting it, I cross the room to meet Hayliel. "Hayliel, meet Gem."

Hayliel's eyes go wide. Not with shock; she's known about Gem for a while now. It was hardly the kind of thing I could keep from the person I spend most of my time with, especially after my mother and Rikeet died. I had to tell someone. But, even though Hayliel has known about Gem, she has never met her. After everything I told her, about how my father kept her a secret, about the small cleft in her lip, I don't think she ever thought she would meet her.

"This is Gem?" she asks sweetly. Practically floating, Hayliel glides over to the bed. She falls to her knees just as Gem rolls over to her, their faces almost nose-to-nose. "It's so nice to meet you."

"Hi!" Gem beams, before bounding off to the next dazzling thing she can find.

As Hayliel stands from the floor, I watch Gem, admiring the light she brings everywhere she goes and cursing my father for ever trying to snuff it out. The thought reminds me that we have no time to dally. I rush to the wardrobe and swing the doors back so quickly I almost knock Hayliel in the face.

"I thought she wasn't allowed to leave her tower?" she asks, barely dodging the blow.

I sigh. "She's not."

"Oh?" My head is buried too deep inside the wardrobe to actually see her smile falter, but I hear it. Oh, I hear it. I feel her peer around me too, looking over my back to see what it is I'm searching for. "What's wrong? Why is she here then? And what are you looking for?"

"This!" I shout, pulling out an old leather satchel that used to belong to my mother's father.

Hayliel frowns up at my raised arm, the empty bag dangling before her. Gently, she reaches it, cusping her hand over mine, and lowers my arm.

"What's wrong?"

I sigh, shuffling over to my bed and plopping down atop it. This will be the last time I ever sit on this bed, the last time I will ever see this room. It might be the last time I ever see Hayliel.

"My father has called a Reaper to..." I don't finish what I'm saying. Instead I nod in Gem's direction. She's found a decanter of fresh water and the matching goblets that go with it and is pouring herself a drink. A half dozen, so it seems.

Hayliel sits down beside me. Out of the corner of my eye, I see her hand hover over my knee, but by the time I look, she's let it rest in her lap instead.

"There's nothing you can do then. If a Reaper has been sent, they will find her—"

I pull the pouch of memory tree leaves from my waist.

"What is it?" Hayliel asks, and when I loosen the drawstrings and pull out the creased pieces of parchment inside, she reaches for them. She wastes no time in unfolding them, revealing the Guardian Tamzal, and the story of the War of Divinity. I am emboldened again by their stories, but more than that I am terrified of what lies ahead for us. Gem's *only* problem is that she was born with a crack in her lip, and the Law of Mother's Love says that people like her don't deserve to live. If the imperfection was healed, she wouldn't have to die. And the Guardians are the only ones who can heal her.

Hayliel is still turning the parchment over in her hands when I finally muster enough courage to look her in her meadow-green eyes. "I have to find a Guardian. They're the only ones who can save her."

"These...are pages from history books."

"I know."

"You don't know if they even exist anymore."

"I know that too. I mean, I know that I *don't* know. But—" I take the pages back from Hayliel, tucking them inside the safety of pouch. Biting my lower lip, I stare across the room at Gem again.

With her tongue sticking out, she climbs into the chair before the mirror where Hayliel groomed my hair this morning. The second she sees her reflection, the triumph falls from her face. She leans forward, as far as she can without actually falling to the floor and examines the crack in her lip with curiosity. I'm not sure she's even seen her own face before.

"She's my sister," I say to Hayliel, my voice nearly a whisper. When I stand from the bed, my strides are slow but assured as I make my way to Gem. "I'm scared, and I don't really have a plan, but...I can't just do nothing."

There's a knock on my door before anyone else can say anything, and the hand I was about to place on my sister's shoulder flies over her mouth instead. I reach my other arm over the chair and around her waist, hoisting her into the air as I tuck our bodies beside the vanity and out of sight.

My chamber door swings open.

"My apologies," I hear Borgravid's gruff voice as he addresses Hayliel. "Have you seen the prince?"

Our existing friendship clouds my judgment. I feel the urge to ease out from our place tucked in the shadows, to tell him about Gem and the Reaper, to run to his side and ask him for help.

But then I realize how strange it is that he's here and start to wonder why he's looking for me. The only logical explanation I can create is of course riddled with paranoia, but it's all I can think of: my father must've sent him. He probably knows I have Gem, and the Reaper is here looking for her, but she's not in her tower, so now they're looking for me because they know once they find me, they'll find Gem too.

That can't happen.

As Borgravid examines the room, I scoot Gem and myself even tighter against the side of the vanity. He might be able to see us from where he stands; I don't know. I'm sure my feet are sticking out, or Gem's coarse, unruly hair is, or that our two bodies are casting a shadow across the floor, or *something*. Any second now, Borgravid will march over to us—not because he *wants* to, but because he's been *commanded* to—and he'll yank Gem from my arms and drag her to the Reaper to be killed.

I clamp my mouth so tightly that my teeth hurt.

"I haven't seen him since this morning," Hayliel says, and I'm pretty sure only I can hear the tightness in her voice. "I think he said he had plans to soak in the baths. When he returns, I can tell him you were looking for him—"

"No. There's no need. I will go to him. Thank you."

Borgravid's cape ripples like a flag in the wind as he turns, leaving the room just as abruptly as he entered.

I exhale the breath I was holding and free Gem from my lap.

Hayliel says, rushing across the room, the layers of her skirt heavy against her quickened steps, "I didn't know what to say to him."

Wiggling out of my lap, Gem squeals, "My turn, Cari! I hide."

My hand flies to my mouth, hissing at her to be quiet. Anyone in the hallway outside could've heard her, but hopefully Borgravid was in as much of a hurry as he seemed and was already gone. When Gem shrinks away from me, I instantly feel guilty. "I'm sorry, Gem. I just can't play right now. We need to be quiet, okay?"

Defeated but obliging, Gem bobs her head.

"What you said was perfect," I tell Hayliel, taking the hand she offers to pull me up to my feet. "At least he'll be one less guard I have to worry about."

"Do you think he knows you have Gem?"

"He has to. There's no other reason why he'd come for me. I saw him this morning stationed at the Forbidden Garden. He should've been there the rest of the day. I think the Reaper is already here, and I think my father knows I took Gem."

Bringing her hands to her chest, Hayliel clasps her fingers tightly, not daring to take her eyes off the door. "It's not safe here. If the Reaper is already here, and your father has already sent the guards for you, then the palace is about to be swarming. If you really plan on finding a Guardian, then you have to leave, now."

I reach for the satchel I left on the bed. "I need to finish gathering supplies first—"

Hayliel spins me around, her hands firmly against my back as she nudges me toward the door. "I'll get them for you. You and Gem have to get out of here, and you have to do it unseen. The guards are looking for you both now."

Taking Gem's hand in my own, I twist over my shoulder. "There's a secret escape chamber. It's not far from here, next to the Forbidden Garden. You know the painting of—never mind; that's not what matters. What matters is, it'll take us to the northern side of the palace, on the other side of the wall. Can you meet us there?"

"Of course," Hayliel says.

I wince, preparing to ask for the impossible. "Would it be too much to ask for a horse?"

Her confidence wilts like a flower in the sun. "The stableman isn't going to give me a horse."

I glance around the room, twisting from Gem's grasp to scurry to the desk on the other side of my bed. I open a drawer to take out a piece of paper, dab a quill in some ink, and start to write.

"I'll send you with a request, sealed by the prince himself," I say with sheepish bravado. When I'm done scribbling a brief note instructing the stableman to provide Hayliel—although in the letter, I just call her my handmaiden—with a saddled horse, I retrieve my seal, melt some wax over the folded edges, and make it official. "Tell him that I'm finally taking my royal duties and image seriously."

She doesn't smile in return. She can't, not when so much worry is straining her muscles instead.

I hand her the letter. "Thank you, Hayliel. You mean—*this means* more to me than you know."

She nods, wrapping her fingers around the parchment and clutching it against her chest like she'll drop it if she doesn't hold it tighter. "I'll be seeing you soon, then."

Together, the three of us exit the room. Hayliel turns down the first hallway we come across, leaving us with one final, "Be careful," before racing, skirts in hand, out of sight.

Fortunately for Gem's and my covert escape plan, Aracari Wing is always less populated than the rest of the palace. Not only my chambers, but also my father's—and my mother's and brother's when they were still alive—are situated in this section of the palace, and considering my father and the rest of the royal family spend most of their time in the throne room this time of year, preparing for the festival, none of the usual guards and servants are around, increasing the likeliness that Gem and I will actually be able to escape unnoticed.

We're just one hallway away from the secret exit when the raspy voice of my father shoots bolts of ice into my heart.

"Tell me, how long have you been a Reaper?"

Before Gem can step past the doorway and inadvertently announce our presence, I grab her shoulders, tucking her against me as I slam us both against the wall.

A Reaper—*the* Reaper—the one that's been sent to kill my sister is here, is just on the other side of this wall.

My heart is beating so fast that I think I feel it vibrating my entire body. Gem blinks up at me, her mouth opening like she's about to ask a question that will surely get us both killed, but thankfully at the frantic shaking of my head, or maybe from the fear bulging in my eyes, she stops herself.

When the Reaper finally responds, I am surprised to hear a feminine, smoky voice. "We don't have to have a conversation."

Her voice alone has me inching my head around the corner to catch a better glimpse of her, despite every warning bell in my body telling me to stay put. But I've never seen a Reaper before. I didn't even know they could be girls—although, in retrospect, I guess that was kind of ridiculous of me. Anyone who commits murder becomes a Reaper, and I'm sure, in the entire history of Tayaraan, there have been at least a few women to do so.

But a Reaper's gender aside, more than anything I just want to see if the depictions were correct. Besides, they sound like they're halfway through the Hall of Altúyur, which means their backs are probably to us. No one will see me.

Holding my breath, I tilt my head past the marble archway.

It's my father who comes into view first, and I was wrong, his back is *not* to me. To my surprise, he's stopped in the middle of the room, facing the Reaper, like he had been expecting their conversation to carry on longer than it had.

Every one of my muscles tightens, afraid what will happen if he sees me. I keep telling myself that I should turn back, that I should retreat to the other side of this wall where Gem and I can hide until they are gone, but I catch the Reaper's red cloak just out of view, and I truly can't help myself.

I lean a little closer. Just a little. Just enough to see...

There are no signs of the talons, beak, or shadowy bodies that were illustrated in Gem's history book. Instead, I find a girl about my age, in a red tunic that hugs her hips so tightly that I can't stop staring.

My father shifts uncomfortably, and I can't help but smirk at the impact this Reaper has on him. He does a good job of hiding it, but it's so obvious that he is intimidated by her—a *girl*, someone who might be even less muscular than me.

"Yes. Fine," my father says, forcing a laugh. "Focused and direct. I can appreciate that. Right this way—" Everything is cut off by his sudden frown. "Acari?"

He turns toward me before I have a chance to slink back behind the doorway, but when he catches my eyes, I throw myself back, nonetheless. My heart pounds in my chest, threating to shatter it like glass. I know he saw me. I'm hiding for nothing.

"What are you doing? Step forward if you are so curious," his voice thunders.

I dare not disobey a direct order from the king, let alone my father, and so I take a timid step into the open, leaving Gem behind with a cautionary glare.

"Our future king." My father blows out a caustic breath. "What a disgrace. Hiding in the shadows like some thief."

I stiffen at his choice of words because he's right and I don't think he knows it yet. I am a thief. I'm stealing his daughter away from him. I guess in a way I'm stealing his last remaining heir too.

Despite straightening and trying to appear the nobleman he wishes me to be, I tremble in the open archway, nothing to hide behind beside my own cowardice. Although I had wanted to see a Reaper, I didn't want it to see me too. Call it superstition, but I have the dreadful suspicion that if I lay eyes on it—on *her*—I will lose my soul for trying to steal Gem away from her.

"Curse you, son," my father says, managing to make our relation sound vile. "If the Divine Lorik could see you..."

My father has no idea how right he is. The Divine Lorik, the embodiment of bravery, would never run away like I am. He would face his battles head on, maybe even challenge the Reaper outright. But thank the Altúyur that I don't carry his name, and so I don't really feel the need to be brave.

However, I can hardly stand any more public scorn. Especially not in front of Gem. She needs to be able to trust that I am strong enough to protect her, no matter what.

My bones shift slowly, cautiously, as I will my trembling bones to stiffen. I clasp my hands behind my back in our standard, respectful greeting, grateful that no one can see my fingers turning blue from my constricting grip.

Stubborn and terrified, my head lifts, meeting the gaze of the Reaper.

I'm surprised not to find the fiery red eyes of a demon. Instead, hers are gray, the irises of a normal human girl. Instead of having a curved beak, sharpened to a point, she has a thin and pointed nose. The Reapers claws have been replaced by normal, white-tipped fingernails that, although jagged and unclean like the savage bandits that dwell in the forest, otherwise seem harmless.

The only resemblance I can find between her and the depictions I've seen is that she is accompanied by a crow, black as ink, perched on her shoulder.

"Y—you're a Reaper."

She cocks an eyebrow and addresses my father. "You sure it's the other heir you've hired me for?"

I swallow air that goes down like dust when my father doesn't object.

"Do you wish to come with us?" he asks, taking a step toward the entryway I'm standing in.

It's then that I realize just how big of a mistake I've made. There are two exits from this hall that would lead to Gem's tower: the one that Gem and I were hiding at, and the one my father seemed to be headed toward. Only, now that I've drawn his attention, he seems to be shifting his course.

I glance at Gem who has plopped herself on the floor and is gnawing on a chunk of her tangled hair.

They can't go that way. If they do, they'll see her for certain.

I leap inside the hall.

"Why don't we…" I draw the syllable out, thinking for an excuse, an idea, anything that might lead them out another exit. My throat grows hoarse and I extend an arm, pointing at the other exit in this room, the one that leads to the southern side of the palace, back to Macaw Wing where most of the servants reside and Dove Plaza, by far one of the most exquisite places in the entire palace. "We should walk through the guardians in—I mean the gardens in Dove Plaza."

I'm about to break off into senseless ramblings about how drab the corridor behind me is and how a Reaper would likely rather have some fresh air. I'm about to tell her that her crow will be happier too, going the way that allows it to stretch its wings and soar.

But I don't get to open my mouth for another syllable, because behind me, I hear the pitter-patter of tiny bare feet, and the excitable gasp of my sister shriek the word, "Gardenens!"

The three of us turn around as quickly as spring shifts to summer.

I watch my father as he deciphers what Gem's presence means. He swivels his scornful gaze back to me. "You would commit treason against the crown? Against your own father!"

I jump in front of him, my hands splayed. "What if there's another way? If we can just find a Guardian, maybe they can fix her—"

"A Guardian?" he barks, his eyes swiveling inside his skull, likely drafting out the verbal lashings I am about to receive.

But it isn't him who speaks.

The cry of the crow draws silence. It seems to confirm that it has spotted the Reaper's target because she strides forward, a viper focused on her kill; on my sister.

"It's too late," the Reaper says, each word deadly. "Once a request is sent, she belongs to us."

I'm not breathing.

Actually, yes, I am. I'm just breathing way too fast to be able to tell one breathe apart from another.

Black, tarry liquid wraps around the Reaper's hands like ballroom gloves, only if ballroom gloves were made of poison. Smoke wafts, ever so slightly from her fingertips, and although I've never seen a Reaper, let alone witnessed their power, I know what will happen if that substance touches Gem.

I don't think. I just lunge. And it's the most reckless and impulsive thing I've ever done.

The crow lets out a warning call, but it's too late for the Reaper to react. I barrel into her stomach with my shoulder, and the two of us stumble to the patterned marble floor. As limbs collide, I clamber over her and myself, scrambling to make my way back to Gem. I fully expect the Reaper to grab my ankle and swing me back to the floor, for her to leech the life from me so she can then deal with my sister, but to my utterly astonished and grateful surprise, she doesn't.

I dash to my sister, and with one swoop, I take her into my arms, and we race out of the room.

7

RUN

SINISA

As the prince charges into me, I curse under my breath. I collapse to the cold, polished floor and expect his lifeless body to follow. I just hope the Council doesn't blame me for his brashness. What did he expect but death when touching a Reaper? It is why we aren't allowed to live in the realm of the living, why we are forbidden any contact with the living outside of the assignments Veltuur provides us, and why it is heavily advised not to eat anything other than butchered meat or baked breads—no one likes taking a bite of a deliciously red apple just to have it decay on their tongue.

Everyone knows this about us, even the mortals, so this guy either has a death wish or he is an utter idiot who's going to get me in trouble.

But, when I feel his limbs flailing against mine, our boots thudding against each other's as he crawls to his feet, I'm so entirely surprised that I'm rendered frozen. This boy *touched* me and yet he still lives.

Once the prince is upright, he makes a mad dash for the girl, leaving me blinking dumbly up at them both, analyzing, reviewing the chain of events in my mind. It's then that I notice the regal fabrics bundled on his shoulder and realize that, although he did barrel into me, I can't say for certain that our skin actually touched. I guess it must not have since he's still breathing.

Still, it's more contact with a human than I've ever had, at least with one I was killing.

Caw! Caw!

I scowl at Crow flapping its wings madly in the air as it swoops down beside me, nailing me in the eyes with each frantic flutter of feathers. Recovering from my stupor, I swat at it with one hand as I push myself off the ground with the other.

The king is pacing, mumbling something to himself that I can't hear. When he sees me, he stops, his face beating as red as blood.

He charges me, a finger outstretched like a spear meant to jab me in the chest. "This is a disaster. Now look what you've done! I thought you were a professional."

When I raise an eyebrow, he stops, cowering a few paces back.

"You have to fix this," he says.

The statement is so unnecessary that I scoff. Of course, I'll fix this. A Reaper cannot, under any circumstances, break a contract, unless they are eager to face punishment from the Council. And I am not. Punishment is always either one of two things: to be tortured by the Wraiths, soulless, mindless demons that feeds on torment, or to became a Wraith themselves, never again allowed to leave the bowels of Veltuur, and certainly never permitted ascension as a Shade.

No thank you.

I've worked too hard to get where I am, and I'm not about to let some bratty prince and his sister stop me from becoming a Shade.

"If you can't," the king continues, taking my silence as an omission. "Then, I will demand a new Reaper."

"You will not," I sneer, trying but failing to conceal my annoyance. "I *am* your Reaper, and I *will* complete the contract just as I have completed all four thousand nine hundred and ninety-nine before."

I leap from the floor and give chase.

But when I round the corner, headed down the hallway the prince has just fled, I find it long and empty.

In the distance, I can see the courtyard it leads into, and the people that have flocked to it, but none of them are disturbed. They meander about their day like most people do, smiling politely at one another, strolling down the pathways without a care in the world. They don't look like how people look when someone desperate and frantic has just run by them.

Which means, the prince never left this corridor.

My steps slow so I can examine the hallway. It's only then that I notice I'm back in front of the garden that called me before. It's silent now, but I'm still tempted to see what's inside it, to figure out what was calling me.

Crow's squawking draws my attention down the hallway though. Hopping on the floor, it seems to be pointing at a particularly large painting that stretches from floor to ceiling. As I make my way over to it, it is easier to tell that the shadow behind it is more than just a shadow, but a breezeway, hastily concealed.

I slide the opening farther ajar, Crow swooping just over my head, and we plunge into darkness.

Inside the hidden passage, the space narrows and dips. It feels like the walls are collapsing in on me and I can't help but struggle against them. I'm used to the open spaces of Veltuur, not the confinement of being buried beneath stone. The deeper I descend, the thicker the air becomes, reeking of dampness. Every breath I draw is strained, my lungs wanting to mimic the walls closing in on me, but with each new breath I draw, I will them open.

I focus instead on Crow's cawing as it guides us beneath the palace and through the jagged rocks.

Then I feel the faint tug at my chest. With a sigh of relief, I recognize the soul is calling to me again. I can feel it, and it's getting stronger, which means we're getting closer.

Just a little farther now.

I push forward, the stone scraping against my shoulders and the top of my head. For what feels like an eternity, I fight through the enclosed space, but with my last reserves of determination, I claw through the final stretch with hastened speed.

I shove the wooden door up, and it crashes backward to the forest floor. Crow glides out first, and by the time I finally climb my way out of the underground chamber, it's already perched atop a rock grooming through its feathers like it's been waiting for me for hours. There's an annoying glint in its eyes.

"Which way did they go?" I ask no one, finding the forest empty.

Caw.

"You're useless! You know that?"

I search the ground for any signs of the prince and his sister, and I find exactly what I need. One trail, heading west.

My lungs and limbs are relieved for the open air, and I make quick use of both of them as I jog along the palace's walls. The soul is so close now, I can *feel* it, a tingling sensation that ripples throughout my entire body. I'm so thoroughly distracted by it, that it takes me longer than it should to realize how odd it is that the prince's path is following the sides of the palace, instead of bolting into the woods.

"Why would I need that?" I hear the prince say, and I assume to his sister.

They're just around the corner. A few more strides and I'll have her. Just one more death, that's all I need, and then it's bye-bye to this Reaper business, and hello to a life with a little more freedom. No more daily quotas. No more living in the Veltuur forest, sleeping on the floor with the fog and crow excrement. I'll be a Shade, respected and feared.

"I don't know. I just thought—"

The earthy scent of hay and manure cause me to sneeze, interrupting the young woman who sounds far too old to be the prince's little sister, and inadvertently announcing my arrival just as I'm rounding the corner.

I see the princess first, sitting atop a horse and hugging its neck fiercely. There's another woman steadying her, someone I don't recognize. She's clearly not a guard, nor a noblewoman, judging from the scrap of fabric tied in her hair and the apron around her waist. I notice the prince last, blinking at me in horror.

But I don't stare too long. Neither him, nor the other woman, matter. My mark is the princess, and she is now in my line of sight.

Arm outstretched, I charge for her.

I'm clueless to the shovel in the prince's hands until it whacks me in the back of the head. Everything flashes white as the object collides with my skull. Everything fades black when my face crashes into the dirt.

8

FAREWELL

ACARI

"I told you it might come in handy," Hayliel says with a guilty smile.

I rub my forehead. "Flightless birds. What am I supposed to do with her now?"

Using my toe, I tap the Reaper in the ribs to see if she's actually unconscious. She doesn't stir, and I am still in shock that hitting her in the head worked. I didn't know Reapers could be rendered unconscious. I guess I always just thought they were invulnerable to everything.

"You don't do anything," Hayliel says, pulling me away from the Reaper. "You get on your horse and you ride hard. You go to every city, town, and village; you talk to every living person if you must. You do whatever you have to do to find the Guardians, and you, Acari Halaud, will save your sister."

I meet her gaze, note the sad smile on her lips, and nod. If she believes I can do it, then maybe there's a small chance we're both right.

As Hayliel hands me the bag of supplies she's procured, Gem begins to wail.

"Not want leave." Gem wiggles in the saddle, trying to jump off.

I jog to the horse and steady her, climbing up behind her. "We have to, Gem. It's the only way to..." My words trail and I swallow hard, pretending she doesn't notice. I don't know how much she's pieced together yet or how much Gem really knows about Reapers. I guess she *did* have the history books in her tower, so maybe she knows more than me. But I'm not convinced she understands just how close to death she came today, and I don't want to be the one who has to explain that to a toddler. "Think of it as an adventure. You've never been to any of the other towns. There's a whole world out there waiting to meet you."

That seems to put a smile on her face.

While Gem shifts back into the saddle, turning her back into my chest, I give one final look at Hayliel. With the sun shining through the trees of Owlena Forest around us, its rays bathe her in a glow that makes her beauty shine, and I struggle even more to leave. I don't want to leave my home, my friends, everything I've ever known.

But black smoke billows around the Reaper, and before I can see what happens next, before I risk her awakening and laying a single finger on Gem, I snap the horse's reins and we are galloping through the forest.

9

JUDGMENT PASSES

SINISA

B y the time I blink my eyes open, I am no longer in the realm of the living. I can tell as much by the damp scent of the air, by the way its coolness fills my lungs like a mountain stream, and by the rise and fall of the ground that has always made me wonder if Veltuur is alive.

Crow's head twitches left and then right, its beak tapping my nose with each angle. I am weary, and my head throbs worse than anything I've ever felt before, but I force myself up.

Caw, Crow cries at my sudden movement and flies somewhere away, but not too far because I can hear the ruffling of its feathers as it settles.

From hands and knees, I can see that although I was still lying, I am no longer on the ground. I expected if Crow fazed us back to Veltuur that I would find myself under the comfort of my tree. Instead of gnarled roots and blackened blades of grass though, beneath my fingers is the smooth surface of stone.

I jump to my feet, staggering at the sudden introduction of vertigo and nausea as I wait for the world to level in my vision. As my surroundings come into focus, I find myself standing in the pit of a dungeon, encircled by nothing but stone walls too smooth to climb.

Not walls, I realize as my gaze travels upward. Seven staggered platforms rise above me, one after another, until the circle is completed with seven thrones. Each stage is lit by dozens of thick, dripping candles, though they are unnecessary as the room itself is illuminated in green by hundreds of glowing abyss flies.

Completing a full circle from the center of my dungeon, I discern the black dot that is Crow, among six larger shadowed figures in every seat but one.

"Councilspirits," I say, addressing my elders. The word is warbled on my tongue, and my attempt at a bow is cut short when my body almost tumbles forward. Thankfully, I catch myself before I crash fully, my head still throbbing.

"Sinisa," the sickly sweet voice of a woman spits. "So kind of you to arise."

I recognize the voice before I locate Nymane among the Council. Second from the left, wedged between two behemoths of rotten flesh and boils, she would otherwise be easy to miss, except that once she is seen, she's impossible to remove from memory. Age has not wrecked her in the same ways it has the others. Her skin does not droop or hang from the bone like candlewax, nor is it hole-riddled from rot, or bloated by gases. Instead, she dawns the pallor of a china doll, and just as fragile, as if she suffered a shattering fall, deep and jagged cracks cover her face and hands.

"You know where you are?" The man who speaks this time is the same one that approached me during my initiation, Leumas, the same mentor who's guided me this far. Though today, he looks as frail and ominous as ever.

Though it is not spoken as a question, I feel as though I am expected to answer.

"No," I say at first. We are in Veltuur, of that I have no doubt, but I have never been *here* before. But a previous visit is not required for me to recognize where I must be standing. "I mean, yes, Councilspirit. I can guess. We are in the Pit of Judgment. I am on trial."

"And do you know why?" Nymane asks, tapping her fingers on the podium of bones in front of her.

My memory is foggy at first. All I can remember is seeing Crow upon waking. But then my head throbs with the pulse of my heart and I remember the impact that caused it. The prince must've ambushed me, striking me so I would not be able to follow him and his sister. *My* target.

"I didn't complete a contract," I say, standing straighter. There is no point in arguing otherwise, in telling the Council that the prince thwarted me, incapacitated me, and then fled before I could follow. There'd be no pride in sniveling about being outsmarted by a mortal. The bottom line is I failed to claim a life for Veltuur. I let down my realm.

Caw. Caw.

A scowl churns my features, and I send it toward Crow's mockery, though it appears unaffected. As if to console it, Gazara, another of the Council, picks a mushroom from the sludgy, moss-encrusted skin beneath her red cloak and feeds it to Crow, before giving it a soothing pat on the head. When she smiles at me, teeth like long, yellowed nails jut from her upper and lower jaw, it gives her an almost beaver-like appearance. The tusks prevent her from speaking clearly, so she leans forward, looking to Leumas with another idle pat to Crow's back.

Leumas nods knowingly. I find being in the dark unsettling, especially in the courtroom, but I am willing to take whatever punishment they deem necessary. I failed in my mission today and there is no excuse. Bested by a bumbling prince and a slobbering toddler—it's a disgrace.

"Tell us," Leumas says, his voice as smooth and low as a crocodile's. "What happened today?"

All but Gazara snaps their necks to face him, though only Nymane speaks. Her shrill, witchy hiss echoes in the chamber. "We know what happened. She did not fulfill her duties. It's to the Wraiths with her. Thirty years, minimum sentence."

For once, we are in agreement.

"I don't wish to plead," I say, my brow tightening. "My task was incomplete. I will accept the punishment."

Inside, my heart flickers in the faintest drumming. It is the first time, I think, that I have experienced fear in the three years since becoming a Reaper. In that time, never once have I broken a rule that required reprimand, so I have no firsthand knowledge of what the Wraiths will do to me. But I've heard the eerie howls that populate the foggy woods, I've felt the chills of someone's presence who wasn't actually there, and I've seen the claws lurking in the shadows. It's not like I've been *dying* to find out for myself, but if this is the way things have to go, then so be it.

What do I care about thirty years? This life—my servitude—ends when Veltuur has no further need for me.

Leumas holds up his hand.

Nymane grits her teeth, the sound of glass on glass, and I swear I see a crack in her skin shatter anew. Annoyed, she settles back into her chair, clasping her hands together on the bone podium again. "Answer the question, Reaper."

Leumas doesn't take his eyes off me. I can feel his gaze like a hot iron, the way I can always feel it. It has followed me since my initiation, and the only reason I have ever been able to come up with is that he didn't trust me at first. As the youngest person to ever become a Reaper, I was seen as a risk. A liability. Now though, I think his suspicion has grown into fondness, and I've often felt like he is grooming me for something bigger.

Dare I hold hope that the empty throne among the seven above me contains my future.

I turn to him then. My patience is wearing thin; I just want this to end. I don't want any special treatment, just to serve my time, and be done with it. But the way he holds my eyes tells me I won't get out of this without telling him everything first.

Making sure my groan is audible from their high seats above, I throw my hands onto my hips. "Crow and I arrived at the palace, and it was the opposite of helpful once we got there. It took me awhile to figure out where we needed to go, but once we found the throne room, we greeted the king, who introduced us to his son—"

Caw! Caw!

"Please," Leumas purrs. "Don't leave out any details. Your crow says that the introduction to the prince was not the king's intent."

I cock my head, remembering. The blow to my skull might've done more damage than I thought because the details are still foggy though, even to me.

"It wasn't," I say slowly, recalling everything piece by piece. "I don't think. The prince was spying on us—or hiding or something. But the king saw him and forced him out of the shadows for an introduction. The sister—my target—stepped out with him."

"Your target was in the same room as you, and you still let it get away? A mere mortal child, for that matter," spits Nymane.

The two blubbery Councilspirits on either side of her, Pillox and Bhascht, nod, their podgy bodies rippling in agreement. Though they are both large, they are each a different kind of plump. Bhascht looks as if he might've spent years floating in Kallinei Swamp. His bloated skin is a muted green, and his eyes are so swollen that they are permanently closed. Pillox, on the other hand, is more drooping than bloated. His flaccid skin makes him appear as if the candles surrounding him are melting him to a vat of lard.

The only Councilspirit who hasn't spoken or moved is Wex. I know little about them, as they mostly keep to themself, but they remind me of someone who spent the entire stretch of history abusing opium in the dark shelter of a cave. Their skin is so pale, it's translucent, the blue veins bulging every so often as they work tirelessly to pump blood through the Councilspirit's decrepit body.

"And then," Leumas says, urging me to continue.

I'm about to tell him I'd rather skip over the humiliating details of chasing after someone with no tactical or strategic skills and losing someone who hadn't even earned their third speech rune yet, when I remember what it was that brought the sister out of hiding.

"The prince mentioned wanting the help of Guardians."

A collective gasp hisses from every member of the Council, except for Wex—whose black eyes become shiftier—and Leumas, who darts his attention briefly to the empty throne.

Clearly, I've given him what he was looking for, even if I have no idea what it means. I don't know what is so important about Guardians. I'm not even sure I've heard the name before today.

"That's impossible," Nymane screeches, her porcelain exterior cracking into more spiderweb fissures. "The Guardians have been dead for centuries."

"We killed them ourselves," Bhascht adds, his bulbous lips quivering.

"Perhaps we missed a few," Leumas says with an air authority, like the answer doesn't surprise him at all. "Perhaps some of them went into hiding before we could reach them."

It is the first time that I realize Leumas already knew this information. This entire time, he's been fishing for it, trying to get me to say it in front of the rest of the Council. As soon as the thought enters my mind though, I'm shaking it away. There's no way he could've known. The only people in the room when the prince mentioned the Guardians were the king, the princess, me, and the prince. And Crow.

A chill licks my spine. Leumas' watchful eye suddenly feels much closer than I ever knew.

"You can't think that. We were thorough," Nymane squawks. She looks back to me. "What else was said about the Guardians?"

"I—nothing," I say, more confused than ever. Not only do I not know what a Guardian is, the sudden interest of the Council makes me uneasy, compounding the caution growing inside me for my relationship with Leumas. It's the first time I've ever felt unsafe in Veltuur, in my home. "The king brushed it off like it was nonsense."

Nymane crosses her arms, shimmying herself deeper into her throne. "That's because it *is* nonsense."

"But if they have come back," Wex begins, and the room falls silent. Their voice is like the chill of wind, blowing over everyone with a shiver. It is rare they ever speak, but when they do, the Council listens. "It is imperative we find them."

Leumas is nodding, his eyes closed. There is the tiniest hint of a smile tickling the corners of his mouth, but it disappears when he opens his eyes and takes me in.

"Reaper Sinisa, the Council thanks you for this pertinent information. We have heard your case and will determine a verdict fitting of the offense."

Bowing my head, I stare at my toes, waiting for the claws of the Wraiths to snag me through the stone floor and into the abyss below. I am ready. I can do this. Thirty years in darkness should go by in a blink for an immortal. Right?

The Council turns to one another to talk among themselves above me. Despite my best straining, I am unable to discern anything of what they're saying; they speak in the language of Veltuur, using the wind and fog and something else I'm not aware of, to communicate in secret. It is a conversation of sizzles and whispers that my ears are not trained to understand. But I can still read body language, and it is clear they are divided on the matter: Nymane, Pillox, and Gazara for one option, and Leumas, Wex, and Bhascht for another.

It seems like now would be a good time for that seventh member to be sitting with them, and yet, the throne remains empty.

"I have decided," Leumas says at last.

Nymane counters, "The final verdict is not yours to make unless—"

"It is done!" he yells, the thick chamber air reverberating.

The Council falls silent. Everyone but Leumas and Nymane remain standing, but it doesn't take the female Councilspirit long to acquiesce. When she does, Leumas peers over his podium down at me.

"We are reassigning you, Reaper Sinisa. Your contract on Princess Gem Halaud of Oakfall will be temporarily suspended."

My body is pricked by ice. I've never heard of a temporary suspension on any contract before. Ever. It just isn't done. We are expected to claim the lives that Veltuur instructs us to claim, and if we don't, then we're sent to the Wraiths. Even then, the contract isn't suspended. It's generally given to another Reaper to perform the task that the other Reaper failed. About a hundred of my kills were passed-on contracts.

"Instead," he continues. "Your new mission is to aid the Halaud boy in locating a Guardian."

My eyebrow raises. "You're joking." The words slip past my tongue before I can stop them, but Leumas doesn't flinch.

"You will return to the land of the living at once and follow the prince on his journey. Befriend him if you must. In fact, I encourage it. Find out what he knows about the Guardians and see if he can lead you to one."

The word *befriend* slides around in my mind like an eel. I've never had a friend, none that I remember anyway. I wouldn't know how to *befriend* someone even if they were forced to endure my company. Take Crow, for example. We've been working together for a few years, and it *still* hates being around me.

Although I'm not sure where friendships even begin, the thought does start to intrigue me, surprisingly, in a weird, experimental kind of way. How do mortals enlist each other's devotion and trust? Probably not by trying to execute their kin.

Suddenly, I remember how protective he was of the little girl. The prince was by no standard convention a fighter. In fact, he gave off more of an impression of a frightened baby bear cub. Even still, he'd stood up for the princess, despite her malformities and mortals' customary revulsion toward defects. I don't know what would possess someone to risk their life for another, but I'm told it's called *love*.

"He's never going to trust me," I say. "He knows I'm the Reaper that's contracted to kill his sister."

Leumas' voice becomes tight and deadly. "Then lie to him. Make him believe he can trust you. Make him believe that you are no longer contracted to kill her."

Lying seems easy enough. I am a Reaper of Veltuur after all, a daughter of darkness and death; why not throw lying into the mix? I can do this. No problem.

"After you find the location of the Guardian," Leumas continues. "You are to report back to the Council."

I nod more eagerly than I anticipated. I hadn't realized it, but I guess I'm sort of relieved. If what Leumas is telling me is the same as what I'm understanding, I just dodged thirty years of torture.

There is one downside though...

"What about Veltuur? Will I be given other contracts in the meantime?"

"No. This is your main objective now, and the only thing that matters."

There's a twinge in my chest as I realize what he's saying: I will not become a Shade until this is finished. But I'm not one to wallow in self-pity. The sooner I can find the Guardian, the sooner I can have what I want.

"But the princess, she is still mine, once this is done?"

The smile that spreads across Leumas' face is pure poison. "Yes. Once you deliver the information on the Guardians, you may return to the realm of the living and claim your five thousandth soul."

The wicked gleam in his eyes is contagious as I feel it spark like a flame behind my own.

I snap to Crow, who glides over begrudgingly to land on my shoulder.

"Come, Crow. Let us befriend a prince."

We disappear from the Pit of Judgment in a noxious cloud of black smoke.

10

RUNNING FROM SHADOWS
ACARI

My lungs strain for air, making me feel ridiculous because I'm not the one that's been galloping for half the day. Maybe it's just being on a horse in general that has left me winded. Ever since I was a child, I never trusted them. The abyss of their eyes always made them difficult to read, not to mention their erratic behavior. One second, the horses would be calm, but then the next one of them would dash away with you helplessly on top of it, begging for your brother to help you down, but he can't hear you because he's laughing too hard at how your foot's stuck in the stirrup, and so you're just flailing around while your horse tries rearing you off.

Not that that ever happened to me.

When Gem and I come across the small town of Ngal, I can't contain my sigh of relief. Yes, because I'm ready to take a break from the sheer terror I experience while riding, but also because we need to change into something less...conspicuous. It's not like I woke up this morning, knowing I was going to be fleeing the palace and trying to blend in with common folk, so I preemptively put on my simplest clothes.

Thankfully, Gem stopped crying a while ago and fell asleep in my arms. I think once we climbed onto the horse, she finally started to understand what was happening. I can't blame her. Even though she's spent most of her life in that tower, it was still her home. Just because she can't speak fluently, doesn't mean she doesn't understand things, and I'm sure she knows now that we will never see any of those people—not our father, not Esabel—ever again.

Not even Hayliel.

The clip-clop of the horse's hooves slows to a rhythmic beat, and Gem's eyes flutter open with a yawn.

"Hey, little Gem," I say gently, moving the hair from her eyes. "Are you hungry? I was thinking we could get some food."

As if in response, her belly grumbles beneath the regal—albeit dingy—silk of her gown.

"Maybe we should also buy some new clothes," I say idly, giving a nervous nod at the ever-growing awareness of our presence.

As our steed slows, the townspeople gather.

"Is that the prince?"

"What brings 'im to Ngal?"

"Maybe 'e's come 'cause of the Festival of Wings?"

I clamber down first, my foot catching on the stirrup so that I'm stuck hopping on one leg until I can get it free. Quiet snickers spread through the modest crowd, but most avert their eyes out of courtesy.

While I'm stabilizing myself, someone nearby helps Gem off the horse, and it's only then that the group seems to notice the snare in her lip. There is a collective gasp and a roar of whispers.

"It's 'ideous! Cover your eyes."

"It should be killed!"

"What is the Prince of Oakfall doing with that creature?"

It's that question that detonates Gem again into a hysterical screech of tears. I whisk her up into my arms, wishing I'd had the forethought to do so sooner, and run for the nearest shop, not even bothering to tie off our horse. My shoulder is already drenched within the few strides it takes for me to get to the door and close it behind us.

"It's okay, Gem. They won't follow us in here."

"Mean," she whimpers.

"I know. I know."

Leaning my back into the door, I let out a sigh, when a woman stirs from behind a counter. I jump, my heart pounding in my chest.

She eyes us both with a hand over her shoulder. Beneath it I can discern three thick bands around her bicep and, between the bottom two, two fragmented ones, the runic tell that someone has lost two children.

I am tempted to tell her of Gem's fate. If anyone would understand, it would likely be a mother who's already lost her own. But then I remind myself that we've already left quite the trail behind us. I don't know what's taking the Reaper so long, but I'm sure she will reappear soon, and when she does, the less anyone here knows about us, the better.

I run my eyes over the shop's offerings and can't believe our luck. Bundles of differently dyed cottons line the walls, along with tunics, hoses, and a few miscellaneous items made from the same fabric.

When I turn back to the shopkeeper to ask for her prices, she looks at us with pity, staring mostly at Gem's lip. "I feel the Divine Iracara presence today."

Iracara—the Divine Altúyur I am named after—is the deity of compassion. So, what she's trying to say is that she empathizes with us, likely because Gem doesn't meet society's standards of acceptability and because she heard the commotion outside that led us into her shop. But her empathy offends me. What is there to be sorry about? Gem is a happy, curious, and beautiful child, despite what everyone says. This woman's pity does nothing but reinforce my father's atrocious outlook on Gem's existence, continuing the tradition of murdering children born with...differences.

Part of me wonders if that's how two of her own children died, though I would never have the gall to ask as such.

"Thank you," I force out, the words sour on my tongue. "We would like to purchase some clothing."

I rummage through my satchel for a pouch of rupees, but no jingle sounds. My face drains of color. I should've been more specific when Hayliel offered to gather some things for us. I don't know what I expected, or where I thought she'd find rupees, but I guess I just assumed she would've packed *some*.

Chagrined, I cover my forehead with a hand. "I seem to have forgotten my curse—I mean purse, the one that has my rupees."

"It's all right, my prince," the woman says. "I will accept a trade instead."

My stomach flips. "A trade?"

"A fair one," she says, nodding. "Select the outfits you would like and give me the ones you wear in return."

Without consciously doing so, my hand floats protectively to my tunic. The one I'd chosen to wear this morning was one of my favorites, a gift from my mother before she passed. I'm only just now realizing it will be the last time I wear it or anything like it again.

I'm about to agree when Gem's stomach growls again. I've never bargained before, but for Gem, I must.

"That's not a fair trade. Our clothes are spun from the finest silks and leathers from all the kingdoms. They likely cost more than your entire stock." My heir of indignation disgusts me, but I continue projecting my voice and pacing with my hands clasped behind my back. The only reason it comes so naturally is because I've seen my father act just this way hundreds of times, so I funnel his pompous and arrogant energy like I am him. "However, we are only in need of an outfit for each of us, and a couple warm meals."

The shopkeeper narrows her view, working through the unspoken request. "I don't provide sustenance here. My wares are of cloth only."

"Then perhaps you could give us rupees in exchange. Not a lot," I'm quick to say, eager to seal the deal. "But enough for a meal each."

She curtsies. "Of course, my prince. Find what suits you both, and I will gather some rupees to make the bargain even."

It takes longer than I expect to wrangle Gem into a dirt-brown tunic, with her squirming and complaining about the fabric itching the entire time. Once she's dressed and I begin to put my own new clothes on, I start to understand her plight. I'm not sure I've ever worn anything so coarse before.

When the shopkeeper returns with the rupees and a pouch, I accept it with a gracious bow and shuffle Gem back onto the street.

The crowd that was once there has mostly subsided, moving on to the next spectacle just down the path—a man walking across hot coals—and allowing us to walk freely among the people without detection as royalty. It's liberating, in a way to be seen as normal. I've spent my entire life under the scrutiny of others, never amounting to the prince I was expected to be, but here, among the people, I feel, oddly, like I belong.

If I'm being entirely honest though, it's also slightly disappointing how easily I can go from being the future king, noticed by everyone, to just another commoner walking the streets. I guess I'll have to get used to it though.

Caw!

The guttural cry of a crow locks my knees mid-step, causing me to trip into someone in front of me. I apologize, or at least I try to, the words jumbling together as I search fretfully for the source of the sound. Finally, after looking atop every rooftop and shop sign, I spy the black creature on a barrel, almost within arm's reach.

Gem sees it too, her bottom lip quivering. I pull her behind me and search the street frantically for the Reaper.

There's no sign of her though. Only the bird. I guess it's possible —although doubtful—that it isn't *her* crow. Maybe it's not even a crow at all, but some regular black bird that my non-bird-eye is mistaking for a crow.

For once, my optimistic hope isn't worth the risk.

I yank Gem into a nearby building, one I recognize from my previous visits to Ngal. Upon our abrupt and lurching entrance, people shift their focus on us. My cheeks redden at the attention, but I try ignoring it, pushing through the populated tavern with my head down, taking Gem to a door at the back.

A large hand comes down on my shoulder, and the barkeep stops me in my tracks. "Can I help you, kid?"

I peek past him, the door almost within my grasp. "No. No help needed here. I was just...coming to ask you for an ale."

He eyes me from head to toe. "Don't look like much of a drinker, and that one there," he says, nodding at Gem, "shouldn't be in here."

"Oh, sorry. My mistake," I say, turning away from him. I take a step back in the direction we came, feeling him resuming his duties behind me.

When the crow caws again, I look down at Gem, apologizing for what's about to be a bumpy, possibly dangerous ride, before twisting back around and rushing for the door.

"Hey!" the man yells. "This ain't the place for—"

Bursting through the back door, Gem and I find ourselves staggering at the edge of the woods surrounding the town. Our options are limited: go through the woods or try to go back into town for our horse.

We don't have time to go back for our horse though, not if that crow really belongs to the Reaper. In fact, we don't have time to sit here thinking about the time we don't have.

I squeeze Gem's hand and run.

White-barked trunks blur past us. Neither Gem nor I are sure-footed, but we manage to stay upright as we flee, dodging roots, tree trunks, and low-hanging branches. Or at least trying to. Once or twice I run face-first into a low-hanging branch, or worse, a spider-web. I try not to think about the hideous creature that is most certainly somewhere in my hair and keep pushing forward.

When Gem's legs tire, I heave her into my arms, feeling the light weight of her like a boulder atop my own legs. My lungs ache, my legs burn, but I can't stop. Stopping means the Reaper will catch us. Stopping means with one touch, Gem will die.

It is the only thought I need to keep me going.

Just then, an arrow whizzes past my head, a rapid stream of air following, as the bolt plants itself into a nearby tree with a thud. Since it came from the direction we are heading, I stop running, thinking to myself that running at full speed toward something with a bow and arrow might not actually be a smart idea.

As we stand there in the clearing though, I feel like a clueless rabbit being stalked by a leopard while a pack of wolves closes in from the front. My heart is pounding so hard that I think I can taste blood.

"Fine afternoon for a jog," a voice like a bear's rumbles from the woods.

As if having conflict with one stranger in the woods wasn't bad enough, five additional menacing characters step into view alongside the first, each dressed in leathers and furs, covered head-to-toe in dirt. No introduction is needed, as I recognize them immediately. Woodland bandits.

I've heard stories about bandits during some of my meetings with Father. They prey on travelers journeying through the woods to steal their belongings and valuables. But from the stories I've heard, they usually ambush roads where there is likely to be a lot of traffic, not people in the middle of the forest.

They surround us almost entirely, leaving only the direct path back to Ngal unblocked.

"Why are you in such a hurry?" another man says with a smile. He's missing a tooth, so he whistles on the word *such*. But that is the least surprising detail about him. Outlining his right eye, nose, and half of his cheek, his face is covered with a tan splash of skin. Considering such deformities are generally *dealt with* at birth, I'm surprised that someone with such a large birthmark has lived as long as he has.

"I—we're not—no one's hurrying." It is my meager attempt at a lie, and I regret it immediately.

The first man pins me down with his amber eyes that seem to glow against his midnight skin. "Do not lie to us, Prince Acari."

Fear dizzies me. I guess I had more faith in our disguises than I should've, but it's still surprising. No one else in the town seemed to notice me once we changed our garments, so why would these bandits be able to spot me from a distance? And so instantly?

Unless...unless they've been following us.

I am trembling more fiercely than my sister is, but I squeeze her closer once again pretending to be strong for her.

"Is that the girl you saw?" the bandit asks, turning to another of his gang.

A young girl, probably not too far from me in age, steps forward, taking Gem's face in hand. It happens so quickly that I don't have time to pull her away, but I do notice that one of the girl's fingers is cut down to the knuckle, scarred over.

"Yes. This is her," the bandit girl says, nodding back to the bear-of-a-bandit leader.

"Hand over the princess willingly, and we'll let you go freely."

Dread freezes me. He said *princess*, as if he knew who Gem was. But he can't possibly know *that*. No one knows. Gem has been a well-kept secret her entire life. No one was allowed to see or meet her when she was born, and since my father forced my mother to wear clothes of mourning for the first month after Gem's birth, everyone just assumed the baby didn't survive. Only six people knew about her: my father, myself, my late mother, my late brother, Hayliel, and Esabel.

My eyes fall to Gem only to find her staring up at me, fear wide in her pupils. Her unbrushed locks fall away from her face and down her back, coarse like the coat of a black wolf. I suppose if they looked hard enough, they could see the resemblance between the two of us, our skin the same tawny shade, our hair black as night, our eyes the same shape, although where hers matches her hair, mine are green like our mother's.

Regardless of how they know she is the princess, I decide it's best not to argue the point. I'd only be lying, and I'm neither great at it, nor do we have the time. What I am great at though—or at least what I've been trained to do—is rely on my privileged upbringing.

"Our family is rather influent—"

The man's face contorts as he looks at me like I'm speaking a different language.

"I mean, I can pay you well," I blurt, realizing I don't even know how much rupees the shopkeeper gave us. Likely not as much as I'm used to carrying.

The bandit bear shrugs. "I have a better idea. We take the rupees *and* the girl."

"I—I can pardon your crimes. Whatever forced you into the life of a bandit, I—I can make it go away. You wouldn't have to live in the woods anymore. You wouldn't have to be afraid of getting caught. You could pursue professions, make a living, have families, live normal lives."

They're silent for a moment, so long I start to think my bargain has worked. A prideful, though uneasy smile breaks free from my hold. Then they burst into laughter, everyone except the bear bandit who remains stoic and menacing.

"Nice try, kid," chuckles the man with a birthmark. "But no one could've made that life sound more boring than you." He pauses for another hearty bout of laughter before returning his attention to me, joy vanishing from his expression. "Besides, what we run from, you can't pardon."

The solemnness becomes contagious, as each bandit turns inward in their reflection. It's a moment that I'm sure we can use to our advantage, if only I knew just what they were talking about. Surely, I can offer them *something*. Anything would be more important to them than a princess that no one knows exists.

But I don't have time to think of anything else. The bandit bear steps forward, reaching into his pocket. Gem and I recoil, but he holds up his other hand in a somehow trustworthy gesture. I stand still, letting him approach.

When he pulls his hand out, he raises a closed fist to his mouth. "Enough chitchat. It's time to sleep now."

My eyes widen when I realize what he's about to do.

He opens his palm face-up and blows on the dust inside. Pollen from the daminila flower sifts into the air on a direct path to mine and Gem's faces. I don't even have to inhale; it just works its way up my nostrils, and I fall asleep before my body thuds to the ground.

11

CONVERGING PATHS

SINISA

"**G**o! Fly ahead," I command Crow when we emerge in the realm of the living. Once again, the people around us shirk, but I have no time to toy with them now. "Find them. We have a job to do."

Crow spreads its wings and, with a gust, propels itself into the air, flying down the narrow road, just above the headline. I stride in the opposite direction, aware that Crow has fazed us nearby, but not directly atop who we seek. They can't be hard to find though. A prince and a princess would not go unnoticed.

"You should know," someone growls from the shadows. His voice is clawing, like a tree branch scratching against the window on a howling night. "I've been sent to keep an eye on you. Certain members of the Council don't believe you're as loyal as you say."

My hackles raised, I spin to face the Shade that's been sent to keep an eye on me. The second I spot his blond hair, I know exactly who he is. Though Veltuur is an infinite realm, Councilspirit Nymane has one Shade in particular whom she enjoys as a pet.

"Well, Nerul," I say, sounding bored. "I hate to disappoint you... Oh wait, no, I don't. The sooner I can complete this task, the sooner I can kill the princess, and the sooner I get to become a Shade and never have to deal with the likes of you again."

He snorts. "Like they'd let you ascend." Though the words are venomous, there's fear behind his eyes. He knows just as much as I do that Leumas has had high hopes for me from the start.

I shrug, turning back to the road and leaving him to the alley. "I guess we'll find out."

People shudder and close shop as I pass, otherwise I'd ask if any of them had seen the missing heirs. Not *missing*, fleeing. And somehow managing to do it well. This prince was becoming a royal pain in my—

"No way it was the prince. 'E's not scheduled to visit Ngal for... well, never that I know of."

The conversation draws my attention, and I squeeze into an alleyway to avoid being seen, lest the couple stops gossiping.

A man answers, presumably the woman's husband. "I'm telling you, I saw 'im with me own eyes. It was 'im all right. And 'e was with a girl. She looked just like 'im!"

The woman barks a laugh. "Well 'e ain't have no children, now did 'e."

"No, I don't s'pose 'e did. But she was 'is some'ow. Maybe a cousin or somet'ing. They were in a state, I tell you. Barged right into the tavern and out the back door."

With two powerful strides, I glide back into the road, blocking the couple from continuing further.

"No," the woman sobs, drowning on her words as if they were tears themselves. "I'm not ready."

I roll my eyes. "I'm not here for you." Stretching my arm out, I reach for her husband and let the black magic swirl in my palm. An empty threat, but an effective one since they don't know that. "I need you to tell me where the tavern is."

There is no hesitation. The man's arm springs up from around the woman's shoulders, casting a shadow back down the road from where they came.

"Y-you can't miss it," he stammers. "Got a sign out front with a fat 'ippo on it. S'called the *'Ippo-critic Tankard*."

This causes me to snort a laugh, causing the woman to whimper and the man to flee from my presence, dragging her with him. I sigh and make my way down the road he suggested, the one I'd sent Crow down.

The man was right—the establishment is easy to find. A carved image of a hippopotamus leaning onto a barrel with a stein in hand would be difficult to miss. By the time I arrive, Crow is flying around in disproportional circles overhead. It flies down to me when it spots me.

"You lost them, didn't you?"

Crow doesn't answer with an argumentative squawk. Instead it fluffs its feathers, as if to say that it's not its fault.

"None of this would've happened if you would ever just faze us where we need to be instead of making me run around all over the place.

"Faze us again," I growl. "And this time, take me directly to the girl."

Crow squawks, flying in a circle over my head as it usually does before a faze. But to my confusion, this time we don't move. Sure, Crow likes to play games and make me work for my kills, but it *always* fazes us, even if it's not exact. After being in Veltuur for so long, I'm fairly certain that a Reaper's crow can't outright disobey them actually.

So when Crow and I don't dissipate to smoke and mist, my brow furrows.

"I said take me to the girl."

Caw-caw.

This is a first. Though I can't understand Crow's squawking exactly, there's something about its tone that gives me the impression that its telling me it can't faze us. Never, in the history of Reapers, has a Crow been unable to faze to its mark. It is what crows do: a contract is created, the contract is given to a Reaper to fulfill, binding the Crow and Reaper to their target, and then the Crow fazes its Reaper to where they need to be.

Only, I no longer have an active contract. The contract on the princess' life was postponed, which means Crow is now longer bound to her, and therefore he can't faze to her.

At least, that's the only logical explanation I can come up with: since she's no longer my primary mark, we can't faze to her. Veltuur must've spat us somewhere close though, so that this wouldn't be an impossible task. After all, finding information about a Guardian appears to be something of great importance to the Councilspirits, and so it must be important to Veltuur too.

Without being tethered to the princess' soul though, we're going to have to do this the hard way.

"Come on," I bark, signaling to the tavern door. "A man down the road said they went in here. Maybe they're still around."

As I step through the doorway, Crow glides to my shoulder, its talons not sharp enough to pierce skin, but sharp enough to remind me of its disdain.

No one notices us at first, as if it were every day that a woman in a bloodred tunic and a bird on her shoulder walked through their doors. They carry on in their drunken conversations about family, work, and hard times while the barmaids refill the emptying mugs and put food on the tables.

It's not until I almost run into one of them that the barmaid drops her pitcher and the room silences to ogle the commotion. It's an innocent kind of interest, one that would quickly dwindle so that they could resume doing whatever it was that mattered more before the glass shattered on the floor if they didn't happen to recognize a Reaper in the midst of it all. But when they see me, when they notice the presence of a Reaper among them, the room hushes further, like the settling of fog on a moonlit night.

The merriment shifts so rapidly to fear and hostility that it takes me a second to remember why I'm here.

"I was told the prince and princess came here," I say, hoping to appease their rampant fears before anyone does anything stupid. It's not often someone attacks a Reaper, but when they do, it's always for one of two reasons: they're trying to protect someone they love, or they're inebriated, which means this establishment is a danger zone.

"Princess? We've got no princess 'ere. Maybe yer Crow's broken; took ye to the wrong kingdom."

My eyes flit to Crow, skeptical at first, but I shake the doubt from my mind. Although Crow is an obstinate pest, it has never delivered us so far off our mark that we find ourselves in the wrong kingdom. Not to mention, I *felt* her. Her soul called to me. She was just outside my grasp, but I *knew* the girl on the horse was my mark.

Besides, I'd recognize the streets of Ngal anywhere. I've been sent many times to this town to retrieve lives for Veltuur, so many that I think I even recognize some of the faces in this very tavern, grieving wives and enraged brothers.

"This Crow does my bidding, and I do the bidding of Veltuur, so if I have been sent to claim the life of the princess of Oakfall, then she exists. Her brother—your prince—kidnapped her and fled before I could finish. They were last seen entering this bar. So, before I lose my patience, it will behoove you all if someone just tells me where they're hiding."

Searching the faces of the patrons, I find nothing but silence and stubbornness. These people don't want to help me. They think me evil. But really, it's themselves they should hate. I've completed contracts for many of the people here, and if not me, then it's likely they've hired another Reaper. I recognize a man in the crowd who'd requested an exterminator when a bee colony invaded his home. Another who called upon my services when their ill mother was on the last leg of her life. And that woman there—the lady playing cards at a wobbly table by the hearth—she requested a Reaper to end the suffering of one of her hens who'd been attacked by a wolf.

Mortals are hypocrites. They need us to do their dirty work because they are too afraid of becoming a Reaper themselves.

"We can do this the hard way, if that's what you'd prefer," I snap, crossing through the common space toward a group of seated patrons. They try scattering when they notice my focus is locked in on them, but as knees bump the table, drinks spill, and someone tumbles back in their chair, they stop moving, choosing to cower instead of run.

"Enough," growls the barkeep, a towel working idly on a mug in his hands. "We want no trouble and 'ave no business to stop you from fulfilling yer duties. The prince went out the back about ten minutes ago."

I nod, backing away from the group I was cornering to instead make my way to the door.

Outside once more, I send Crow ahead to search for them. While Crow searches from the air, I crouch to the earth. The prince's clunky footing leaves a distinct trail to follow, and despite my contempt for running, I peddle my feet fast enough that I am working up a light trot. I have to remind myself that the sooner we find the prince and the princess, the sooner we can find a Guardian, and the sooner I can get on with executing the princess and becoming a Shade.

As I run, I squint from the brightness of the sun, despite the cover of the canopy. This forest is shattering and loud with light, and I'd prefer Veltuur over it any day. My eyes remain glued to the ground, carefully watching the path he left behind. Although their footprints are disorganized, I can tell they were running, and at one point, the prince even picked her up because her trail ends and his steps deepen in the moist earth.

Eventually, his pace slows.

The footprints end where a new grouping of footprints appears. Tracks circle his like a crescent moon. An ambush. It would've given him no way out but the way he came. Only, I already know he didn't go back that way because there is no other trail but mine.

A shimmering red powder is peppered over the terrain, and since there are no daminila flowers nearby, it's not difficult to guess what its purpose was in all of this.

Someone ambushed the prince and princess. Someone captured my target.

And that someone is going to have me to answer to.

I'm not an adept tracker, so with so many new footprints, it would be difficult for me to determine which way they all went, so all I can rely on now are other external clues. It's the first time I allow my gaze to rise, searching the surrounding area for any signs of where they might've gone. I spy Crow hopping across the earth floor, a series of three-pronged scratches disturbing the rest of the trail from its talons. It squawks at me, cocking its head before launching into flight. Surprised by its willingness to assist, but certainly not going to make a big deal out of it, I follow.

It's less of a *flight* and more of a long leap though, because almost as soon as it's up in the air, Crow glides back down, landing on an unconscious body lying facedown in the dirt at the base of a nearby tree. The lanky body of the prince would be difficult to mistake, even in his new attire. By the delicate rise and fall of his chest, I am relieved to see he is still breathing. I can't have him dying on me and thwarting yet another of my missions. It would be to the Wraiths with me for certain then.

Careful to avoid the crunch of dried leaves, I tiptoe around him, hoping to find my mark lying underneath him, guarded by his body. He's not large by any standards, but she is small enough that I think she could fit easily beneath him.

When I find that he is only leaning at that angle because his elbow is propped awkwardly beneath him and that there is no girl in sight, I search the other side of the tree. Nothing.

I growl through a white-hot flash of frustration, rounding the tree and coming toe-to-toe with the prince. If anyone knows where the princess is, it's him.

My leg rears back, preparing for a solid blow that will hopefully wake the prince from his catnap, when I remember that I'm not actually sure why my power didn't kill him earlier. Sure, I have a theory, but the truth is I don't have much to test it on. I've literally never had any other contact with a mortal before, so I can't be sure it was the lack of skin-to-skin contact that saved him. For all I know it could've been a special fabric that he's no longer wearing, or perhaps the palace itself was protected by some charm.

If I'm wrong and even touching him through the leather toes of my boots can kill him, then kicking him now will only make my mission take longer. He is my lead to finding the Guardians *and* the girl. I can't afford to test my theories right now.

Instead, I storm to the nearest tree and in its shadow I find a fallen branch longer than my arm and barely thicker than one of my fingers. Dragging my feet, I use the short distance between the tree and the prince to make as much noise as possible, his final warning to wake before I use harsher methods. When I reach his body, I wait half a second.

There are no new signs of consciousness.

I shrug and swing the stick down across his back.

"Time to wake up, prince!" Each word becomes a new thwacking and I manage to get a fifth one in before the prince has opened his eyes and scurries out of reach.

He cowers against the trunk of the tree, cradling his head from any further blows. "Stop! I'm up!"

I lower the branch, but my grip stays strong, ready to strike again if need be. I am willing to do whatever it takes to get the answers I need, to find the Guardian I've been sent to search for.

But I'm suddenly reminded of something Leumas said: *Befriend him if you must. In fact, I encourage it.*

Squinting, I observe the prince. His eyes are wide with bewilderment, but the longer I watch him, the more I realize it's not me he fears. Not right now, anyhow. As his eyes dart around the forest, quick and desperate, I realize he's searching for someone. His sister's absence, the sister he tried to protect, must not be of his own doing.

Me beating him any further will do nothing to rebuild the trust I've been instructed to nurture.

I drop the stick, my hands creaking in protest as I utter a word I'm not sure I've ever said before. "Sorry."

He stiffens, peering up at me with reluctance.

"I didn't know how else to wake you," I continue, unsure of what to say next. In my focused chase, I hadn't constructed a plan to make him believe that I was no longer going to claim his sister's life. I know I need to gain his trust though, and I think in order to do that, I have to show that I care for the same things he does. "Where's the girl?" I ask, realizing the second the words leave my mouth just how suspicious they sound.

Judging from his scoff, he senses it too. "I hid her. You'll find her anywhere—*won't* find her anywhere," he corrects with a roll of his eyes.

I snort, finding amusement not only in his awkward speech, but also in the fact that he just lied straight to my face. It's not something I experience often, a mortal having the gal to lie to me. They beg and plead, sure, but usually they don't have the power to lie, not when the life I've come to claim is within an arm's reach and my black power is already coiling around me.

Apparently, this prince and I have something in common: neither of us have any intention of telling the truth.

"Oh, I'm sure you did," I say, a poisonous smile hooking the corners of my mouth. "And then afterward, you thought you'd take a long and restful nap in the middle of the woods." I pause long enough to roll my own eyes, and I point back to where his tracks ended. "I followed your trail. I saw where you were ambushed, and I saw the daminila pollen. I know you didn't hide the princess because you didn't have time to. You were surrounded by five, maybe six mortals, and I'm guessing they took her since she's no longer here with you."

The prince blinks at me once, his eyes watery but the levy's unbroken. Throwing his back against the base of the tree, he sighs deeply. Something worse than sorrow darkens his expression. "She was counting on me," he whispers. "She was counting on me, and I— I didn't protect her."

I recognize his vulnerability and know this is a prime moment to prey upon. Something happened to his sister, and he just might be desperate enough to accept my help.

"Who took her?"

He scoffs again, rubbing his eyes. "Oh, right. Like I'm just going to tell you where you can find the girl you've been sent to kill. She's my sister, and I'm not letting you near her. She might've been kidnapped by—whoever, but at least she could still be alive. If you got ahold of her though? She's be dead."

I need a different tactic. Something to make him think that we are on the same side. Perhaps it's time to give him some of the truth.

"I have new orders," I say. "The Council has interest in the Guardians you spoke of. I am to aid you in finding them and report back to Veltuur."

The color drains from his face at the mention of the underrealm. He blinks, recomposing himself, if only slightly. "Who's the Council?"

The question confuses me. "What do you mean? The Council oversees Veltuur and all of the Reapers. You must know that."

"Why would I know that? It's not like I've spent a lot of time down there, consorting with the Reapers and swapping stories about my favorite ways to murder children."

"We don't—" I start, but recognizing the futility of arguing with someone who doesn't understand Veltuur or appreciate the balance of life and death, I stop short. Instead, I focus on the realization that he isn't arguing with me about having new orders, which seems to hint that he at least believes that such a thing is possible. "The Council is who I receive my orders from," I say plainly. A twinge in my side warns me that maybe I have said too much already. I had never thought that the knowledge of Veltuur was meant to be kept a secret, but I begin to wonder now.

"What do they want with the Guardians?" he asks next, pushing himself up on unsteady legs.

It is another fortunate moment where I am not forced to think of a lie.

"I do not know. Questions aren't really permitted when you have an order. You just do it, so that's what I'm doing."

He seems to mull this over, scrutinizing me with a pained expression. "And what makes you think I want to bring you with me? I could just leave you behind and find the Guardian on my own." Though his sentiment is strong, the words wobble in his throat.

Like the predator that I am, I find his weakness tantalizing. An open invitation to strike.

"What makes you think you have a choice? With one touch I could claim your life here and now and search for the Guardian without you."

As I say the words, I see his demeanor change back to the frantic distrust of a mouse. Pinching the bridge of my nose, I curse my instincts. I've just undone what little foundation I'd worked to build. This whole *friending him* business is going to be more difficult than I thought.

"I don't talk to people much," I admit.

I expect nervous laughter from him, but he's too frozen, like a deer before a wolf.

"What I meant is," I say, struggling to add a gentleness to my voice. "I need the Guardian to appease the Council, and you need the Guardian to save your sister. We can search by ourselves, but we might find a Guardian sooner if we helped each other."

"Y—you just said you didn't need to kill her anymore. Why would I still need to save my sister if you're no longer meant to kill her?" he says pointedly.

My eyes slam shut.

"You're lying! You do still want to kill her. You're just trying to lure me into a false sense of safety or whatever, so I'll lead you straight to her. Well, it—it's not happening!"

Caw-caw-caw! Caw-caw-caw!

I kick my heel at Crow, stopping its mocking laughter at once. But it has every right to mock me. The prince has seen right through me, and to no one's fault but my own. I couldn't even make one little lie believable.

From the middle of the woods, suddenly every shadow I see feels like it's watching us. My imagination plays tricks on me, branches becoming claws, leaves rustling like wings. I'm sure that if I can't convince him here and now then Veltuur will summon me back and I'll be forced to accept a fate far worse than the embarrassment of trying to befriend a mortal.

I can't give up now.

"Just because *my* contract has ended, doesn't mean your father can't request another Reaper to finish the job," I reason. "He threatened to do as much back at the palace when you fled with the princess. I reassured him I'd handle it, but now that I've been reassigned, it's only a matter of time before he finds out and decides to request another Reaper. I don't need to remind you how easily a Reaper will be able to find her. They'll faze right to her, and you won't be there to protect her this time."

"Any Reaper can?"

"No, not any—"

"Can you burst to her now, or whatever you called it? You know, poof: you turn us into smoke and then we can find where the bandits took her. Before another Reaper does."

I scowl. He's either really good at sniffing out lies and already knows that I can't actually faze to her, or he's just really lucky. "That's not how it works. A Reaper can only faze to the life they've been bound to by their contract. Since the princess is no longer mine, Crow can no longer faze us to her."

An acquiescent frown. Slowly the prince starts to nod. "I guess that's a good thing. It means you're telling the truth and Gem really isn't your target anymore."

"All I care about is locating this Guardian you spoke of so I can report back to Veltuur."

The prince goes silent, distance growing between us again. He draws inward, a glint of guilt dulling his normally striking brown irises, until he's riddled with dread. "If we found the Guardians—or even just *a* Guardian—and you told your Council about them or her —or whatever—what would happen next? Would they... would they kill her-him-it?"

I think for a moment, unsure what exactly to say to him. I'm not actually sure what will happen to the Guardians after I report them. All I know is what I've been instructed to do, and once I relay the information, the Guardians are no longer my problem.

"I don't know," I say finally. "Does it matter?"

"Yes! Of course it matters. I can't just condemn them to death like that." He buries his face in his hands, swearing. "Flightless bird! If you guys wound up killing them, it would be my fault and I'd be turned into a Reaper and I'd be taken to Veltuur and forced to murder people for the rest of my life!"

Scowling, I pop my hand onto my hip. "That's not how any of it works."

"You don't know that!"

Instead of meeting hysterics with hysterics, I stare at him, dawning my best *are-you-serious* expression.

"Oh," he says, shrinking. "I guess *you* kind of *do* know something about being turned into a Reaper."

"You think?" I say, flashing him a sardonic smile. When he doesn't reply, I think the conversation has ended, but when his watchful eyes fixate on me, I realize he's waiting for something more...for me to relive his worries, I guess. I'm not sure how to do that, exactly, but I've always found comfort in truths so I just tell him what I know. "The Council can't just *decide* who to kill. We rely on requests from mortals to determine who we claim for Veltuur and when. The rest of the deaths are a matter of fate: every living creature has a lifeline with a beginning and an end. When Veltuur senses the natural end of a lifeline, we act. I don't think the Council can just *decide* to kill the Guardians—" Except, I honestly suspect that somehow the normal rules of life and death might not apply to them in this case, though I don't know why— "As for you becoming a Reaper," I say, stifling a laugh. The thought of someone like *him* being a Reaper, without a dark or graceful bone in his body, is perhaps the most ludicrous thing I've ever imagined. "Mortals request the deaths of their friends, their mothers, their children all the time, and they remain in the realm of the living even after a Reaper has completed the task. The only way *you* could ever become a Reaper is if you actively, physically ended a life.

"And finally, for the record, it's not like how you describe it. You call it *murder,* and you act like it's so shameful to be a Reaper, but our role is important in maintaining the balance. Without Reapers, the realm of the living would be overrun with noxious untethered souls, your resources would deplete, and life would be meaningless. We aid people—*and* animals, *and* insects—in completing their journey. They die, Veltuur feeds, and then it breathes life back into Tayaraan. It's circular and necessary."

"It's necessary for you to kill children? Gem's barely even lived more than three years of her life. You cannot convince me that it's her time to go."

"Yeah, well, take it up with your father. He's the one that sent the request, not me. You can't blame me or the other Reapers for doing our jobs, but then not blame the mortals who made the request."

The prince opens his mouth to speak, but then blows through his lips instead. "You're right. My father is just as much a murderer; he's the one who wants Gem killed... I just wish... I don't understand *why* you do it. Sure, okay, it's a balance and the world would overflow with dead souls—although, I'm not actually sure that's true, but whatever —but why not just take a different life then? Gem's just a kid...and I'm sure you get sent to kill—*take* other kids too. Why do you have to follow the orders?"

My eyes snap wide. "Why do I obey Veltuur?"

He nods, clearly not understanding the way the underrealm works like I do. How could he? He doesn't know the terrors that await rogue Reapers, hasn't heard the horrific stories told from one Reaper to another about the few that decide to disobey the orders of Veltuur...

But he *has* heard the stories of the Reapers. To him, those are the cautionary tales that keep him in line.

"I'll make it simple for you to understand. You govern your actions out of fear of becoming a Reaper. Well, Reapers have things that they fear as well."

"They do?" he asks, utterly staggered. When all I do is shrug, he prods further. "Like what?"

"The Wraiths." I'm not meeting his eyes when I say it. Instead, I'm watching the shadows of the forest flicker, like uttering their name is a summons.

"What's a Wraith?"

They writhe again, and this time I think Acari sees it too, how the shadows of the tree branches along the forest floor almost look like spindly limbs climbing up from the earth, how the shadows tucked deep inside bushes almost seem to blink.

"Something terrible," I say, a chill prickling my spine.

Acari runs his fingers through his midnight locks, brushing the length of the hair back and revealing the shaved sides of his head. It also gives me a clearer view of his runes, the color of mint practically glowing from his tanned complexion. It strikes me odd that he has a full set of the common runes. A person of his age—my age, I'd guess —usually has to experience immense pain or struggle to earn the final markings, a line above either eyebrow. Although I've seen children as young as four with those runes, it seems unlikely that a prince, someone born and raised in prosperity and without a care in the world, would know anything about suffering.

Desperate to veer the conversation away from the shadows watching us, I bob my chin at him.

"How did you earn your final common runes?"

He startles, seeming more disturbed by the question than he was of the Wraiths.

"My mother and brother," he finally says, his features darkening more than they already are. It's like a shadow just cast itself over him. "They died recently. I guess it was one of the natural deaths you were talking about, or at least, not a death where someone sent a Reaper. They just came across some aacsi and died. Just like that. An accident. Wrong place, wrong time."

The aacsi—and all of the creatures who rely on the deaths of others to survive—are permitted by the underrealm to kill if it is for survival. Falcons are allowed to hunt. Wolves, granted permission to kill their prey. When the aacsi killed Acari's family, it was a necessary part of their survival and therefore it was already anticipated by the Councilspirits.

However, without a Reaper and a crow present, the souls of the fallen are just...lost. They linger in the mortal realm, wandering and shattered, never to be reborn again. At least, that's what we are told. I've never actually seen one of them with my own eyes, but I understand mine and Crow's roles in this well enough to know it is the truth.

But I say none of this to the prince. There's hardly any reassurance to be had from knowing his loved ones will never be reborn, that they are gone forever, especially since the memory of their deaths clearly still pains him.

I've seen mortals comfort each other during times like these, times of grief and immense sorrow. A pat on the back, some gentle words, and they let each other know that they're not alone and that they're cared for.

For the briefest moment, I'm tempted to try my hand at it. But even in my charade of friendliness, I wouldn't even remotely know how to do it correctly.

I change the subject instead. "Remind me your name, prince."

"Prince? I'm not sure I carry the title anymore," he says with a sad laugh. "My name is Acari. You're...my father called you Sinisa, right?"

I nod, admittedly surprised to find that he already knew my name. I guess one would remember the name of the Reaper who was going to execute their sister though.

"If we're going to work together," I say before the conversation veers down *that* path again. "I think you should tell me what happened to your sister."

12

BY ORDER OF THE KING

ACARI

I know I shouldn't trust her—she's a Reaper for crying out loud, a Reaper who I only met because she was originally sent to kill my sister. Then again, if she's not going to kill her anymore, maybe it's okay to trust her? Especially since she might be my only chance at getting Gem back. It's not like I, alone, can walk into a bandit camp and rescue her. I'll need some muscle, and what better muscle than a Reaper?

"Okay, so, after I hit you over the head—sorry about that, by the way—we took one of the royal steeds. I haven't really ridden a horse in a long time, not since one bucked me off when I was about ten and my brother just sat there laughing at me, so I was kind of terrified about riding one, on top of already being terrified about being chased by a Reaper, but..."

When I peer up from the rolling and twirling of my hands, I find Sinisa staring at me flatly.

Just because I believe she can help me, doesn't mean she doesn't still scare me. She has the power of death. *Death.* Who wouldn't be terrified of someone who all it took was a touch of the skin and, poof, you're dead? Further still, who would want to risk getting on that person's bad side?

"Right. You want me to get to the point. I can do that," I say, folding my hands over themselves to keep them under control. Sometimes it feels like they have free reign; so does my mouth. "Okay, so, we were running through the bandits when a group of forests showed up."

It's only when I finish the sentence that I hear my mistake. I start to correct it, but Sinisa waves me on, apparently already understanding my intent.

But it's here in the story that my recollection becomes fuzzy. I can recall one of the bandits stepping forward to examine Gem, but then nothing else. The memory turns gray and I'm left wading in the mist.

"They used daminila pollen on you," Sinisa says with a shrug. "It's not uncommon for people to fight its effects. I wouldn't be surprised if you fell asleep before the rest of your body did. You probably stumbled over to the tree on your own, while they stowed your sister away." A grin pops up on her face. "It was probably fairly amusing."

Despite knowing how rude it's considered to gawk at someone, I find myself doing it now. To be fair, she started the rudeness. I mean, who makes a joke like that...now?

"What?"

"Don't you know when it's appropriate or not to make a joke?"

Her smile disappears, a thoughtful frown replacing it. "No."

I smack my face. There are about a hundred or more masters of social etiquette in the kingdoms who would better suited to this task than I am, but since we're alone in the middle of nowhere, I'm afraid I might be all she has.

"Well," I say, straining to form a simple explanation that seems all too logical to me. "Here's a general rule for you: when someone's family is in danger, it's probably best to refrain from making a joke. People might find it...tasteless."

"Okay," she says, shrugging before turning around and calling behind her. "Crow!"

The bird spreads its black wings and sails through the fading light of day. I expect it to land on her shoulder like it did in the palace, but it instead chooses to land on the ground between us.

Resisting the urge to jump back, I instead grimace, disgusted and frightened by its proximity.

"Go to Veltuur. Talk with the other crows and see if any of them have heard of bandits in the area. Come back to me as soon as you know something." Before the bird can turn to smoke, she adds, "And if you *don't* learn anything by tomorrow morning, I expect you back regardless. Don't just leave me here like I know you want to."

It croaks, and for a second, I think it sounds like it is in protest, but it disappears seconds later.

"You call your bird Crow?" I ask.

She scowls, angling toward me. "What else would I call it?"

My hands dart up in protest, eager not to be on the receiving end of any of her negative emotions. "S-sorry. It's a great name. I was just asking because, well, I thought it might get crowfusing—*confusing* to always call it Crow."

At that, her head tilts, the brunette waves of her hair shifting in ripples. "Confusing how?"

Disbelief screams in the frenzy of my thoughts. I am having a conversation—a strange conversation, but a conversation nonetheless —with a Reaper. *A Reaper.* And not just *any* Reaper, but the one that was sent to murder my sister. I have to fight the urge to smack myself in the face.

Instead, I clear my throat. "I just meant when you and your Reaper friends are hanging out, talking about your crows or whatever it is you do, doesn't it get confusing to know which crow you're all referring to if the species is called a crow, but you also named your personal crow Crow?"

Though her expression remains blank, discovery and consideration flicker behind her gray eyes. A long silence settles in the space between my words and hers before she finally, simply replies, "No."

"Okay. It doesn't matter," I say, squinting, trying to erase the last few wasteful moments away. The longer we stand here, the farther away Gem could become. "We should get going. We need to find my sister—"

"That's why I sent Crow. It will return with information to help us track her. Until then, well, it will be dark soon. Although staying under the canopy of the woods at night sounds comforting to me, I'm guessing it is not your ideal sleep time arrangement. We should find an inn."

I glance over my shoulder at the bright circle of light, blocked by trees, plummeting below the horizon. We don't have much daylight left, and Sinisa is right: staying in the woods after dark would not be wise.

It's not that I want to wait any longer to go charging after Gem, but the truth is since the bandits that took her left without me seeing which direction they went, I don't have much of a choice but to rely on the insights of a bird.

"There is an inn back in Ngal. We could stay there until your crow returns."

Sinisa inclines her head, holding out her hand. "Lead the way, your highness."

I flinch, seeking shelter from the arm that swings over my head to scratch the back of my neck. "Uh, I think it's just Acari now."

She shrugs again. "Great. I'm bad with mortal formalities anyway."

"I can imagine," I utter.

"What was that?"

"Nothing," I blurt way more suspiciously than I intend. The nape of my neck suddenly itches again, and I angle my gaze downward to avoid her gaze. "Why don't we get going? You know what they say: from pillar to post!"

She scowls at me, but there's the faintest twitch at the corner of her mouth. "You're using that saying completely wrong, but you're right. We should go. Ngal isn't too far, and we can rest there while we wait for Crow to return. Come on."

The walk back isn't long, but by the time we finally enter the outskirts of the town, the sun is hanging low over the horizon. The pastel purple and blue hues of the sky soften the streets with growing shadows, the people making themselves scarce as they turn in for the night.

At least, that was my first impression.

But when I notice Sinisa clenching beside me, burrowing her head down like a horned magrok ready to charge, I realize I've misinterpreted everything. The people aren't fleeing because it's dusk. It's the night before the first of ten days of the Festival of Wings. They should be in the streets celebrating, lighting candles, singing the songs of flight and wind, adorning their altars with cardamom, saffron, lentils, and mustard seeds in hopes that this might be the year when the Divine Altúyur finally return to grace us with their presence.

Instead, they're abandoning their altars half-replenished. The songs they're singing, end mid-note when they see Sinisa and I approaching, but I know it's not me they're looking at. It's her.

"There's the inn," I say, trying to distract us both. I point over the buildings between us and the next road over, up at the dark, hickory wood and not one, but *two* smoking chimneys that are the landmark to the best inn in Ngal.

Silently, almost too quickly for me to perceive, Sinisa jerks her head, the only acknowledgment I get that she sees it too.

With her head still down, she leads us around the corner to the next street, before tucking herself into the shadows of the first alleyway we encounter.

"What are you doing?" I whisper, ducking into the small space beside her.

She shoves me back out into the streets. "I'll wait here while you get us a room."

I don't say anything for a moment. Self-consciously, I glance up and down the street to make sure no one is watching me, only to find that *many* people are. The people we scared away on our way here are beginning to reemerge from their homes, and when they search the street to see if they're safe, they spot me almost instantly.

I smile awkwardly before returning my attention to Sinisa. "I don't understand. Why are you hiding? Why is it important that you go obscene now?"

"*Unseen*," she corrects. "How did you ever earn your third language rune when you still constantly struggle with words?"

"Only when I'm nervous."

"Then you must *always* be nervous."

Sheepishly, I smile. "It's a curse. But you didn't answer my question."

"And you didn't do what I asked," she bites back, though despite her scowl, there's a playful tone in her words. "You saw the way the mortals reacted to me. There are no laws requiring that innkeepers do business with Reapers. I'm hiding to ensure that you're able to get us a room. Unless you'd rather sleep outside?"

Almost as if on command, a pesky stigree buzzes by my ear.

"Not at all," I say, swatting at the air by my ear, in front of my face, and eventually deciding just to flail around my entire body.

But before Sinisa can make fun of me or say anything else, I turn, practically running to the inn. Where there's *one* stigree, there's a dozen, and I have no interest in becoming the next piece of flesh that they decide to burrow into to lay their eggs.

The thought alone makes me shiver, despite walking through the door into the firelit parlor.

As I walk across the room, I draw the attention of most of the patrons socializing inside, and I can't help but wonder if the disguise I chose earlier is woefully terrible, or if they're staring for some other reason.

"Excuse me," I say when I find the innkeeper sitting among some of the patrons. "I-I'd like to rent a room, please?"

The woman flips her hair over her shoulder, using the motion to swing her hand onto her hip. She examines me exactly like my father does, making sure to showcase her lack of approval vividly in her expression. "We're full, kid. Get lost."

"Oh," I stutter, shrinking back and feeling just as childlike as I sound.

I turn around to leave, prepared to deliver the bad news to Sinisa, when I see the rows of key rings on the back wall behind the counter.

Most are empty, sure, but there's at least a half dozen just waiting for a guest.

It doesn't make sense to me why she would turn away a paying customer, why she would rather lose money than serve me. But then I catch sight of the dirt creased in my hands, the scuffs on my trousers, and when I reach up to check my hair, I find a twig ensnared in it. When Gem and I selected our new outfits, I made sure we looked like respectable commoners. But now, I likely look no more affluent than a beggar.

On any other day, I might've continued walking out the door, too embarrassed or nervous to ask again, but I guess after defying my father, outrunning—at least, temporarily—a Reaper, and facing off with bandits, standing up to this burly woman doesn't seem so scary.

"Aren't those keys for guests?" I ask, pointing at the wall before readdressing her.

She readjusts herself, shifting in her chair like all I've managed to do is irritate her more. It's enough to make me lose some of my gusto.

"I'm sorry. Please don't throw me out. I have rupees; I can pay." I grab the pouch from my waist. Although the sound is muted by the parchment and memory leaves, the distinct sound of silver tapping together chimes from my wears.

She eyes me warily a moment longer, but then abruptly stands, nearly knocking the table and a few glasses of drinks over. "All right, we'll see what we can do. What do you need?"

"Well," I say, lowering my voice when we reach the counter. "I have a friend waiting outside, and we kind of need to be discreet."

The woman's eyes light up before she winks at me. "Don't worry, kid. We know how to be discreet."

"Wait, no—I didn't mean like that. We're not—"

She winks again, the grin creeping up one side of her face, feline. "It's all right. No one will say a thing. Honest to the Divine Quetzi herself." She reaches back, grabbing one of the iron keys in hand. It's heavy when she smacks it into my palm. "Here, I'll give you a room just down that hallway. It's the only one on that side of the building, and the two of you should be able to sneak inside without anyone seeing you."

Instead of defending my honor, I tuck the key into my pocket and turn from the innkeeper, just in time to watch two of my father's royal guards enter the main entrance of the inn.

Completely and utterly the opposite of inconspicuous, I shuffle backward, slamming into the counter. The commotion draws the guards' attention, though since there was only four people in this room before they walked in, I'm pretty sure they would've spotted me regardless.

The first guard taps the base of his spear into the floor. "Acari Halaud, by order of the king, you are to return to the palace."

"My prince," the innkeeper gasps behind me.

I hear her drop to her knees in a deep bow, but I don't dare take my gaze off the guards. I guess this means my father isn't done with me. He must've sent his guards after me when I fled with Gem. Although I am a disgrace, I'm *his* disgrace, his only heir.

I can't let them take me back there. Not until I save Gem, and maybe not ever. But my back is quite literally up against a wall here, with no chance at escape. Unless Sinisa saw them enter. Maybe she's hatching some elaborate scheme to come rescue me.

The second I have the thought, I realize how ridiculous I sound. If anything, she likely abandoned me the second she spotted them. Sure, working together makes sense when two people share a common goal, but only if one of them isn't also being tailed and captured by royal guards. She doesn't need me. It's not like I know where I'm going anyway; she could easily find the Guardians without me.

At least my father didn't send Borgravid. Being arrested in front of him—*by* him—would be a lot more humiliating than by some random guards that I don't even recognize.

"Will you go willingly?" the second guard asks.

Seeing no other option, I hold my arms out. They each grab one, yanking me back out of the inn and into the night.

I tell myself not to look at the alley where I left her. I tell myself I already know the answer that will be waiting there: she's gone. She had no reason to stay. But I've always been a glutton for punishment, and so my eyes disobey me, desperately searching the shadows to see if she's still around.

To my dumfounded surprise, I spy her red tunic instantly.

"Sinisa," I breathe, and suddenly I'm reinvigorated with desperation. I can't go back to the palace. If I do, no one will save Gem. I'm her only hope, and my father will surely lock me up in the tower just to ensure I'm out of the way while he finishes the job.

My lungs burst. "Sinisa, help!"

AMONG MORTALS

SINISA

Concealed in the shadows, I wait until Acari has disappeared inside the inn before I casually lean back against one of the alleyway's walls. "I'm not sure you could be more obvious stalking us if you tried," I say, sighing at the figure tucked farther down the corridor.

Nerul's bloodred eyes gleam like rubies dazzling in the depths of a black lake. His skin is so pale, he blends in with the night like a ray of moonlight, but it's his mischievous grin, the canines that puncture his lips as they peel back that truly stand out.

"*Us*?" he asks, taking a step forward and basking in the night sky. "Therein lies your answer. There is no *us*. There is only you. I fear you may be taking this whole *befriend the king* thing a little too far."

"You know what I meant," I grumble, trying to make it sound like his assessment is ludicrous.

"I'm not so sure I do. You were sent back to Tayaraan to find the Guardians and report their whereabouts to the Council—or whatever information you gleaned. And yet, you've made no progress in your mission. Even now, rather than working through the night, instead I find you hiding in an alleyway, waiting for the prince to return so that you two can...what? Share a romantic evening together?"

"It's not—" I cut myself off. A cyclone churns inside me, but I ball my fists together as if my own bare hands are all that's keeping my frustration tethered. I know Nerul's tactics. I know he is only trying to get a rise out of me. I know giving into him will mean he's won, and I've lost.

But as much as I hate losing, my grip is slipping.

Before my irritation can unleash, I remind myself that Nerul—as infuriating as he is—is my superior, someone I am expected to obey and respect, someone who will one day soon be my colleague.

My eyes flutter with a forced bow of acquiescence. "I apologize for the misunderstanding, Shade Nerul, but I assure you that I have no romantic intentions with the prince."

"Pray tell then, why are the two of you back in Ngal instead of seeking the Guardians?"

Unable to control my nostrils flaring, I turn my head away, and instead focus on the celebrations carrying on in the street.

It's not often I'm in Tayaraan long enough to witness the festivities preluding the Festival of Wings. My duty is to perform my task and return to Veltuur, so it's rare I am ever around long enough to actually *see* the celebrations unfolding.

Tonight is mild compared to what is to come, but there are still a few citizens dazzling in outfits of charms and gemstones, their masks vibrant with red and yellow and blue feathers. Some people finish decorating the altars they created with a different bird figurine, color of fabric, or feather, to denote one of the eight Divine Altúyur, in hopes of earning their blessing for the year:

The macaw for intellect.

The lorikeet for bravery.

The quetzal for integrity.

The peacock for inspiration.

The sungem for memory.

The dove for peace.

The owl for fate.

The aracari for compassion.

It's no surprise that for every two altars I spy one of them is dedicated to the Divine Iracara. For a people terrified of becoming Reapers, compassion is one of their most coveted virtues. To them, compassion is what Reapers lack.

I'm not so sure that's true.

With a deep breath, I explain myself to Nerul.

"The prince encountered daminila pollen earlier in the day and is still suffering its side effects. As he is my only lead to finding the Guardians, I need him level-headed, and so I suggested we rest in Ngal while we await word from Crow about the whereabouts of his sister—whom he lost to a group of bandits just outside of town. Since the prince would likely not have given me the information I needed if I didn't first help him retrieve the girl, and since I'd like to keep her close by for when all of this is over, I decided helping him retrieve her —albeit time-consuming—is necessary.

"Secondly, I am *not* hiding. I was creating an opportunity for a conversation with you so I could tell you to be more careful with how closely you're following me. If the prince sees you, he'll start to think something is wrong, and if that happens, he might not tell me what he knows, and then you can explain to the Council how we lost their lead."

"Watch your tone, Reaper Sinisa," Nerul warns, his voice as cool as the night. The crow on his shoulder squawks at me too, like even it holds authority over me. Nerul reaches up to stroke the creature's beak, his robes falling past his elbow to reveal the dark veins beneath his skin. "No one enjoys being under surveillance, but it is a necessary precaution, and one you would do well to accept."

"It doesn't bother me. I'm not doing anything wrong." Although true, the words sound like a lie, even to me. "I just don't want someone else ruining my mission."

"And I commit to doing no such thing. If you are as devoted to Veltuur as you say you are, then I will loosen my leash, so to speak, and allow you to complete the task you've been delegated. But take heed. Not many Reapers are granted extended visits in Tayaraan. There is reason for that."

I'd ask him why, but I know he wouldn't answer me. It might also make me sound like I'm focusing on the wrong thing here, and thus undo the ounce of trust I just received from him.

"Of course, Shade Nerul. I have no desire to make this take longer than necessary."

"Very well." Nerul sweeps his arm out, his crow hopping to his upturned hand as he steps out of the alley.

Of the denizens remaining outside, almost all share a collective shriek at the smoke collecting around him, at the death that seems to live beneath his skin.

Before he is consumed in coalescing shadows, he calls over his shoulder and I can only just barely see his nose and red eyes from beneath his hood. "If you're committed to haste, I'd suggest checking on your prince. It seems the royal guard are intent on intervention."

"What?" I say, breaking for the street.

Just as Nerul disappears, I fill the space where he was standing, the black clouds clearing around me, the dry stench of moss and woods lingering in the air. But through the clearing, I see the guards he spoke of, each of them holding on to one of Acari's arms and steering him out of the inn.

Our eyes lock, and for the briefest moment, I have to consider whether rescuing him is worth it. With him out of the way, killing his sister will be immensely easier. The only problem is I can't kill her until I find her, I can't find her until Crow returns, and even once he does, I'm not allowed to claim her soul until the prince tells me what I need to know about the Guardians.

But even before I reach my inevitable conclusion, Acari shouts my name.

"Sinisa, help!"

There's something about his desperation that ignites me. There's something familiar about seeing him dragged against his will, and if I never knew this about myself before, I know it now that I don't believe anyone should be forced to do something they don't want to do.

This prince does not want to be taken back to his home, and right now he is calling on me to intervene.

I'm sprinting before I even notice it, leaving behind the questions I have about why I feel so compelled to help this boy when I could just as easily avoid the trouble.

The guards struggle against his squirming. One of them takes both his arms while the other unlatches one of the carriage doors. They push and pull him forward, trying to force him into the vehicle, and I know if I don't reach them before he's inside that he will likely be gone. I know men like the king. If he's sent for him, it is to teach him a lesson, one that the prince will likely be "learning" for a long time. He will be imprisoned at the palace, or at the very least forbidden from fulfilling his quest.

Fortunately, I don't have to worry about any of that though, and neither does the prince. In strides, I cut the distance between us like a hawk diving after its prey. The guards notice me one at a time, stiffening at the sight of me, a Reaper, charging full speed for them.

The one holding Acari releases him instantly. In one great leap, he takes shelter behind the carriage, a terrified moan escaping him. The other guard freezes, door still in hand, eyes as wide and white as the moon.

Stumbling forward, Acari scrambles as far away from them as he can until we are side-by-side. I ignore his grateful yet bewildered gape, sensing his questions but uninterested in answering them.

"You will tell your king that he is no one's to claim," I bark.

The guard before me remains motionless aside from a slight quiver to his bones, while the guard hiding behind the carriage pokes his head out from behind the wheel.

"M-my apologies, R-Reaper. But the king commanded—"

"I don't care what your king commanded. Is he mightier and scarier than a Reaper?" When the guard shrinks back from the challenge burning in my eyes, I know I've made my point. "The prince will return when he decides to return—*if* he decides to return. And until then, the king won't send anyone else after him, or so help me, I will kill each and every one of them. Do I make myself clear?"

"Y-yes."

"Good. Now, be gone."

I flick my wrist, and a tuft of black smoke puffs from my fingertips. The guard behind the carriage yelps, but to his credit, instead of fleeing and leaving his comrade, he steps from around the back wheel just enough to grab the other guard by the shoulders and pull him away. The jerking motion seems to be enough to snap the other guard back to himself, and together they scramble into the carriage. There's a crack of a whip before the horse bellows and bolts down the road.

Left standing in the dust, Acari coughs into his hand. When his lungs are cleared, he eyes me warily. "Th-thank you. I wasn't sure you'd help—not to sound mean or anything. I just wasn't sure a Reaper—I mean, someone like you—would...you know?"

As I stand there watching the carriage rock from side to side as it barrels down the cobblestone road, I'm not sure if I'm relishing in my victory or just avoiding the prince's unspoken question. There's a very logical, rational explanation for why I helped him, but I'm not so sure it alone is why I did. I can't remember ever making a decision like that before, a choice between helping someone or standing idly by. Then again, even though I can't remember one, I can *feel* it, a flash of a memory that I can't quite piece together, and I can't help but wonder if this has something to do with Nerul's warning. He said there was a reason Reapers weren't allowed to stay in Tayaraan too long. Maybe it has something to do with our memories.

"Let's just get to our rooms," I say, feeling strangely vulnerable all of a sudden in the middle of the street. I turn back around, to start making my way to the inn entrance, but I stop short when I see him running a hand through his hair. "What is it?"

"Uh, well, you said *rooms*. But, for all intensive purposes, I just got us the one room. It cost less, and I just figured we'd want to stay close,

so that once your crow returns, we could leave as quickly as possible
—what? Why are you smiling?"

My lopsided grin twitches higher. For a moment, I consider
telling him he's confused his words yet again, but I find it too
amusing to risk making him correct the habit.

"Nothing," I say with a breathy laugh. "Just lead the way."

14

BETTER LEFT FORGOTTEN

ACARI

My cheeks burn red when I push the door open and find that the patrons inside are still staring at the main entrance. I swing a hand over my head to scratch my neck and wave awkwardly with the other. "Hello again. Looks like I'll be staying here after all."

"Blessed by the Divine Lorik himself," the innkeeper says, something between feral hunger and excited wonderment burgeoning in her eyes. She stands from her table to greet me and makes it two full steps before staggering still, her expression collapsing.

The screeching sound of a chair grinding against the wood floor causes me to wince, and a man grunts from behind the innkeeper. "Unless this is official business, *she's* not welcome here."

The innkeeper nods, backing away from me as the Reaper steps beside me.

From the corner of my eye, I see Sinisa smile. But it's not the polite kind of smile a guest greets a host with. It's the kind of smile that reminds me of a poisonous flower, something that looks so beautiful but is utterly deadly.

"Oh, I'm here for business," she says.

My hands fly up when the color drains from their faces. "She doesn't mean like that. We're on a quest, of sorts. She's not here to kill anyone. We just need a room to stay for a few hours until her crow returns with information from Veltuur about where we can find my sister."

Everyone in the group blinks at me like I've just grown a second head, and then a third. I can't say I blame them. The statement that just came out of my mouth isn't something I *ever* thought I'd say. I'm working alongside a *Reaper*.

After silence lingers between our two groups for a moment, the man standing—the one who I'm suddenly realizing is as thick-skinned and bulky as a magrok—strides over to us in two steps. He towers above us both so high that he has to crane his neck to look down at us. I quake so thoroughly that the table beside me practically starts rocking. Sinisa, on the other hand, doesn't even budge. She stands her ground, one hand on her hip, completely immersed in his shadow.

"If you're not here to kill someone, then you need to leave before there's trouble."

I make for the door without further protest. No accommodation is worth a quarrel with a man built like a Ghamayan Mountain and a Reaper.

But as I twist around, I see the black tendrils of magic curling just beneath Sinisa's fingertips.

"Sinisa," I say cautiously, unsure where I find the confidence to say anything. "Please don't—"

But she either doesn't hear me, or like everyone else in my life, she has already perfected the art of ignoring me. "Come any closer and we'll see what kind of trouble there is."

Pinching the brim of my nose, I spin back around. When I look past the mountain of flesh in front of me, red and angry, I find the innkeeper clutching her bosom, staring at us in horror.

"Look," I say, trying to channel every lesson I ever received on debating with foreign dignitaries. "We don't want any trouble, despite what she says. We just need a room while we wait. You won't even know we're here, and we'll be gone by sunset. Please."

I lean into the word like I'm reaching out to Sinisa as she's dangling over a cliff. *Take my hand. Help me, help you.*

"Fine. One night."

Before the innkeeper can change her mind, or before her brutish friend can decide to take matters into his own hands, I motion Sinisa to the hallway behind us where we find our room.

If I thought I'd find comfort from being behind the closed door, I am sadly mistaken. Trapped inside a locked room with a Reaper manages to have the opposite effect. Instantly, I am on edge. I don't know where to walk, whether I should sit on the bed or stand, how to cross my arms—or if they should be kept relaxed at my sides. Mostly though, I don't know how I'm going to pass the time while we wait for news from her crow.

Sinisa takes soft, timid steps around the room, taking everything in. Her gaze falls to the hearth, then floats to the bed, the candlestick beside it, and finally to the window. She contains her astonishment, if only barely, and I can't help but wonder what has her so impressed. Everything in here is made out of wood—and none of impressive quality. There's dust on the hearth, and the table in the center of the room shakes with each footstep.

"I've never stayed in an inn before," she breathes almost inaudibly. But when she notices me staring, her expression hardens. "You should rest for the journey ahead. The bed is yours."

"I—uh..." I find myself intrigued by her awe, but aware of her bristling, I don't want to pry. "Thanks, but I don't think I'll be doing much sleeping."

Almost on cue, a shiny, black spider creeps from the bedpost to the corner of the room. I bump into the door with a thud. Yep, definitely won't be sleeping tonight. Not with that thing sharing a room with us.

"Why not?" she asks.

Maybe I'm already used to her lack of manners and improper socializing etiquette, or maybe I'm just exhausted, but I'm not offended by her tone. "Because my sister almost died today, and then, while I'm in the middle of rescuing her, she is kidnapped by bandits, and I'm worded—*worried* about what will happen to her."

Assessing me with eyes as gray as stone, Sinisa says flatly, "Well, at least you know they're not going to kill her. Otherwise they would become Reapers too, and that's a fate no one chooses."

There's sadness in her words, but I'm not sure why. From everything I've seen so far, it doesn't seem like she's unhappy being a Reaper.

"Is it not what you wanted?" I hear myself asking, wishing I knew how to keep my mouth shut instead. I'm pretty sure if my father was here—and if he cared anything about hurting a Reaper's feelings—he'd tell me this is exactly the kind of question you *don't* ask someone.

To my surprise though, she isn't offended. The question actually almost seems welcomed. And because I tend to put my foot in my mouth so often, it's a welcome change.

"Who knows. I have no memory of what I wanted before becoming a Reaper," she answers plainly. There is no feeling behind her words whatsoever. No remorse, no doubt, no anger. It's as if she just told me the color of the sun or sky.

"You what? Really? How can you not remember?"

She shrugs. "I just don't. It's like I was born anew the day I was initiated."

I blink, mulling over the information. Although it seems like common knowledge to her, this is something I've never heard before and I doubt many people know.

"But...why not?" I ask finally. "How—why would you lose your memories? Why would that be part of your initiation?"

The more I think about it though, the more it actually does start to make sense. Without their memories, Reapers would be completely disconnected from their past lives. They'd have no friends or family, absolutely nothing to connect them to the mortals they were sent to kill. Killing a human would be just like killing a hog or even a stigree; it would mean nothing. The death would be weightless because they wouldn't be able to see their sister's face in the person they killed, let alone be able to sympathize with the families they were taking these people from.

Without their memories, they'd become perfect assassins.

"I don't know," she answers, sounding bored. "Perhaps it's just how Veltuur works. An exchange or something."

I nod, pulling a chair away from the small table. Before I can bring myself to sit down though, I search underneath it for more spiders like the one in the corner of the room. When I find none, I position it so that I can keep one eye on the spider in the corner while still being able to face Sinisa.

Only, my gaze doesn't settle on her or the spider. Instead, I can't stop myself from staring at the pouch resting against my leg.

"Would you want to remember if you could?" I ask her, wiggling the pouch free and setting it on the table. Idly, I twirl the drawstrings around my fingers, waiting for an answer as the subtly, earthy aroma of the memory tree's leaves fills the space between me and my restless fingers.

"Maybe. I guess it would be interesting."

She doesn't seem to notice that I'm suggesting it is an actual possibility. She says it the way I say something that, when given the opportunity, I back out of. Like when I told my mother that I'd think about accompanying them to the ball, but then when the day finally came, I said no, just like I always knew I would.

There's a moment when I realize I could just let all of this talk about reliving the past go, and Sinisa wouldn't know the difference. I could keep the memory leaves to myself and use them for seeing my family in the moments when it was hardest to be without them. After all, since I don't think I'll be going back to the palace any time soon, this batch of memory leaves is all I'll have for a long, *long* while.

Then again, the thought of withholding an opportunity for her to be able to learn about her past doesn't sit well with me.

"It wasn't a hypothetical question," I say finally. "If you really wanted to know, you could. I have some—well, there's this tree; it's sort of forbidden? It's at the palace, but before I left, I sort of... grabbed some of its leaves and—"

"*You* stole something that was forbidden?" she asked, bemused.

My head sinks into my shoulders, and my smile is guilty. "Maybe? I know. I shouldn't have. I mean, the tree is basically extinct, and I know it's not a toy to be digging into memories but..." When the topic becomes too painful, I let my words fade out, and I redirect the conversation to the possibility I'm presenting her. "The leaves help people recall things, so, if you really *are* interested, then you could try some. And it's totally safe. I promise. I'm not trying to like poison you or anything."

Sinisa jerks back, looking at me like I'm the most ridiculous and insane and goofy person she knows. I may be all of those things, come to think of it.

"Which, I'm realizing now sounds completely auspicious—sorry. Um... *suspicious.* I just mean that I've done it before, so I know what it's like."

Something about the way she's staring at me, like she's analyzing every single muscle in my face as it shifts, makes me stop talking. I swallow what little saliva is left in my mouth, but it goes down like I've just grabbed one of the cold coals from the hearth and swallowed it instead.

"Why did you take some of the memory leaves?" Sinisa asks.

She inches closer, still scrutinizing me like I'm a trellis and she's trying to figure out the best way to climb up me—not that she's thinking about climbing me, not in *that* way or anything, she's just—

"Why would a prince..." she continues but stops short with a slow dawning of recognition. It takes her awhile to say anything more, to tell me what realization she came across, and I'm dying to know if she's right. I never find out though. Instead, Sinisa returns to my original question. "Sure. Why not? It might be awhile before we hear from Crow. I will try the memory leaves. Just tell me how they work."

There's a moment where I'm almost tempted to ask her what made her decide, but the exciting prospect of helping her uncover her past, and subsequently learning more about her myself, is too much to ignore.

"It's simple. I make a tea and you drink from it." I glance at the fireplace, the dry logs and kindling stacked inside beneath a charred iron pot. "We can't make tea without boiled water though, and we can't boil water without a fire—"

"Then make a fire," she says with a flick of her wrist, flinging herself back onto the bed.

"I—I don't know how." The only fire I can muster is the one burning in my cheeks.

Sinisa props herself up on her elbows. "Don't they teach princes anything?"

With another guilty grin, I shake my head. It's true that growing up as royalty means I have limited life experiences in some ways—okay, *many* ways. It's true that I was never taught how to cook a meal, how to make anything useful like clothes or weapons, and I was certainly never shown how to build a fire.

I don't bother telling her all of the things I *was* taught though: how to manage the royal bank, how to speak to foreign dignitaries in all of the main languages of the lands, how to dance the four kingdoms', um, dances. I don't tell her any of this because none of it will really help us right now anyway. The fact of the matter is that I was never meant to leave the palace unless accompanied by the royal guard, my servants, and my handmaiden...

Hayliel...

It's the first time I've thought about her all day, and I'm not sure why that particular thought brings with it so much heartache. It's probably for the best that she won't be accompanying me around the realm as my handmaiden, forced to wait on my every whim while I socialize, fraternize, and selectinize a queen to rule by my side.

I never wanted that life and I certainly never wanted to drag Hayliel around for it all.

If anything, I just wanted...wanted...I know I shouldn't even think it, but I guess I'm not a future king anymore, and I'm certainly no longer the Prince of Oakfall, so what does it really matter if I dare think what I truly feel?

All I wanted was, well, *her*. To be with Hayliel.

And I guess that's why it hurts, because even though we could've never *been* together, at least we would've *been* together, as friends. And now, I'm not sure I'll even ever see her again.

With a growl, Sinisa swings her legs back over the side of the bed and charges by me to rearrange the logs in the former fire's ashes. And honestly, I'm grateful for the wake she creates, the one that jostles me from my own mind; I can get lost in there for hours if I'm not careful.

I take a seat at the edge of the bed and watch, trying to learn anything that might actually prove useful now that I'm going to live the rest of my days as a commoner. Before I can see much though, sparks have already caught the kindling.

As warmth fills the room, I start to settle back against the pillow when I remember the spider and I bolt up straight instead and practically hop back to the table. The pouch of memory leaves shifts, reminding me that I can make myself useful while Sinisa gets the flames going.

There is one mug in the center of the circular table. I blow into it, a cloud of dust pluming back into my face. When I start coughing, Sinisa looks back at me, snorts the briefest of laughs, and turns back to the fire. It's odd to me how human she can seem in some moments. Strange, yes. But that could be said about anyone who comes from a different land with different customs.

I can't help but wonder what she was like before she was a Reaper.

"How long have you been...uh...Reaping?"

Using an iron rod she finds nearby, Sinisa pokes the embers around, her eyes trained on the task before her. "Three years, I think."

My eyes pop wide. I'm glad she's not looking at me because I have no control over my face. "That...can't be. You're not even that old now. What were you, like...like—"

"Thirteen."

My stomach plummets. I know how people become Reapers. Take a life and Veltuur claims you as their servant. I guess I just always imagined them as hardened criminals, people with a lifelong darkness that one day plummeted when they finally snapped and killed someone. I mean, sure, I have also heard that sometimes Reapers are created out of accident. All it takes is one slight misstep onto a bug you didn't see on the path, or like that spider in the corner of the room. If it crawled onto the bed in the middle of the night while I was sleeping and I rolled on top of it and squished it, I'd be suffocated in a cloud of ash and then disappear until one day I came back as a Reaper.

So, at thirteen years old, I can only imagine that her fate was accidental. It had to be. Maybe she swatted a bee or something.

I almost ask her again how she became a Reaper, but considering she's already told me she doesn't remember, I manage to bite my tongue and wait for the memory tea to tell us the rest.

Not wanting to waste another second, I take the pot outside to the spigot and fill it with water.

By the time I come back in, Sinisa is standing on the bed, staring at the spider.

"What are you doing?" I ask, lugging the heavy pot over to the fire. I set it into the circular holder with a slosh, a splash of water sizzling in the fire below.

Staring at the black creature, she cocks her head. "You don't like spiders. Why?"

My chin wrinkles. "I just don't. They're...frightening. The way they can kill you with one bite, it creeps me out."

Not dissimilar to the way Reapers kill with just one touch, I catch myself thinking.

"Very few can do that," she says, casting me a look over her shoulder.

"So?" I say in defense, retrieving the pouch of leaves from the table and carrying them to the pot. "Even if it's only one in a hundred, that's still a big chance and I'd rather not die. I think that's a fairly normal desire in life: not to die."

Rolling her eyes, she turns back to the spider, hand raising. The shadow it casts looms over the spider like a dark cloud. "Would you like me to kill it for you then? So you can stop worrying about it?"

I almost spill the tea leaves everywhere at the suggestion. "What? No! Don't!"

Her hand stills. "Why not?"

I approach the bed, ready to tug her away, but we both recoil when black smoke spirals from her hands at my proximity. Instead, I clear my throat, backing away steadily, slow enough that I catch her glaring down at her hand before I turn back to the pot. I pluck a leaf from the pouch and pinch it between my fingers into the water. Behind me, the mattress creaks and squeaks, and Sinisa plops down away from the spider to sit on the bed.

When the tea starts to boil, I pour enough into the cup to fill it halfway. The memory leaves can last a long time and provide many memories, if prepared correctly and used sparingly. The trick is not to use too much but also not to dilute the dose more than necessary. I've kind of mastered it after these last few weeks. Actually, maybe that isn't something I should be so proud of.

Rather than handing the cup to her directly and risking evoking her dark power again, I slide it across the table. "It's ready when you are."

Sinisa approaches the table and cup like a snake getting ready to coil around its prey, as if she thinks if she doesn't strike first, it might attack her. It's the first time I realize how terrifying the position she's in must be—so much for being named after the Divine Altúyur of compassion, I hadn't even once considered what she might be going through right now. Every time I drink the memory tea, I at least know the ghosts that haunt me and am willingly welcoming them back. But she is going in blind. She has no idea what the memory tea will unlock for her.

She brings the mug up to her mouth, steam rising to her nose.

"You don't have to do this if you don't want to—"

"I want to," she says, and she sounds so unequivocally sure that I'm actually jealous. If only I could ever make choices so easily.

"Well then, all you do now is focus on a memory from before."

Her eyes flick up from the mug. "I don't *have* any memories from before. Isn't that the whole point of this?"

"Oh, right." My hands find their familiar place intertwined before my face as I draw out a thoughtful but utterly useless, "Uh. So, it doesn't have to be a full memory. It can be anything. Like if there's a scent you remember, or a song, or a name, an object. Something like that."

"I remember blood," she says, and my skin runs cold.

"Oh. Okay, well, that might be—"

Before I can finish, she dumps the mug back into her throat. In one great gulp, she drains the tea and bangs the cup onto the wooden table.

From experience, I know that the tea doesn't take long to work. Once the warmth reaches her stomach, the memory will come to life around her. She will be transported to her past, and considering this is her first time, she might even believe it's real.

It's entirely possible that we should've both been more afraid of what she was about to unlock.

Shivering, like the room is made from ice, I sink back against the wall, trying to get as far away from her as possible. If blood is her only memory, whatever she's about to experience is likely to be hostile...

I should've warned her more, should've given her some tips on how to remain grounded in the midst of an illusion.

Distance hollows her features, the tea snatching her away.

I watch her with cautious curiosity, like a field mouse eyeing whatever it is that field mice eye from their safe distance away so that they aren't devoured by a fox. I open my mouth, prepared to say something she might find helpful, but before I can, she collapses.

I take a step toward her, thinking the worst. I've never heard of anyone having an allergic reaction to the memory tree leaves, but I've also not heard many stories of people using them. The tree has been under protection for centuries.

"Sinisa? Are you o—"

"No. No-no-no-no." Writhing on the floor, Sinisa wails, her voice years younger than before.

She tries crawling backward, away from something horrific that I can't see but I know is all too real to her. Tears ripple down her cheeks like rivers as her body stops abruptly. She stares at her leg, kicking it relentlessly, trying to free it from a grip that is a ghost to me.

"Let go of me! Let go!" she sobs, her voice harsh.

Something's not right. Something can't be right. She's thirteen years old. This memory should be one of fondness, one of playing with other children, and doing chores, not of...*this*. No child should endure *this*.

Especially not a second time over.

My knees crash to the floor beside her, my mouth almost pressed against her ear. "It's not real. It's just a memory."

The sobs grow more frantic, her fingers grasping desperately for the fabric around her legs. But when they lose their grip, she loses her resolve. She whimpers as her hands find a new place to latch onto, digging into the floorboards, no longer looking forward, but instead, as far away as she can see.

When I realize what I'm witnessing, my hands fly to her shoulders, prepared to shake her free from the illusion plaguing her mind. "Sinisa! Sinisa, wake up! It's not real! It's not real! It's just a memory. I-it's not happening again. You're safe. You're..."

I find fault in everything I say, switching directions only to find another dead end. It *is* real. I mean, it did happen. All of what she's going through right now, she's already been through, and I can't do anything to help her. I can't do anything to undo it because she's reliving it all again.

And if it wasn't for me, she would've never even known. She would've never had to go through this violation ever again.

It's all my fault.

I reach out to her again, this time to take her cheeks into my hands, but I stop short. Poison oozes from her skin when I get too close, and it sends me scuttling backward across the floor like a scared child. I rock myself against the wall, helpless to what I'm watching. I keep looking over her, like I'll see the man on top of her, hoping I might be able to tackle him away and end all of this.

But all I see is air. No one can stop what's happening.

Except, that's not entirely true.

Suddenly, Sinisa's hand clenches onto something cylindrical, though all I see is air. I perk up just as she swings whatever down into whoever was atop her. Cheering her on, I inch closer, eager to see her triumph.

Sinisa shuffles to her feet, sniffling but with a wildfire burning in her eyes. Her entire body shaking, her breathing rapid, she releases a guttural battle cry and lunges forward atop her assailant. The invisible object in her hand strikes again and again, her empty fist crashing into the floor five times in total before slowing, panting on hands and knees. But she's not done. Her eyes flick up like she sees a sudden movement and she delivers one final blow, seeming to leave her weapon behind inside her target before she scrambles back, hugging her knees to her chest as her breath grows ragged again.

I don't need to see the memory to know that she is covered in blood.

I don't need to see the memory to know that Sinisa's only crime was wanting to protect herself.

15

SINISTER MEMORIES
SINISA

I stand from the pool of blood I am sitting in just as it disappears, replaced by a room I don't recognize. Not at first. I am too distracted, left haunted by the encounter. Though he is dead, though his body has somehow vanished, I still feel the rough, unwanted grasp of his hands on me.

Trembling, I am frozen solid despite the warmth from the fire. It is like I am a ghost, here but somewhere else.

It's not until I see Acari perched nearby, gaping at me with remorse, that I remember where I am and what just happened. Self-consciously, my hands fly to cover my exposed body, only to find that I am clothed in a red tunic. *My* red tunic. The clothes of a Reaper. I find the comfort I need in that thought. I am a Reaper, and that was nothing more than a memory. A nightmare. Something I was meant to have left behind.

My throat is dry, and my cackles are raised. I'm ready to maul the next person that utters one wrong word in my direction. There's a rawness in my chest that can't be undone, like my heart has been ripped clean out of me. No, wait. Perhaps the opposite. Retrieving that memory has set my body ablaze with emotion. I want to scream and cry. I want to be alone and I want to be comforted. I am terrified and brave, enraged and relieved, proud and ashamed.

And all of these things are familiar, like they belonged to me before I became who I am, before I was reborn.

I look down at my hands as if seeing them for the first time. Darkness pools at my fingertips, lurking like deadly poison beneath my skin. But for the first time in three years, I don't feel so dead.

By the time I look up, Acari has inched even closer. "I'm—I'm so sorry. I didn't know—I should've warned you—I couldn't…"

"It's not your fault," I bite out, anger rising within me. I shouldn't be the one comforting him. He didn't just experience the worst night of his life. "You should get some rest. When Crow returns, we should be ready to head out as soon as possible."

"But you—" Acari holds out his hands, stuck there for a moment. When he swallows though, closing his eyes, he rotates his shaking hands in an attempt at composing himself. "Are you all right?"

It is a dumb question and I'm tempted to tell him as much. I don't know exactly how the tea he gave me works, so I don't know if he actually *saw* it all or what, but I know he knows enough to realize I am not okay. Far from it. *That* had been my life, every week, sometimes every night, for *years*. It had taken everything in me to make it stop and I knew the consequences. Being a Reaper was far more preferable than having to endure another second of that man's unwanted glances and grazes.

It still is.

But having the memory of it fresh in my mind is dizzying. It's like I'm thirteen again, and I'm back in the orphanage, back in my bed, shaking, wondering if he will be coming for me tonight or if he'll take one of the other girls.

I *know* he's dead, otherwise the Wraiths wouldn't have taken me to Veltuur, but I can't shake the feeling that he is still alive, waiting to take me again, as he had so many times before.

I'd kill him again if I could.

Sharply, I stand and stride to the fire, staring into it before Acari can see the pools of tears held at bay only by my eyelashes.

I sharpen the edge of my voice like steel and cut through the uncomfortable silence. "I am fine. You should rest."

"I don't think I can..."

I know what he's about to say, but I can't stomach to hear it. Instead, I pretend like he's talking about something other than my past.

With a stomp of my boot, I spin around. I storm over back across the room and stomp onto the bed, ignoring the dried mud crumbling from my boots onto the flannel blanket and instead focus on the black creature nested in the corner where the ceiling meets the walls.

"I didn't mean—" Acari pleads, but he is too late.

I know who I am.

I am not some weak, little child.

I am a Reaper.

All it would take is a simple touch and this spider would end. But I don't want to just touch it. There's too many years of anguish and rage built up inside me, and I only got to kill my abuser once for it.

Instead, I ball my hand into a first and smash the spider against the wall.

Without Crow there to act as the conduit between here and Veltuur, the soul of the spider dissolves into the ether.

Instantly, shadows writhe in the room in protest. Veltuur does not like when a life is claimed without its permission or instruction, but I do not care. Let the Wraiths tell the Council. Let them summon me and punish me for an eternity. See if I care.

When the ripples of darkness settle, and I am *not* snatched back to Veltuur, I jump down from the bed to resume my gazing at the fire. Numbly, I realize I've just completed my five thousandth kill. I doubt it counts, but still. I expected it to feel more victorious.

Acari argues no more. Instead, he shuffles onto the bed in complete silence and rolls onto his side once he's under the covers. Despite his earlier assumptions that sleep would deny him tonight, he succumbs to it almost instantly. There's so much on my mind that I don't even care. In fact, I am grateful for the solitude in the dying dimness of the fire's glow. Being alone is comforting, or at least it always had been, ever since my initiation. Now I can't help but wonder what I preferred before. Though some things have come back, my past still feels largely unclear.

While I was in the memory, I felt like a completely different person, someone wide-eyed and excitable. Of course, some things remained the same between us: I am still as determined as ever, and my sense of humor likely always was and always will be an acquired taste, but there was something tragic about reliving my past self, outside of the experience I was dropped into, and that was realizing that the girl I used to be is dead. I never took the time to mourn her; I never really thought to. But I do now. In my own way, I guess. I play with my power, calling the black spirals forth into a sphere of black flames mimicking the fire in front of me, just to send them back beneath my skin again.

This darkness, I fear, has always been inside me. That memory dredged up a whole lot more than just one terrible night. Not individual memories, just mostly the things I was thinking about when I killed that man. I thought about how if my parents had never died, I would've never been sent to the orphanage and none of this would've happened. I thought about the friends I was leaving behind, about a boy I had a crush on.

I bring forth my black power, swirling it around in my hands. It's no wonder Veltuur strips Reapers of their pasts. Now that I have all these memories, I am tempted to find my old friends, to sink my teeth into pears and apples and peaches again, to fall in love.

But a Reaper can't do any of those things. My power will leave fruit rotten in my hands. It makes everyone afraid of me, and even if someone wasn't, getting too close would only hurt the people we care about.

I was better off without my memories.

Caw.

"Crow!" I say, spinning around to find the bird perched on the backside of one of the rickety chairs. It couldn't have been better timing. I need to get out of this inn. I need to distract myself from all of these emotions and remind myself what is really important: restoring my reputation with the Council and becoming a Shade.

"What did you find?"

Before it can answer, I shake my head, remembering how the game works with it. Direct commands only. "Blink once if you know the whereabouts of the bandits, twice if you don't."

Crow blinks, one time. I wait for a second motion, just to be sure, but when it doesn't come, I sigh in relief.

I kick the bed and Acari stirs.

"Come on," I say with a jerk of my head. "Crow is going to take us to the bandits. It knows where to find your sister."

16

CUDDLY AS A FIREFUR

SINISA

Neither of us take long to vacate the room as we both have very little in the way of belongings, but I watch skeptically as Acari retrieves the pouch of memory leaves from the table. I hate to admit it, but part of me is still intrigued by them and curious to uncover more, even if the louder, more stubborn side of me tells me that I'm never going near the stuff again. I can't imagine any memory being worth it.

By the time we leave the inn, the streets are vacant. My first thought is that it is because people have fled inside at my presence, but for once this is not the case. The glow of the moon above reminds me that it is the middle of the night and therefore most of the denizens of this town are fast asleep. Even Acari yawns, wiping sleep lazily from his eyes, despite the crispness of the night air.

I, on the other hand, am emboldened by the night. The absence of people, the glow of the moon, it fuels me with focus.

Something about the shadows between the houses makes my hair stand on end though. Without bringing alarm to Acari—who is probably too aloof to notice, even if I was being obvious about my suspicions—I scrutinize every obscurity we pass. When one of them moves, a human form sulking deeper into darkness, I am not surprised by Nerul's presence, even if I am frustrated by it.

Having him so nearby adds pressure to my every action, and part of me had hoped we'd leave without his knowing.

I can't mess this up—any of it—otherwise Nerul will return to the Council and report me. I've already delivered one unsanctioned kill. I don't need any other infractions during this mission.

With Crow as our guide overhead, we make our way to the woods again, heading in the same direction where Acari and the princess were ambushed. It's not surprising. Bandits tend to stay close enough to towns so they don't have to travel far to obtain what they need, but not so close that anyone would stumble upon them. Though the site of the ambush would likely be designated as "too close," my guess is their camp is not far from it. We might've even been able to find them on our own if we'd wanted to scour every inch of the woods without a care for time. But I don't think time is something either of us are interested in wasting.

We pass by the tree of our initial encounter, then dozens more, until we've walked past so many stumps and branches and leaves that I can no longer keep count. My legs ache, an unfamiliar sensation wrenching them with each step. Walking for extended periods of time isn't something I do often. Normally I just have Crow faze me wherever I am needed. But with Crow being severed from its connection to the princess, I am forced to do it the mortal way.

I watch the moon nestle behind the trees with each hour that passes.

When I hear leaves rustling nearby, I crouch on light feet. I am a leaf, blending in soundlessly with my surroundings. The prince, on the other hand, is as loud as a dog. Though he stops alongside me, he inadvertently kicks a rock and sends it skipping along the path into a tree.

I glare at him, but he seems confused and utterly unaware of the ruckus he's making. When I pinch my own lips together, he seems to get the hint and at least tries to walk more quietly.

Eyes wide, ears open, I tug all of my senses to search the woods surrounding us. The trees are so dense in this part of the woods though that they act as a buffer between us and anything beyond the trees directly surrounding us. The silence is like a void. And my view is so encumbered, that I can't even see Crow overhead.

But then, something shuffles just out of my sight. On one toe, I spin to face it, hands out, power ready. If we are under attack, then I have no choice but to let my Reaper magic flow so that I can complete my task. The Council will just have to get over it.

But it's not something malicious and deadly, I find. Instead, an orange, glowing ball of fur with two alert ears and a swiveling tail hops from beneath the underbrush. I lower my guard at the sight of the harmless firefur, grateful for the light it brings into the dark woods. Although carnivorous, firefurs pose no threat to us, as they only eat the carcasses discarded by other predators.

"I've never seen a firefur before," Acari says beside me, gazing at the creature with childlike wonder. "Not in person anyway, just the pictures they have in books, but even those don't do it justice. Look at it! It's fur really does look like it's on fire. How do they do that?"

His eagerness ushers him forward, and the creature skitters back a handful of hops. At the same time that I realize the creature isn't supposed to be hopping, at least not lopsided like that, Acari seems to as well.

"Oh no. It's limping. I think its leg's hurt." Trying to get a better look, Acari squats low to the ground, his hand outstretched. "Come here, little guy, we can help—"

Before he can finish, the firefur hobbles back through the under-brush, scattering the dirt and fallen leaves on the forest floor and casting the two of us into darkness again.

I let my eyes readjust to the dark, but just as I'm about to resume our original path, Acari plunges forward through the foliage. His entire lower half is already submerged in the bush. He shields his face from the branches hanging overhead with one arm and points forward with the other.

"What are you doing?"

"I'm trying to protect my face from any spiderwebs that might be—"

"No. I don't mean why are you holding your arm out like that. I mean, why are you clawing your way through bushes in the middle of the night?"

His arms flap outward. "We can't just leave it here. It'll die. Or something will come and eat it and *then* it'll die."

"And what about your sister?" I growl, signaling behind me. "Aren't you worried *she* might die?"

There's a pause, one long enough to confirm that he *is* worried about her, but not long enough to confirm that I've convinced him to stop.

"It's like you said," he grunts. I can't see what he's doing, but I can hear the branch he's pulling aside as he tries squirming through a particularly dense patch. "They can't kill her."

It's not like him to be so blasé where the princess' life is concerned, but I'm too frustrated by his negligence to think much about it. Instead, I hold nothing back.

"There are far worse things than death."

Though I leave the horrors of what I endured as a young girl unspoken, when Acari lowers his head, I know I've made my point.

With a roll of my eyes, I approach him, but just before I can grab hold of the sleeve of his shirt and pull him away, I spot the firefur just on the other side of the shrubbery. The fiery flickering of its coat permits enough light for me to see that it *does* appear to be favoring one of its paws. There's no denying that we could desperately use the light it would provide us, and if it's injured, it might actually be easier than I expected to capture.

I release a low, gravely groan. "Fine. We catch the firefur and then we get back to our mission. Just move out of the way so I can get through too."

I place my hand firmly between Acari's shoulder blades prepared to give him a shove, but the warmth I find radiating off him gives me pause. His heat is unlike anything I've ever felt, truly. Every time I've ever touched any living creature, death has already been lurking; it makes their skin sweaty, clammy, and oftentimes cold. But since Acari isn't fearing for his death, since he's not shirking away from my very touch, instead, for once, I feel the rise and fall of his breaths, the heat his life—his blood—circulating throughout his entire body.

I've never wanted to keep touching someone so badly.

And so I shove him all the harder, sending him stumbling into the clearing and startling the firefur anew.

Before I can stop Acari from bolting after it, he chases the fading light and plummets into the woods.

"Don't," I say, trying to warn him, but his bounding steps carry him faster than my voice can reach, "chase it..."

When I finally clamber out of the bushes, I too barrel after them. Branches whip my face and legs, leaving lashings and splinters behind that I am forced to ignore. I guess I can't complain though since I fare better than the trees, who die on contact, their once vital leaves becoming dry and brittle as bones.

Acari is nowhere to be seen, but I follow the sound of his staggering steps, cursing his foolishness. Ignoring the aching in my joints, I clear a log and continue running. When I see leaves swaying before me, I know I'm gaining on them.

It dawns on me then that we're moving too fast for a chase of a creature so small. Especially one that's supposed to be injured. Unless...

Unless it's luring us somewhere...

Still charging at almost full speed, I push through some dense, low-hanging branches and nearly crash into Acari on the other side. My feet catch, veering me out of his path and into the tree beside him instead. As we collide, flesh to bark, the tree and I croak. I push myself off it just as the trunk starts to blacken.

I glare back at Acari, standing still in a new, dimly lit clearing. He's staring straight forward, and I have to push myself off the tree to see that he's staring at the glowing firefur that's wedged itself between some boulders. I recognize its fear by its rapid breaths and cowering body, but it's not until Acari steps to the side, attempting to come at it at an angle instead of directly, that I notice the firefur's eyes don't move with him.

It's not hiding from us.

"Acari," I say, my voice a quiet warning.

But by the time I get his attention, the color drains from his face.

The air reeks of salivating tongues.

Slowly I turn, shielding Acari and the firefur behind me as I face the ravenous snarls of the predators that have surrounded us. Glowing eyes of ochre and amber blink in existence. I spy four sets in total, circling us like the meals we are before the strong bodies of the wolves creep into view, bellies rumbling with anticipation. Their fur, thick to fend off winter nights, twitches with each prowling step. Their steps are nearly inaudible, if not for the random blade of grass or flower that gets shuffled aside. But it's the growling that is most menacing, the upper lip of each of them raising higher the closer they approach, to reveal deadly and glistening fangs that are primed to puncture one of our throats.

A normal person might be afraid. Someone like Acari who quivers as the wolves close us in. But I feel no such thing.

Not for myself, anyhow.

By the alpha's lead, they lift their chins to the moon and sing.

The alpha of the pack leaps first. I meet him mid-air, hands splayed, one reaching for its throat and the other for one of its legs. With jaws snapping in the air, my fingers graze his fur. Darkness swirls on contact. The alpha's pupils become large disks, his jaw hanging limply from his snout, as he crashes to the ground lifeless in a matter of seconds.

The world shudders, Veltuur's growl of disapproval.

I try ignoring it. There's no room to worry about what the Council might do to me for this.

Their alpha dead, the other wolves dive.

My power may be limitless, but I can't take them all on at once. Rolling from the center of the circle, I land in the grass and it dies beneath my hands when I push myself back up. I charge for the two closest canines. They snap at me, more of a warning than anything. I think they might understand that I am not their food, or maybe they know how lethal my touch can be, but they are too bloodthirsty and enraged to back down.

I hold up my hands, one aimed at the creature before me and the other at the one behind me.

"No!" Acari's voice pierces the air like an arrow. "Don't kill them!"

I realize dumbly that he means the wolves. His caution and stupidity nearly makes me lose my focus, almost missing the moment when the wolves pounce. Fortunately, I recover enough to aim my hands in a way that will avoid me being wounded in the process. I aim high and push on one of the wolves' noses. On the other, I lean back and touch its throat as it whirls by me.

Agonized screams tear into the silent night, drowning out Veltuur's roar.

I whip around to find the fourth wolf sinking its teeth into Acari's chest, around his shoulder. The creature shakes him like a ragdoll and Acari's screams sink deeper, wrenching from his belly. As I race toward them, Acari tries shoving the wolf's face away from him, but all he manages to accomplish is making the creature lock his jaw tighter.

I am no hunter, and I have limited experience with wolves or most creatures of the living realm, but I am familiar enough with death to recognize when it's close. One more snap of the wolf's teeth, perhaps a transfer from Acari's shoulder to his throat, and the young prince will die.

I recognize the panic thrashing inside me only because I felt this same sense of desperation the day I killed that man. It's the kind of rushing and heightening of senses that somehow manages to make everything seem like it's moving too fast and too slow at the same time.

If I can just get close enough, I can kill the wolf with one touch. But I'm too far away. It has the time it needs to snap his neck before I'd even get close.

Need courses through me, dark and unbounding, begging for the wolf to die. I can feel my power answer it, agreeing to claim a life that wasn't meant to be mine. Darkness spills inside me, coursing down my legs and arms and up my neck, black and inky, until I am a kettle of boiling water, ready to overflow.

Before the wolf can make its next move, I scream, pushing against my own skin. Smoke, black as night, fires out of my hands with such force that I am knocked backward, but not before I watch the blast hit the wolf in the head, engulfing both its ears and eyes in the opaque beam of concentrated death. The power of it blasts the wolf backward too, its limp body crashing into the trees behind it.

I gape down at my hands like they are foreign. Never before have I seen this kind of power. My magic has always only ever come on contact, never by my own command and never like some projectile at my disposal.

Acari crashes to the ground in a heap of limp limbs.

"Acari!"

There is no restraint when I run to his side, skidding to a stop at my knees. I almost pick up his head to cradle it in my lap, but fortunately I remember myself before inadvertently killing him.

When his eyes flutter, feathers dance inside my chest. They are quickly turned to ice with shame though. What am I doing? Why am I so relieved to see him alive?

Right, my mission. I can't find the Guardians without him. That is his purpose in my life and that is why I need him to stay alive. That's the only reason. Or at least, the only one I am admitting to.

My gaze flickers to his oozing chest. Blood is pulsing freely from his wounds, having drenched his entire shirt already. I lean forward to put pressure on the puncture marks only to lean back again remembering I can't. I can't touch him and not make everything worse.

Since becoming a Reaper, I have never felt so helpless.

Finally, his eyes manage to open. To my surprise, he's not writhing in pain. Instead, his gaze is hollow, directed up at the sky and I don't dare cross its view. Only a second passes before he grimaces, as if the wound is just now causing him pain. His vision settles on me and I smile.

I *actually* smile. At a mortal. Though I don't want to admit it, I am relieved he is alive. Dare I say that maybe this forced, contractual friendship is becoming real for me. I am amused by his bumbling nature, intrigued by his love for his sister.

But my relief fades when I realize he is not looking at me fondly. There is hate behind his eyes.

Letting his head fall to his side, he gazes upon the dead wolf lying so close to him that their bodies are pressed together. With his uninjured arm, he reaches around to the wolf's body, petting it desperately, with a shaky hand.

Though death is so natural for me, I forget that for mortals, who live in a realm where killing something—*anything*—is entirely forbidden, I forget how much value they can place on life.

"If I hadn't killed them, you'd be dead," I say softly, putting some distance between our bodies, even as I remain kneeling beside him.

"I... I know that," he says between hitching breathes. There is a pause, meant to give him time to recover verbal strength, but it only weakens him. He's sobbing by the time he speaks again, his hand tightening in the wolf's mane. "Death just isn't an everyday occurrence for some people, Sinisa."

The words burrow into me like worms writhing in my thoughts. The only people I'd ever mourned had been my parents, but even that I'm only halfway aware of, and only for a few hours now thanks to the memory tea. Before tonight, for the past three years, death had just seemed normal. Necessary. It was either us or the wolves, and I wasn't about to let it be us who died. It doesn't feel like a wrong choice. In fact, I don't regret it at all.

I do regret giving him a reason to look at me like that though. I'm tired of that being the way everyone looks at me.

From the crevice of the nearby boulders, I watch silently as the firefur and a handful of others hop from their hiding spot and approach one of the other fallen wolves with satisfied and celebratory sniffs. They don't realize it yet, but I've just killed their primary source of food. Without the wolves to prowl, the firefurs will have to find another predator to do their hunting for them, or rely on the luck of coming across freshly dead animals on their own.

At least they'll have the corpses of the wolves to survive off, for now.

"We..." I start, unsure of what I'm about to say but needing to fill the silence. "I think we need to get you some help."

Acari nods through a grimace as he pushes his hand down against the bleeding of his chest. "I should've known...what the firefur was doing."

"What do you mean?"

The small rodents radiate, surrounding us in a firelike glow as they devour the remains of the four beasts. I catch Acari trying desperately not to watch them, but it's difficult to ignore their voracious slurping and gnawing as the critters chomp their way through fur, flesh, tendons, and bone.

"It was stupid...to chase after it. I know what firefurs eat..."

"Yeah, but, you didn't know it was luring you to your death. I didn't even know they did that."

Not that that means much, considering I don't know *a lot* about things in the realm of the living, but Acari seems to get whatever reassurance he needs from it because he drops the topic.

Caw.

Coming from seemingly nowhere, Crow swoops in from the sky and lands in between two of the wolves' corpses, illuminated in orange on either side like it was the evil mastermind behind the entire ambush. It squawks a few more times, and I fight the urge to throw a rock at it. I'm not sure why it's mad at me when it's the one that led us into the path of a firefur and then left us to die. I know it saw the wolves. It could've warned me.

Acari tries pushing himself up but slips. As his back thuds against the ground, he winces and groans.

I glance to the woods around us, not really sure what I was hoping to find. He needs a healer, someone who knows the herbs that will prevent infection and death. But there is no such person around.

We'd have to walk back to Ngal, but I'm not even sure where that is from here. We've raced too far from our original path.

"Thank you," Acari croaks, drawing my attention from the trees. "For saving my life."

The words are bittersweet, and I am not sure whether to accept them, but because he's staring at me expectantly, I say, "It needed to be done."

"Maybe," someone mocks from the darkness.

I am on my feet before I can exhale my next breath. Dark power pulses at my fingertips, rippling around my hands while I scan the surrounding foliage.

"Lower your hands so I can help the boy," the voice—a man—says again.

My hearing is usually hyper attuned, but I struggle to locate his precise location. It's maddening. Instead I swivel and spin around Acari's injured body, trying to locate the stranger.

"He's in pain," the man says again when Acari grimaces through another particularly agonizing reminder of his wounds. "And he will die without help. I can save him. You cannot."

His words sting, but I know he's not wrong. As much as I wish I had the power to heal him right now, all I have is the power to kill him.

I waver only a second longer, before finally letting my arms fall to my side.

The man that steps out from the shadows would blend in entirely with the night if not for his amber eyes. They are the eyes of a watchful hawk, and even when he averts his attention to Acari on the ground, I still feel myself under their scrutiny. I bend over Acari with him, not wanting him to get too close without me being right there with him; within arm's reach of this stranger, if need be.

Through clenched teeth, Acari asks, "Is it affected?"

"He means *infected*," I say to the stranger, biting back the smile tugging at my lips before addressing Acari. "And no, it's not. Wounds don't infect that quickly. Don't they teach princes anything?"

His laugh blends in with his next wince.

While the man assesses the damage, I scrutinize every detail I can about him. The purple runes on his forehead are nearly camouflaged against his dark skin, but when the wind blows the branches just right, they shine in the moon's glow. I almost gasp when I see the jagged rune from his eye down his cheek, the one bestowed upon mortals when they are terminally ill.

Instead I avert my eyes to his working hands as they assess the damage done, only to find more runes, ones I've never seen before.

Each of his fingers' nails are inked with beads and swirls. The middle finger alone has a line of them, leading to the back of his hand where a swarm of feathers loop in intricate designs of purple loops.

I can't keep my eyes off his runes as he pulls a jar from a pouch in his belt and applies the gel inside to Acari's puncture holes.

Before I can ask him what he's giving Acari or what the runes on his hands represent, the prince's eyes droop open and he stares straight up at the stranger.

"You," Acari accuses wearily. "What did you do with my sister?"

17

TRICK OF THE BANDITS

ACARI

Whatever the bandit lathered onto my chest is helping diminish the pain a little, but not enough. My arm still throbs, burning as if the wolf's jaw was a brand. I can still feel its fangs like they're permanently plunged into my shoulder.

But when I notice the bandit from earlier, the one who kidnapped Gem, it's almost enough of a shock to allow me to ignore the searing heat. I start to push myself onto my elbows.

Instead, the movement sends a spike of agony tearing through my chest and I crumple back to the earth.

"Take it easy," the bandit says sternly, still avoiding my question.

I ask again, through gritted teeth, and I wish I could claim it's from vigor instead of pain. "What did you do with my sister?"

"She's safe," he says. "That's all that matters."

The vague answer reminds me of something my brother would've said, but the tone is that of my father's, and I'm aggravated all the more.

Before I can demand any real answers though, the bandit lifts me off the ground and hoists me like a sack of potatoes across his shoulder.

"What are you doing?" I manage between winces.

This time, Sinisa steps in. I've never heard her sound so fierce. "Put him down, or—"

"Stop," the bandit says gruffly, cutting her off. He peers over at me, slung over his back. "You plan on living long enough to see your sister again, right?"

The question cuts away any fight I had left.

"That's what I thought. I'm taking you to camp. You'll find her there, safe and unharmed."

With me on his shoulder, he climbs over the rocks and boulders until we reach flat ground again. Sinisa follows closely behind, her hand readied. My brow furrows, and I shake my head at her, and surprisingly, she listens, lowering her arm with a grumble.

Once atop the rocks, I peer over the bandit's shoulders, sensing something ahead. Through the trees, I see glints of campfires for the first time and wonder how we managed to miss them before. The bandit camp was practically right on top of us. It's probably how this bandit found us, likely hearing our screams, maybe even the wolves who howled right before they attacked. Maybe he came to check out the commotion and see if we were all right.

"What are you after?" Sinisa asks, her eyes dark and menacing as she comes around to face him. "First, you kidnap his sister, then you stalk him? If you wanted the prince so badly, why didn't you just take him when you used the daminila pollen?"

The bandit growls, and I feel it rattling against my torso. We're both silent for a moment, waiting for more of an answer, but when it becomes clear he's not giving one, I let my thoughts wander.

Without Sinisa's help, I would be dead. I have no doubt of that. It's a miracle she was able to subdue one wolf, let alone all four. I know I shouldn't guilt her for killing them, but part of me can't help but wonder if there had been another way. All my life I've been told that death is wrong, evil. We're taught growing up that every life is important, every living creature no matter how small has value.

Except for babies born with deformities that they can't help, I guess...which contradicts everything when I think about it. If every life has value, then surely so do the most vulnerable among us. And if

I'm all that stands between Gem's life or death, then maybe it was right that the wolves died. At least it was quick. Painless.

When did everything I've ever known start to seem so backward?

Sinisa leans in close, even though the bandit can likely still hear her. "We can't trust him."

The man snorts. "And I suppose the prince is supposed to trust a Reaper?" Unlike most people, there's no disgust behind the word when he says it. He just seems to be calling her out, challenging her to argue with him. "Tell me, how did your paths cross? Wasn't it the princess you were meant to kill?"

I stiffen, unable to find words. He can't know that, not unless he's been following me a lot longer than just since my arrival in Ngal.

It's obvious his words have disturbed Sinisa as well.

"Who are you?" she asks, the words so forceful that licks of black smoke spark beneath her skin.

I wonder what it would take for her to unleash the same force onto the bandit that she released on the final wolf. I'm not sure I want to find out.

The bandit stops walking and inhales deeply. "The name's Rhetriel. Rhet, if you don't mind."

Turning around, Rhet looks her up and down, grimacing the entire time, as if he found her so hideous to look at, it was hurting him to continue doing so. Don't get me wrong, I know she is a Reaper, but she isn't painful to stare at. Unlike the images of Reapers in Gem's book, Sinisa is actually, admittedly, surprisingly pleasing on the eyes. There's a swagger to her hips when she walks that would be mesmerizing if I stared too long. And her eyes, although the depths of their sadness are a bottomless pit, there's something striking about them, fierce and unyielding. I've also seen her smile, unbound by darkness. Not many people can say they've seen a Reaper smile. It makes me feel privileged, knowing it is all the more special.

I clear my throat and roll my shoulders when I realize I've been staring too long, but thankfully neither of them seem to notice. The movement of my arms makes me also realize that the pain continues to dwindle. In fact, my shoulder feels almost numb now.

"Okay, *Rhet*. Who are you?" she prods further. "Why did you take the princess?"

He grunts. "That's as much as *you* need to know for now."

"Fine. How much farther are we going then?"

The question takes me by surprise. As best I can, I prop myself up to peer around Rhet's head, easily spying the bandit camp just ahead. From a distance, the towering wooden fence would've looked like a cluster of trees, but up this close, there's no mistaking the fortress wall, the torches lighting the path, and the guards patrolling nearby.

When I look back at Sinisa though, her eyes are still searching.

"Don't...you see it?" I ask hesitantly.

The change in her expression is all the answer I need.

"She can't see it," Rhet says with an air of arrogance. "And she can't follow us any farther either."

"What?" The word is low and deadly, but it's not enough to curb the panic rising in her tone.

Sinisa storms forward, only to run into an invisible wall.

Rhet shrugs and uses the momentum to set me on my feet beside him. "I tried to warn you. No Reaper can pass."

Sinisa's eyes widen as she begins pounding against a thick shield of air. She jogs to the left, and then to the right, all the while keeping a hand on the clear barrier.

When she realizes there's no way in, or at least stops searching for one, she fixes me with a desperate look in her eyes. "Please, I have to help you find the Guardian. If I don't..."

Her mouth hangs open, the words refusing to flow so I never actually find out what happens when Reapers don't complete their missions, but I know that Sinisa has already failed once.

I become suddenly aware of Rhet's eyes on me. "There is one way," he says.

Sinisa's eyes cut to him so swiftly I flinch.

"What is it?" I ask, surprisingly interested in hearing our options. I mean, this *is* the Reaper who tried killing Gem. It would be completely reasonable, and perhaps even responsible, to leave her here at this strange, magical barrier.

But I don't *just* see a Reaper when I look at her anymore. I see the little girl who had no choice but to defend herself. I see the friend who just saved my life.

"If you can vouch for her, we'll let her through." Rhet directs his attention to Sinisa, a glare reddening his features. "But remember who and what she is, and how you met her to begin with."

Something tells me it's been years since even she's known who she is. In the past few hours, we've learned more about her than she probably has since becoming a Reaper. I get the impression that all this time she's thought that all she is is a Reaper, someone sent to executions without any other purpose but to bring about death.

But when the wolves attacked us, she protected me. She screamed my name and ran to my side when I was bitten.

Surely, she is *more* than just a Reaper.

"I—I think so, yeah," I hesitate, the words threatening to bolt from my lips while my fear of being horribly wrong about her struggles to hold them back. It doesn't succeed. "Yes, I mean, I vouch for her. She saved my life."

Rhet nods, and rather than seeming grudgeful, it's as if he holds no doubt. It puts me at ease.

Rhet reaches out an open hand. "Take my hand and you may enter."

The gesture freezes her in place. Sinisa gawks down at his palm, eyes incredulous. I too can't help but stare at Rhet like he's lost his mind. His hands are completely bare; no gloves, nothing to protect him from her Reaper power.

But before I can remind him of what she's capable of, and before Sinisa can do anything, a black bird dives between them. Crow swoops back into the air, circling around for another malicious strike at the extended hand. The bird misses, Sinisa startles back, but Rhet remains unmoving, the invitation still there.

The bird hovers in between the two of them, wings flapping like razors, fending off what I guess is a perceived threat.

"Crow," Sinisa warns. "Get out of the way."

The bird does as it's told, flying to the ground so quickly that the leaves beneath it waft in the air.

When she's thoroughly done glaring at the bird, she returns her attention to Rhet, one eyebrow high. "You know I can't. Not unless you have a death wish."

Caw, the bird seems to say in agreement.

"Yes, you can," Rhet says, the words deliberate, each one slow and with meaning. "I am protected, and it's the only way you can cross."

Sinisa stares at his hand, considering it.

A drumming warns in my chest though, trickles of fear coursing through me. If Rhet dies, I'll have to drag myself to the encampment alone. I'll have to beg for the other bandits to bring me my sister, to insist that Rhet had promised to do so before his untimely death. I might also have to beg for Sinisa's life and tell them that it was only after Rhet's insistence that she grabbed his hand.

"Are you sure?" I ask. "If you're wrong, then, well...I would just encourage you to make sure you're not wrong."

"I'm not. I will be fine." His voice resonant, the words like stones, Rhet's arm seems stronger, steadier than ever. "Are you coming, Reaper?"

Sinisa's eyes dart hesitantly to the trees, but only for a second. With a hollow clap, she swings her hand into Rhet's and winces.

Her eyes are shut.

They stay shut, waiting.

But when nothing happens, she opens them one at a time.

We both stare at their hands, interlaced like the moon cradled in the night sky, waiting for the black power to seep out of her fingertips. But it doesn't.

She looks to me with amazement just as Rhet yanks her through the barrier. Her shock grows deeper when she beholds the bandit encampment inside.

Behind her, the crow goes wild, cawing furiously and pecking at the translucent wall.

"Crow can't come?" Sinisa asks, looking over her shoulder. She almost sounds excited about it.

"No."

I look to Sinisa, hoping to give a telepathic apology for our host's lack of explanation, but instead, I am struck with awe as runes the color of lavender blossom on her forehead.

"Sinisa," I breathe her name like it's a cloud floating from my tongue. "Your—your runes."

As if expecting to find her face on fire, her hands fly to her forehead. She runs her fingers over the bumps and grooves, eyes wide with wonderment. I realize how strange it must be for her, like meeting herself for the first time, or, I guess just for the first time in years.

Like myself, and like most people our age, she bears all of the common markings: the star of birth, the three dots for language, a line above either eyebrow to indicate grief, and the splashes of color on either side of the star that mark her first true moment of fear. I try not to think about whether any of her runes came from the night she experienced in that memory.

Noticing our awestricken faces, Rhet calls over his shoulder. "You are not a Reaper here. The camp is protected."

Once again, Sinisa is looking at her hands. It takes me a second to realize she's likely feeling for the power she's grown so accustomed to having.

Shamefully, relief floods me. I want to trust Sinisa, I do, but at least here I know without a doubt that she won't betray me after all. While we are here, Gem is safe. Well, as safe as she can be after being kidnapped and dragged into a bandit camp.

We make our way up to the gate, and the effects of the poultice start fading rapidly. I expect it to come on as slowly as it dissipated, but I am not so fortunate. The pain in my shoulder thickens, searing through my chest and shoulder like I'm being torn into by a predatory maw all over again.

I gasp and start blinking in and out of pain-induced consciousness.

Rhet slings me back over his shoulder as the gate opens. The conversation he shares with the person on guard is muffled, but I think I recognize him too, the one with the birthmark covering half of his face.

Once inside, we pass by a dozen or so eager onlookers, memorable mostly because so many of them seem to be missing limbs or have scarred eyes; the life of a bandit must be more dangerous than I ever imagined. But when I see children, daughters and sons who look as if they are happy, and I notice the disfigurements on them too, I begin to question the stronghold we've stumbled into.

"He needs to see a healer," Sinisa says through gritted teeth.

"Where do you think it is I'm taking him?" Rhet replies, quickening his steps.

"I thought you were taking me to my sister?" I try to say through bites of pain. But just as I manage to groan out the first few words, Rhet stops at a person draped in fox hide, and when they blow a crimson powder into my face, the sparsely populated camp disappears into nothing.

18

THE PRINCESS AND THE REAPER
SINISA

"Hey! What are you doing—" I yell at the bandit woman blowing daminila pollen at Acari.

"The healer needs him sedated," Rhet says, shifting his hold on Acari with a bounce. He addresses the woman. "Bring the girl to us."

The woman disperses, as does Rhet, and I'm left with no choice but to follow him. People stare at us as we walk by the different dwellings, but it's not with fear like I'm used to. My hand floats up to my forehead again, and to the runes that shouldn't be there but somehow are. I can't explain my joy at feeling their raised edges, but something about them makes me feel lighter, like perhaps I'm really not the monster that everyone sees me as. As we walk, I trace the markings, getting to know myself with what little information I'm provided. They tell the story of my life, but it's like they're in a language I don't know how to read. I don't know which words earned me the dots beneath the star on my forehead, I don't know which moment earned me my first marking of true fear.

Rhet leads us into a hut at the center of the encampment, lowering Acari's unconscious body onto a cot made of woven leaves.

The healer approaches him, and the two of them share a hushed conversation as I watch them silently from the edge of the room.

He leaves her to begin her work, a needle and thread in her hands, and grabs something from a nearby table before crossing the room to me.

"Here, eat." Without further warning, Rhet throws something circular at me.

I barely catch it in time, and I'm just about to tell him I don't want anything from him, when the words dry up in my mouth. With the fruit in hand, my fingers glide over its soft skin and nothing happens. Poison does not seep from my fingertips. The life of the luscious apricot is not drained before my eyes.

My eyes flit to Rhet, who nods.

The apricot is in my mouth in the next second. Its juicy sweetness drips onto my tongue and I practically melt. It's been...I don't even know how long it's been since I've been able to eat a fruit. Years. It's been at least years.

I roll my head back, savoring the sugary nectar, but I'm interrupted by a burst of light as the door opens.

"Cari!" cries the little girl who rushes inside. The princess sees her brother first, and the healer at his side. When she notices me, she shrinks behind Rhet.

He pats her head once, then twice, awkward and yet somehow fatherly. "Don't worry. She can't harm you here." Then, inching past Gem and her clawing arms, he walks to the door. With the doorknob in hand, he snorts at me. "Don't get any ideas about this one. I'll be back soon."

Without another word, Rhet cranks the door ajar and sinks into early morning light.

Slowly, Gem turns to face me. Her lips pinch together as she assesses me.

I sink my teeth into the apricot again, the sound magnified in the quiet hut.

Gem steps cautiously toward me. "Nice?"

Still chewing, I glance at the door. "Rhet? I don't think so. He's got this air about him like he thinks he's better than everyone."

"No," Gem insists, peering up at me through eyes as wide as stones. "Nice?"

I realize then that she's talking about me.

"Oh," is all I can manage.

This is a great opportunity for me to lure her to a false sense of security with me. I've never needed to rely on such tactics before, but now that my mission is a little more complex, it might behoove me to get on her good side as well.

But the way she blinks up at me makes me feel like my stomach is twisted in knots. Like somehow it would be worse to lie to her about being a friend than it would be just to take her young soul.

"No," I hear myself reply, quiet but firm. "Not nice."

Her frown deepens, and I turn away, burying myself deeper into the dark confines of the room, in shadows, in blackness where I belong.

19

CAUGHT IN A LIE

SINISA

Two hours pass and Gem's black, curious eyes still blink over at me. Every time I look away and look back, she is still staring at me, expectantly, but for what, I do not know. I can only take life, not give it, and even *that* I seem unable to do right now. Not as long as I'm here.

If anything goes wrong, I won't be able to protect myself, let alone her brother. The only one able to save the prince now is the healer before us.

The woman unwrapping the sodden bandages around Acari's shoulder bears the same hand markings as Rhet. As she works though, cleaning the wound, applying poultices, and securing new dressings, it's easier to ignore her runes and to focus instead on whether the prince is still breathing.

He's hardly moved since Rhet brought him in. He does not flinch or wince when the healer applies pressure to the teeth marks marring his shoulder. His chest simply rises and falls in a soft, peaceful rhythm.

I, on the other hand, am anything but peaceful. Patience has never been my strongest virtue, and although Rhet has been gone only a few hours, his absence carries the weight of an eternity.

I am on edge. I can't shake the feeling like we have walked willingly into a trap, and the small child's gaze-of-guilt isn't helping any. Without my Reaper power, I feel more vulnerable than I have ever felt. What's worse is having my target staring at me like she knows what I still plan to do to her. It's like she can see right through everything, and the longer we share a room together, the more difficult it becomes to think about.

"Stop staring," I snap at her finally, and then groan when she doesn't listen.

I wrench my thoughts away from her and to the encampment. A place like this shouldn't even exist. There has never been a place where a Reaper could not go. We are the bringers of death, and death knows no limits.

So, how is it that a group of bandits live in a place where Reapers cannot reach? How did I become mortal again—even if temporarily—when I crossed the barrier? Does the Council know this place is here?

I saw Nerul in the woods, just before we crossed over the boundary, so maybe they *do* know. If the Council knows though, Nerul sure didn't. He looked just as surprised as I was when I grabbed Rhet's hand and the encampment flashed into view. I wonder what it looked like from Nerul's perspective, to watch all three of us disappear. I wonder if he's still standing there, pondering how it works, the same way I am. Probably not. He's probably already in the Pit of Judgment telling the Council all about it.

After tucking the dressing inside itself, the healer bows without a word and disappears from the tent, leaving Acari with just his sister and me.

A few moments pass and not a single one of us moves a muscle—not Gem, not Acari, and certainly not me. But when Acari begins to stir in the cot made of banana leaves, I perk up and draw closer to his side.

"Acari?" I whisper in the quiet room.

I can tell it's an effort to open his eyes, the side effects of the daminila pollen likely still in effect, but he manages to peel one eye open drowsily, followed by the other. He finds me instantly.

"Sinisa?" he asks, his voice hoarse with exhaustion. "Where's Gem?"

"Cari!" Gem shrieks, racing across the room and squeezing in beside me. She's so small that she can barely see over the cot. "I here, Cari!"

"Gem," he rasps, her name almost entirely a sob. His eyes close as he cups her cheek, a happy kind of sadness curving his lips. "I thought they... I thought you... Are you all right?"

Leaning into his hand, she nods vigorously. "Rhet nice."

I snort, crossing my arms. "He can't be that nice if he kidnapped you."

Acari flicks his gaze to mine, a mixture of agreement and warning. "Let's not talk about that. I'm just glad you're safe."

"You have very low standards for what you call safe," I snort again. "We don't know these people, and we don't know what they want. Now that you have awoken, and since your wounds have been tended, we should go. Before they come back."

"Rhet said stay," Gem pouts. She doesn't look at me when she says it though.

Caught in between us both, Acari glances from one of us to the other. He examines the cloth wrapped around his shoulder and timidly tests his arm's mobility. He winces at the slightest use of his muscles, but he's able to raise it from the cot at least one hand high. Lowering it back down gently, he turns to us both.

"Maybe we should hear what they have to say first. They didn't harm Gem and they helped me. They even made you human again."

"I have always been human," I growl.

"Sorry, *mortal*," he amends. "Don't you want to know how they did it? Or why it's possible? They seem to know a lot that we don't. Like, they even knew who Gem was—*no one* knows who Gem is. How did they find out? How did they know where to find us? If they know all of this, maybe they know about the Guardians too."

It's a possibility I had not yet considered, but one that would have great value. If they know anything about the Guardians, it would help me complete my mission more quickly so I could finally return to the Council and become a Shade...

But why doesn't that excite me like it used to?

"Fine," I say, backing away from his bedside to sit on a stool nearby. "If that's what you want, we stay."

While Acari and his sister catch up like two excited squirrel kits, I try ignoring them and sinking into my own thoughts, but it's of no use. Every time Acari mentions our journey to save her, I can't help but notice the prideful and heroic ways in which he recalls it. Valiantly, I fought off the royal guard, I protected him from a pack of starving wolves, and when it came to stepping over the barrier and into the bandit encampment, I did so bravely, unwilling to let him continue the journey without me.

I wish I felt as heroic and selfless as he saw me. Instead, I feel nothing more than a traitor. My mission is going exactly as planned. I befriended the prince and now I have his blind trust. Together we will seek a Guardian, I will report back to Veltuur, and then I will be sent to claim the princess' life. I should feel triumphant and clever. Instead, I feel like I have just stepped out of a lagoon and I can't rid myself of its slimy waters.

I remember having friends before I became a Reaper; I thought about them while I killed my attacker. But that was the friendship of children, of carefree joy and limitless imagination. Acari's friendship is something more. He has seen me in my most vulnerable moments, and I have seen his as well. When the Council sent me into the mortal realm, I viewed this conquest like a game, like something to be won. It no longer feels like a game though. To betray Acari means to lose his friendship, and to my surprise that feels an awful lot like losing. But if I don't complete my task, I will have the Council to answer to, and that too will be a great loss.

Once we find a Guardian, once I return to the Council and my contract is reinstated, I will have a very difficult decision to make.

Silence pierces my ears and I realize their conversation has ended. I peer over to find Gem has snuggled up beside her brother and is already fast asleep.

When Acari sees me staring, he clears his throat.

"Thank you," he says.

"For what?" I dare ask.

"For everything. For getting me here. For not killing my sister," he adds with a soft chuckle.

Feeling more cynical than ever, I retort, "It wasn't by choice, you know. You hit me over the head and the Council took her contract away from me. I would have claimed her life, otherwise."

Acari's lips purse together and he stares up at the thatched ceiling. "Maybe you would've then, but you're not now. So, thank you for not trying to kill her now."

I don't remind him that I am without my Reaper powers for the time being and therefore he does not know *what* I will do. He should not trust me, someone who has been deceiving him all this time. I am not worthy of his faith.

"After my mother and brothe—" He pauses and sighs the heaviness away, before running his fingers through the princess' crow-black hair. "Gem's all I have."

It stings to hear him say it, but I know it's the truth. Though we've come to know each other, this partnership will end. One way or another. A Reaper has no place in the mortal world, and a mortal has no interest in a Reaper as a friend.

"What happened to the rest of your family?" I ask before my thoughts can spiral further.

Acari's eyes tighten, wrinkles appearing at their sides. The pause that follows is one of grief and longing. I'm about to tell him not to worry about telling me anything, to rest instead so that he'll have the energy he needs for when we leave the camp, but his eyes open.

"They were traveling to a royal ball in Ghamaya to represent our family. My father was ill, and I was too frightened to go with them—I never really liked the idea of having to travel outside the safety of our palace, let alone our kingdom. I even worried about what it would be like to be high up in the mountains and wondered what we'd do if there was an avalanche. I was distraught, as you can imagine. So, they let me stay in Oakfall."

It is all too easy to believe. I imagine there are many things that terrify the anxious prince. Spiders, grime, bandits, wolves—and those are just the things we have encountered during our short time together. The list is probably in the hundreds.

"The wheel of their carriage was apparently in need of repair, and so they were forced to make an unexpected stop along the path, in between towns on the outskirts of Oakfall. While they waited for the wheel to be replaced, my brother decided to take a stroll through the woods. He came across an aacsi nest. We don't have them in Oakfall —well, at least we *didn't*—so Rikeet didn't know how dangerous they were, or how to avoid them."

They are not unknown to me. I remember hearing about them recently. The Council had received a request to enact genocide on the creatures, which was denied. Not only does Veltuur have stipulations for the lives it grants to pass, but aacsi are considered brethren to the Reapers. They attribute many lives to Veltuur, given their nature.

"I'm told he died instantly," Acari says with a hard swallow.

I am not sure what comes over me, but I find myself compelled to try to ease his pain. "He would have. The aacsi are swift in their kills."

Just like Reapers, I think.

"I know," he says, sighing.

"What of your mother?" I ask, fairly certain his pain is only about to grow deeper.

"After he'd been gone awhile, they went searching for him, everyone including my mother, despite her guards' protests. Call it mother's intuition, but she knew something was wrong and she couldn't just sit around and wait for the bad news.

"She was the first one to find him. And like Rikeet, she had no previous knowledge of the aacsi. Before the guard stationed with her could warn her, she was batting them away from Rikeet's dead body and they...they killed her too."

When Acari starts to sob, I don't offer any words of comfort, for I don't have any to give. None that could ease his suffering or bring back his loved ones. But I find myself wanting to try. I have a sudden urge to place my hand on his shoulder when I realize, for the first time in three years, I actually can without risking his life.

Before I can act on my impulse though, a ray of light blinds all of us, as the door opens, revealing that the night is fading to day. From inside the darkness of the hut, I can barely make out the vague outline of two figures in the entryway.

Acari and I share a cautious look as the two figures enter.

"Sorry for the intrusion," calls a woman, her voice as bright as the sun shining inside. "But we've been expecting you, and despite the young prince needing his rest, I was too thrilled to wait any longer."

When she steps inside, letting the door hang ajar for light, I first notice her hair, the color of pumpkins, stretched as long as vines. She has fair, plain features, but they are speckled, somehow matching her cheery disposition.

In stark contrast, Rhet pushes in beside her, hunched and judgmental.

"I'll cut straight to it," she says with a warm smile. "My name is Aulow. I may share my title with you yet, but for now all you need to know is I am in charge here."

I almost don't hear her though, my focus searing into Rhet. "What took you so long?"

"People, places, patience," Aulow says with a wave of her hand, and I might've mulled over her vague words if it weren't for the designs I saw on her hands, the same ones that mark both Rhet and the healer. It doesn't seem possible to see runes that I've never seen before today on three different people within the same hour, within the same confines. I become even more transfixed by them and what their runes might mean.

But Aulow carries the conversation onward. "Because he was speaking with me and the other—" She clamps her lips tight, seemingly catching herself before she can accidentally reveal something she doesn't want to. "The other leaders. We needed to discuss what to do with you now that you have arrived and we have decided to give you the test. To prove you are worthy and safe."

"Worthy?" Acari groans. "Rhet said I just needed to vouch for her, which I did."

"And that was the first trial: to have a mortal's trust," Aulow confirms, her voice as sweet as sugarcane. "But there are other trials she must complete."

"Like what?" I ask, my eyes flicking to the top of their sockets.

This time, it's Rhet that speaks. "Why did you come here?"

I don't back down from Rhet's intense glare. In fact, I have perfected one of my own that I send his way. But when I hear Acari shift in his cot to prop himself up, I turn toward him. Our eyes meet and I see that he too is waiting for my answer, like he has the same question. I am not sure why I find it so insulting. It's not like I have been honest with him about my intentions.

I narrow my eyes and look back at Aulow and Rhet. "I am helping Acari find a Guardian to heal his sister."

Rhet scoffs, his folded arms flexing as he shifts, but Aulow holds up a decorated hand. "You seek nothing else from the Guardians?"

"I didn't say that. I have been tasked by the Council to report back to Veltuur with the whereabouts of the Guardian."

"*The* Guardian?" Aulow asks, though there is bemusement behind her eyes. "There is only one that the Council is interested in?"

"There's more than one Guardian?" Acari interjects, pushing higher up onto his arm. When he moves too quickly though, the pain bites into him again and he hisses, lowering himself back down onto his back.

My eyes do not leave Aulow's. I recognize the bait for what it is, but I'm not sure why she has thrown it out before me. Why does it matter how many Guardians I am seeking?

"I don't know how many Guardians there are, only that I have been asked to deliver information about them. Before yesterday, I was not even aware that such things as Guardians existed."

"*Things?*" Aulow balks, a playful glint in her eyes. "You believe the Guardians are artifacts or sigils or something of the like?"

Beside her, Rhet's low laugh sounds more like a growl.

She is toying with me. They both are. But why? I do not yet know.

After scrutinizing me for a long moment, Aulow nods. "I appreciate your honesty this far, Sinisa. Thank you. I have only one more question for you." Her tone is nothing but warm and friendly, but the finality of the statement causes my throat to tighten. "Would you like to end your contract on the princess, or do you intend to carry it out?"

The question cracks through me like a whip. I feel the searing sting of it lash across my heart. She knows. *They* know.

But worst of all, Acari is about to know now too.

The prince blows out a laugh. "You've got it wrong. The Council ended Sinisa's contract on Gem when they heard about the Guardians."

"Did they?" Rhet says flatly. "Strange. The Council has never ended a contract before."

Another short laugh, one that seems to drain the smile from Acari's lips as he considers what Rhet is suggesting. "But...Sinisa said that they wanted to learn about the Guardians." Beside me, I sense him pushing himself up again, turning toward me to gauge for himself whether or not what he is realizing is true. "You said they don't want you to kill Gem anymore. That's true, right?"

I don't dare meet his eyes, though I feel my betrayal crashing into him all the same. My eyes are fixated on the ground, but no matter how hard I try focusing them, my vision blurs through tears I have not shed in years.

"Choices. Consequences. Change," Aulow mutters.

"What?" Acari and I ask in unison.

A soft smile tugs at her. "Sometimes we make the wrong choice. Sometimes the consequences feel too great at the time, but later we change our minds about our previous decision."

There's a calm knowingness in her tone but it does nothing to ease my nerves. I feel as if she's talking straight to my soul, like she already knows everything I've done or thought of doing.

"I will ask the question again. Would you like to end your contract on the princess, or do you intend to carry it out?"

My voice is hoarse, and I bristle more than I mean to. "What do you mean do I want to end my contract? No Reaper can."

"You lied!" Acari roars, startling his sister awake. Sitting upright, his legs dangling over the edge, he cradles her closer against him. "You lied to me. You made me believe you were good. You tricked me! You said—"

Aulow holds up her hand. "There will be time for that later. For now though," she says, bringing her attention back to me. A grin broadens between her cheeks, practically illuminating the room. "You have given the correct answer." She turns, cocking her head back to look up at the tree of a man beside her. "I think she's ready, Rhetriel."

"I disagree," Rhet grunts, looking me up and down.

But Aulow waves him off. "As ready as she can be without *knowing*."

"Knowing what?" I ask, cautiously.

Aulow draws closer, taking my hands into hers. I can't help but marvel at her touch, still not sure how it is even possible that I can touch a mortal and they survive it. As my fingers delicately trace over the runes on her hand, my eyes linger on the designs.

She giggles. "Soon you'll understand, if you haven't pieced it together already."

My attention snaps to her, questions lurking behind my eyes.

"Brace yourselves," Aulow says to all of us with a radiant grin. "Your worlds are about to come undone."

20

THE MARK OF PROPHECY
ACARI

"This realm is full of secrets, kept from everyone but those who seek the truth," Aulow begins.

I'm learning the truth of *that* more quickly than I'd like. All this time I thought Sinisa was trying to help me, when really nothing had changed. She is still the Reaper meant to kill Gem, and I've led her directly to her. At least I know that as long as we're here, she can't touch Gem—which is probably why she wanted us to leave so badly. As long as Sinisa can't use her power, she can't complete her contract.

I won't let Sinisa do it. I don't care what it takes, but I will keep Gem protected for the rest of her life. No matter what.

"Secrets," I say with a dark laugh, hugging Gem tighter. "All and sundry present seem to have lots of those, and I'm sorry to be so direct or rude, but I don't know how many more secrets and riddles I can take. So can we just get to the part where you tell us what you know about Sinisa's contract on my sister? Is that why you took Gem? Is that how you knew who she was?"

"Not exactly." Aulow tilts her head. "We knew about Gem because she is one of those secrets I mentioned. Your sister is marked by prophecy."

My focus wavers, first to Sinisa, but when she meets my gaze, I'm reminded of her betrayal, and I look upon Gem instead. She peers up at me from her big, curious eyes. I trace my finger over the scar in her lip.

"Like all of the others who are born misshapen, Gem was born a Prophet. Long ago, people feared the Prophets, declaring their visions dangerous and immoral. It is why it's customary to have them executed now when they are born. It's a barbaric practice that has been carried on, even though most people don't know why they do it anymore."

Awe for my sister only grows the longer I stare down at her. I've always known she was special; I just never knew how.

"A Prophet," I whisper to her like I'm telling her an enchanting fairytale. When she giggles, I'm taken aback by the beauty I see in her that my father fails to notice, and the smile fades from my face. "Does my father know?"

"I would have no way of knowing," Aulow admits, a gentleness to her. "But my guess is no. As far as we can tell, we are the only people living that know of them."

I could be wrong, but I sense the intentionality she uses with her words, and wonder if she's suggesting that people *not* living might know about the Prophets too. Maybe the Council Sinisa works for knows. Maybe she even knew. Why else would they be so determined to kill her?

"What does this have to do with breaking my contract?" Sinisa asks finally, and I hate that I convince myself that there's real remorse in her voice.

"One thing at a time," Aulow says sweetly before continuing. "There was a time when the Prophets were all-knowing. They would have visions of droughts impacting entire kingdoms. They would see the births of children three towns over.

"But that was long ago. Over time, these visions became fewer, more specialized."

"What do you mean?" I ask.

This time, it's Rhet who answers. "They only see each other now."

At the risk of sounding repetitive, I ask again, "What do you mean?"

Aulow begins pacing the room, in slow and meticulous circles, her gaze drifting to the floor. "The Prophets only see the future where each other are involved, and only when a life hangs in the balance. They can only see each other if there is a possibility that the Prophet can be saved. We believe they send each other a kind of signal when they're in danger.

"Your sister called to our Prophets the day you fled the palace."

"She did?" I ask before looking back down at my sister. "You did? Did you know?"

Gem doesn't answer. Instead she buries her head into my chest.

"Hey, it's okay. I'm not mad or anything. I think it's kind of incredible."

That earns me the briefest glimpses of a smile before she slowly pulls her face back up for air.

"How long have you known you could do it?"

"I no know," she whines, tilting her head and looking up at me through self-conscious eyelashes.

"Oh," I say dumbly. "Th-that's okay. I do lots of things that I don't know I'm doing too. Like, just the other day when I was studying with the language tutor, I was so focused that I actually passed gas, completely forgetting the tutor was even in the...room." As Gem erupts with laughter, I glance around the hut, realizing that I'd yet again forgotten that there were other people around me.

I clear my throat, hoping someone will change the subject. To my great relief, Aulow does.

"It's unlikely that your sister has seen much of her talents yet. Most Prophets don't have true visions until they're a little older. Some children her age will have nightmares though, ones that they don't realize are real, but even that is rare for someone so young."

"Okay, great," Sinisa says, forcing an unfriendly smile. "So, you kidnap Prophets and what? Use them to help you find more Prophets? Is that supposed to make us trust you?"

I swallow, straightening my back like I asked the question myself, even though deep down I am far too naive to have ever thought of it. I look to her with a kind of self-abashed gratefulness. It's the first time I chance meeting her eyes since she admitted to still being contracted to kill my sister, and it's the first time since then that I realize: I don't believe she's bad.

She's interrogating these bandits like her only purpose is to protect Gem. And earlier, she saved me from those wolves. She could've easily killed me. She could've just as easily left me at the inn when her Crow returned with the bandits' whereabouts, but instead, she woke me up and we left together.

Maybe it's like Aulow said. Maybe at first, Sinisa made the wrong choice, or maybe she'd planned on doing something that would've been terrible, but now? Now she's asking these people what they know about getting out of a Reaper contract.

"By the dove, no!" Aulow says in a fit of laughter. "You misunderstand."

"We rescue them from Reapers," Rhet barks, arms still crossed against his chest, the thick ropes of his hair resting over his chest. "We provide them safety."

"No Reaper can cross the protective barrier. Not without a blessing from one of us, of course," Aulow explains.

"Yeah, why is that?" I blurt, drawing my gaze from Sinisa. "How does that work anyway? Can Prophets create barriers like that too?"

Another chuckle from Aulow. "I'm afraid not. A Prophet's gift is prophecy. But we"—she points from herself to Rhet—"are not Prophets."

My heart sinks into my stomach.

"Then...what are you?" I ask cautiously, the hope that's growing inside me too much to contain.

Aulow's smile beams again. "I wondered when one of you would ask. It is my pleasure to inform you both that the task you set out to accomplish is complete. I will make no bones about it. We are not bandits. We are not Prophets. We are the Guardians."

21

THE FIRST SOUL

SINISA

Everything seems to slow as the significance of what she's saying hits me.

We found a Guardian. Two, in fact.

We completed our task, and now Gem can have the opportunity at a life that Acari so desperately wants for her.

And for the briefest moment, I am living in triumph.

We did it. We completed our task.

But that bubbly sensation of elation doesn't last when I remember what I am supposed to do next, the decision I have to make.

Claim the life I was set to take, or accept my fate among the Wraiths.

For as long as I can remember, all I've wanted was to become a Shade, to serve Veltuur dutifully, and to help maintain the balance between life and death. I have a place in the underrealm, a purpose. But my goals there seemed a lot more preferable before I knew what the realm of the living had in store. Though regaining one of my memories has proven that there is evil in this realm just as horrific as the Wraiths, more than anything my time here has shown me that this place has far greater things to offer than just suffering.

The night I killed my attacker, I'd done so to protect my friends as much as myself. I felt the same kind of protectiveness toward Acari when we found ourselves surrounded by wolves. I saw it in him too when he realized that I had been lying about my contract for Gem's life.

That kind of connection, that level of love, does not exist in the underrealm.

Completing my mission, returning to Veltuur, means giving up the mortal realm. Again. Only this time, I'd remember what I am giving up. I'd remember losing a friend.

Although Aulow's suggestion was cryptic, and sounded far too good to be true, I am all the more eager to hear what she has to say about ending a Reaper's contract.

But Acari breaks the silence before I can.

"That means..." he says slowly, staring at Aulow. His unhinged jaw widens into a grin as the realization dawns on him. "You can save my sister. The book said that the Guardians healed people—they were able to grow back people's legs and cure them of the worst diseases. That means you can heal Gem's lip. Then my father won't have to...you know, send a Reaper after her. She'll be safe. She'll be able to live a normal life."

Rhet shifts uncomfortably, sharing a dubious look with Aulow who inhales sharply.

"I'm afraid not," she says to him, clasping her hands at her waist. "Not in the way you think."

"But...the stories, they said that the Guardians healed people like her, that they helped protect them and keep them safe. That's why I was searching for you. If you can't save her, then..."

Tutting sweetly, Aulow approaches Acari on the cot, placing a gentle hand to his forehead, and her other to Gem's cheek. "I'm afraid it doesn't work that way. The only way *we* can save her is by bringing her here, under the protection of the boundary, which we have done. But in order to hide her from the contract out on her life, she'd have to stay here with us. Forever." Almost as if to prove her point, she expands further. "Living here, although we make it as normal as can be, it's not like living a normal life. And, any time Gem would leave the encampment, she'd be at risk of a Reaper finding her."

Glaring doesn't begin to describe the way Acari's eyes dart to me. I've never seen such hurt and betrayal in someone as I see now in him. "Not if her Reaper let her live," he begs. "I know you don't want this. You don't have to do it. You could just let her live—"

"No, she can't," Rhet says flatly.

"Well, if she wants to stay a Reaper, she can't. But there *is* another way," Aulow continues, ignoring the other Guardian to stroke Gem's and Acari's faces. "A way for your sister's contract to be terminated with her life still intact."

Aulow shifts her gaze to mine, as if I have the answer and she knows I will explain it.

"What?" I shrug. "Become a Wraith?"

"Waife?" Gem asks, looking up at Acari expectantly, but with a cautionary glance up at me, he shakes his head at his sister and puts a finger to his lip.

"That is one way, I suppose, and perhaps it's best to consider them all before you make your choice." She straightens from the siblings, crossing the room back toward me. "You know the three ways to terminate a contract. Yes?"

"Three?" I protest, growing more doubtful by the second. I don't know why I thought this person, this Guardian would know more about the ways of the Reapers than I do. Only those of us who have lived in Veltuur and lived by its rules will ever truly understand it... "There are only two."

"Yes, well, it would be bad for business for them to tell you there were more, wouldn't it?"

Though I'm still skeptical, I'll admit her confidence intrigues me. I lean in closer, ready to hear whatever she is willing to share.

"The first," she says, looking over her shoulder at Acari. "Is to claim the life—not really the outcome we're looking for though as it in no way saves your sister. The second is to—"

"Kill the person who requested the execution," I answer before she can finish. "But Reapers can't take the life of someone with an active request out. The king would be immune to my touch until I kill the princess."

"Correct," Aulow says, tilting her head toward me before waving a hand in the air. "But that's not important either."

"Get to it, Aulow," Rhet barks, and for the first time since meeting him, I find myself warming to him. I, too, dislike waiting.

"There is a third way, but it is more challenging than all of the others." At this, Aulow reaches out to me and takes my hands into hers. At first, her eyes remain closed, as she squeezes my fingers gently. When she finally looks up at me, the sorrow I see reflected in her gaze makes me wonder if I want to hear what she's about to tell me. "The only way for you to destroy the contract out on Gem, and not to become a Wraith in the process, is to sever your bond to Veltuur."

For a moment, all I can do is blink. Just a moment though, before the roiling bubbling brew deep down in my stomach forces itself out in a bark of laughter. "There is no way out of being a Reaper. Once someone becomes a Reaper, they are indebted to Veltuur for life. I do not know who played this trick on you, but it is false."

My laughter fades only when I see Aulow's seriousness deepen. She and Rhet share a moment, one without words, but the meaning is palpable enough that I understand it. Rhet still thinks I'm not ready, and Aulow is beginning to worry the same.

I do not like people doubting me. I guess I'm stubborn like that.

My teeth grind together before I decide to indulge her. "How do I stop being a Reaper?"

Aulow blinks at me with growing delight. "Retrospection. Reconciliation. Reprieve."

I'm at the peak of an eyeball, a growl low in my throat, when Aulow clarifies.

"All you have to do is make peace with your past."

My eyes stop rolling. Instead, they glare over at her, liquid fire burning within them. Make peace with my past? There is only one thing I remember about my life before, and she certainly can't mean for me to make peace with that.

I shrug, trying to play it off. "What does that even mean?"

"I know it's hard because when you became a Reaper, Veltuur stole your memories. It's how they keep you enslaved to them. Without knowing your past, you can't accept it, and therefore, you can't escape from them."

"But you remember," Rhet growls. "Every Reaper remembers something."

Dread starts to build inside me. Everything had been erased after I'd become a Reaper. Everything except the blood that I now know belonged to the man who abused me for years.

There's a pause, and with it, my anger builds. I can tell by the remorseful incline of Aulow's head exactly what she is going to say before she says it and a voice is already screaming inside me that I can *never* do what she is suggesting. He doesn't deserve my forgiveness.

"Reapers must make peace with the person they killed. That's how they make peace with their past. It's how they move on."

The room starts to spin, and suddenly I am slammed back into the quivering body of that thirteen-year-old girl. I am alone and scared, shivering with fear and rage. I am naked and raw, a puddle of blood surrounding me. Blood that I unleashed. Tainted blood from a man who I was supposed to be able to trust but couldn't.

But I do not regret the decision I made that day. I decided that he would no longer overpower me, at whatever the cost.

"I have made peace with my past. It happened. I can't undo it, but he won't ever hurt me or anyone else ever again, and that is all the knowledge I need to be at peace."

The disdain in my voice makes Aulow wince, even from behind her persistent smile.

"Says the child with a crow," chides Rhet.

I meet his gaze. "What is that supposed to mean? What does my crow have anything to do with it?"

A hand cradles either of my shoulders, pulling my vision back to

Aulow and the speckles on her cheeks. It is difficult to remain combative when looking at her serene expression, but Rhet's words are like seeds planted inside me. They haven't sprouted yet, but I fear they are about to.

"Taking the life of another, even someone who did horrible, awful things to us or those we love, haunts us."

The words stop flowing from her, as she gives them time to sink in. When the pause lingers longer than the others though, I realize she wants me to figure the rest out on my own. Fear quickens my blood. Whatever truth remaining is something so awful that she is hoping she won't have to be the one to say it.

But I don't understand what I am trying to figure out. They are claiming that I have yet to make peace with my past, but I did what had to be done.

These two Guardians do not know me, and they certainly do not know what it was like living as I did. The constant state of shame and disgust. Going to bed every night in sheer terror that he would come for me, or one of the others, and feeling guilty when I had secretly hoped it would be someone else's turn.

What I did, killing him, was the best thing that ever happened to me, to the other children in the orphanage, and to him. My only regret is that he didn't suffer longer.

So, they are wrong. I have made peace with my past, or rather, there is nothing to make peace about. Unlike what Aulow suggested, nothing haunts me. I sleep just fine at night. And yes, I have a crow, but so does every other Reaper so...

My eyes widen with sinking realization.

"No," I breathe, soundlessly. "You are wrong. I chose my crow. It didn't..."

A memory fills my vision, the one of my first night in the Veltuur woods. I was standing before the trees when Leumas told me to go forward and *choose* my crow. I am certain he said it was *me* choosing. But, though I have never questioned it, the more I replay the scene in my mind, the more I remember that walking among the trees felt a lot like fate guiding me to the knotted gnarl of a trunk, drawing my attention up to a single crow waiting in the branches.

"No." The word comes out as a gasp of air, and I start to pant.

In the dim light of the hut, recognition and empathy bloom in Aulow's face, but it is not enough to heal the slash ripping open my chest.

"You're saying..." I try to put my scrambled thoughts into words between shattered breaths, but each one hurts more than the last. The effort to speak at all makes me nauseous. "The man I killed...he is my...my crow. The same crow I have been with...been working with for three years. The same crow that...sleeps over me at night and—" My breaths become too ragged for me to continue.

The room starts to spin again, and I am unsure how long my legs will hold me, how long my lungs will keep me conscious.

"Breathe. It'll be okay," Aulow says sweetly, rubbing both of my shoulders, likely as much to soothe me as to keep me steady. "You will be rid of him as soon as you're able to make amends for taking his life."

The world snaps still.

"Make amends?" My teeth bare as I unleash the wolf inside me. "I did nothing wrong!"

"You killed a man," Aulow says calmly, a voice of reason and sympathy. "Do you feel no remorse for that?"

"No! He deserved it!"

A tidal wave of ice burns through me, so cold that I am left shivering, but so hot I am sweating. From its depths, I'm drowned in a silent rage, wave after wave of fury rolling through me. I was just a child. I didn't deserve any of the things he did to me, but he *did* deserve death. I don't ever, *ever* have to forgive him for what he did.

When I finally blink back into reality, all eyes are fixed on me and I feel the pity in the room like an odious smog. The contents of my stomach threaten me, but it's my rage that sends me bursting for the door like a ravaging tornado. Rhet does nothing to stop me. He only steps aside.

As I race into the blinding light of day, I am bombarded by more scrutinizing eyes. Everywhere I turn, more stare back.

My legs are heavy with lead, but they propel me back toward the wood. Distantly, I hear my name being shouted from behind me, but I don't stop, and I never look back. I can't take any more unraveling today. I just want to be back in the peace and quiet of the woods, some place where I can think.

As I cross the invisible boundary, I feel a surge of power course through me and I find the relief I was searching for. Death lingers beneath my skin once more like a welcomed friend. It is the calm chill that I so desperately needed.

I suck in a few ragged breathes and rub my hands over my face.

But in the same moment that I find relief in its presence, I am also struck by the loneliness it carries. Being a Reaper again means my touch will kill. No more grazes of skin, no more holding hands. The intimacy I was starting to learn about in the healer's hut is ripped from my reality.

I look back over my shoulder. Now, out from the confines of the camp, all I see are trees. Once again a Reaper, the bandit camp evades me, even if I know it lays just beyond the disguise. I reach my hand out, afraid I might not actually be able to return, even if I wanted to.

Caw!

I freeze. Every hair on my body stiffens. My breathing becomes ragged again as I rotate so slowly back around to find Crow on a branch at eye level. It croaks again, and this time I actually flinch.

Not *it*, I realize, catching myself. *He.*

For someone who hasn't felt much of anything for the past three years, I recognize all nine thousand emotions as they trample me.

He was my abuser.

He was supposed to be dead.

He has been at my side all this time doing everything in his power to make my life as miserable as possible.

He.

Still.

Controls.

Me.

But I can't scream, or cry, or laugh, or do whatever it is the emotions inside of me are roaring to do, because a gray haze builds around me like a ring of fire. The fumes lift up and over me until I am enveloped in a cocoon of black smoke.

They have come for me. The Councilspirits are summoning me back to Veltuur.

22

A LIFE IN THE BALANCE

ACARI

My eyes are peeled open with horror as Sinisa bolts from the healer's hut. Her crow. Her actual *crow*... I can't even pretend to understand how she must be feeling right now, but I know it's got to be horrible. She's spent the last three years with that *thing* with her the whole time, the man she thought she escaped that night she finally killed him and became a Reaper.

Aulow doesn't know what she's asking of Sinisa...

Gem scoots from my lap to the edge of the bed and blinks up at me. Her life flashes before me, the one where she is stuck inside this small camp for the rest of her life because Reapers are after her, never able to visit the mountaintops of Ghamaya, the deserts of Marágros, or the beaches of the Coast of Dreams. I know it's selfish and unappreciative to want more for her after we've found safety and her life has been spared, at least for now, but I can't help it. I *do* want more for her. I never wanted her to live all of her days in a tower, and being trapped here will be almost the same.

If we can't convince Sinisa she's strong enough to forgive her past, then Gem's future is condemned. And maybe Sinisa *is* strong enough. What other thirteen-year-old girl has done what she's done and had no regrets? What other young woman has faced off with a pack of wolves and lived to tell the tale?

My smile is lopsided as I nod at Gem one last time before springing from the cot.

The hut tilts one way, then the other, so that I feel as if I'm being carried out to sea on bobbing waves. Before I fall, Aulow steadies me. Despite the throbbing in my shoulder, I lean into her hold until everything settles, before making my way to the door.

With an audible thud, Rhet's hand grasps my good shoulder within his mighty grip. "If she isn't willing, then your sister is only safe here with us."

"You don't know that she's not willing," I protest. "You just don't know what you're asking of her."

A dark shadow rolls over him like a cloud, but I push through the door before he can explain what he knows. There will be time for that later. I just need to get Sinisa back here. She is Gem's only hope, and honestly, I guess I just don't want her to leave. Not like this.

"Sinisa!" I yell, incidentally drawing everyone's attention outside.

My name becomes a hushed murmur among them. It's only been a day or more and somehow I've already forgotten that I am—*was* a prince, and therefore known by all. As I swivel my head searching for signs of Sinisa's path, I'm surrounded by doting and wishful faces, some with scars, some with birthmarks, some missing limbs, and some with none of those. A mixture of Prophets *and* Guardians, I realize.

Before I get distracted by marveling at just how many of them there are, my hands float up in the air. Surely someone here saw her.

"Uh," I stammer, addressing the crowd. "A girl just ran through here. Did any of you, by any chance, see which way she went?"

Almost as one, the small crowd points to an exit. I can just barely see a smudge of red mixed with the trees—Sinisa's tunic. My legs react before I can think and I start sprinting through the camp. I only make it a few steps before the swinging motion of my arms sends a new jolt of pain across my chest, and I fold over in a hunch, cradling it.

When I stand back up, the red smudge is gone. A hollow pit grows in my chest. My feet are desperate, scurrying over rocks and through the compacted dirt until I'm outside of the gate.

As I draw closer to the boundary, I become more aware that the forest is missing its normal sounds. Birds chirping, leaves rustling, there's nothing. There's an eerie quiet that has befallen the trees here and it has me all the more worried about Sinisa.

I don't dare cross the boundary though.

"Sinisa?" I ask in a low whisper.

Just when I think it can't get any quieter, the air stills.

"I'm afraid she's gone," calls a man from somewhere behind the trees.

His voice is so cold that hearing it sends a shiver through me. My neck cranes, searching beyond each tree before a shadowy figure finally steps out from behind a thick oak and leans his back against the bark.

If I thought his voice was cold, he himself radiates it. His skin is as white as ice, and I don't need to see the forehead beneath his hood to know that I'll find no runes there.

I blink, rubbing my eyes. "Are you a pigment of my imagination?"

"I believe the word you're searching for is *figment*. And no, I am not. I assure you, I am entirely real."

"Y-you're a Reaper."

The stranger shrugs. "Something like that."

Tears sting my eyes. Not because I am about to die—because I'm not; no Reaper can cross the boundary. But I am heartbroken, none-theless. There's no doubt in my mind that this Reaper's presence means my father really has taken a contract out in my name. He would rather be childless than have a daughter with a birth defect and a son who defied him.

Shoving himself off the tree, the Reaper slinks toward me like a snake.

I stagger back, farther behind the boundary, away from the approaching Reaper, and closer toward safety. I guess Gem and I might be joining the bandits—I mean, the Prophets and Guardians —together.

It's then that I remember something I'd forgotten, and I become emboldened: Sinisa couldn't see past the barrier, which means he can't either. Though I don't dare turn my back on him, I feel safer as I shuffle backward.

"Oh, I wouldn't leave if I were you," he says, nodding at the distance growing between us. "I'm not here to harm *you*."

At the accuracy with which he addresses me, I stop dead in my tracks. Maybe he can just hear me—maybe Reapers have really good hearing or something... Or maybe he really *can* see me. And if he can see me, then maybe he can cross over.

"If you're not here to harm me, then why are you here? Did my father send you?"

"Dear boy, there are those far more powerful than a meager king. You have upset the balance. A mortal requested a Reaper, Veltuur sent one, and you meddled in their affairs, and now there is one more abomination running around."

"She's not an abomination! She's a Prophet—" My hands fly to my mouth. Although no one told me not to tell anyone, it's only just now that I'm realizing that Aulow said this was a secret as old as time. Sinisa hadn't even seemed to know about them, which probably means I'm not supposed to go around telling everyone about them either, *especially* not the Reapers who are already trying to break in.

A wicked grin creeps from his face.

I purse my lips together. "It doesn't matter. You can't get in here anyway. She's protected, and you'll never get her."

As the man reaches the barrier, he tosses the hood away from his face, revealing bloodred eyes and hair like wheat. He raises an eyebrow. "For now, maybe."

"For—forever! You can't come in here. Reapers aren't able to cross unless—"

"You mean like dear Sinisa couldn't?"

My eyes narrow. "That was different. She was invited."

"Ah. And she's the only Reaper ever to get invited into Guardian territory?"

I find myself staggering backward again, but I can't tell which piece of the statement is more staggering, the fact that this Reaper knows about the Guardians or the suggestion that other Reapers could get through.

"That's...that's not true. You're lying."

I tell myself that Gem is safe. Gem is safe. Gem is safe. She has to be. With Sinisa gone, this is our only hope.

"What you ought to be worrying yourself with is whether or not you believe that a Reaper, if determined enough, could infiltrate the encampment," he says, taking one final step forward. He taps the invisible shield, a cruel curve of his lips. "And I'll give you a hint—we can."

If she's not safe here, then she's not safe anywhere. Not until the contract on her life has been ended. I refuse to let it end in her death, and if Sinisa won't help us then...that only leaves one other option.

"You know the only real way to keep your sister safe," the Reaper says.

And I *do* know. Thanks to Aulow and Rhet, I have all the answers I need to be the one to save her myself. And for once, I don't have to think about it. I will do anything to save Gem.

"I have to kill my father."

23

BETRAYAL

SINISA

The darkness I am encased in holds longer than I expect. I have taken a hundred breaths while I float here, maybe a thousand, and still I linger in the black nothingness. Never before has a trip to Veltuur taken this long. Part of me wonders if the Council has decided to skip a conversation and has gone straight to sending me to the Wraiths.

At least Crow is nowhere in sight. I seem to be free of him, at least while I am stuck here. That realization alone is enough to make me wish I could be stuck here forever, even if the Wraiths are coming.

Not a moment later, Veltuur pulls me into its thrall.

I slap onto the stone floor on hands and knees. Somehow, as I stand in the Pit of Judgment to face the Council, I am even less prepared than the last time I was here.

I know *why* I have been summoned. They expect answers about the Guardians that I was sent to find, though I am no longer sure what I want to share. Telling them anything will lead them straight to Acari and Gem. I may have fled from them, but it was never my intention to run straight into the Council's arms and toward Gem and Acari's damnation, not until I had a plan at least.

And now that I am here, there is no time to think of one. The

Council will expect full cooperation, and I am a loyal servant of Veltuur, so why wouldn't I give it to them? But I'm surprised to find I don't want to. Somehow, keeping all of this a secret from Acari is starting to feel like a greater betrayal than omitting anything from the Council.

The chamber of council seats is exactly as I last saw it. The six Councilspirits sit in their respective thrones, towering over the pit I am standing in. The most ornate throne of all though is still empty, and even as all of the eyes in the room aim at me like daggers, I can't help but speculate where the seventh Councilspirit is. Perhaps they too betrayed Veltuur and were sent to the Wraiths. Perhaps there is a fate worse than that.

"You smell like the living," Nymane says, addressing me with a scrunched nose that causes more cracks to fissure her porcelain skin.

Decrepitly slow, Leumas stands, his arms stretched as wide as his grin. "A welcomed return, Reaper Sinisa. I believe what my fellow Councilspirit means is that you have spent much time in the realm of the living and your sacrifice for our cause is much appreciated."

"Your fellow Councilspirit said exactly what she meant," Nymane sneers. "Let's skip the formalities and theatrics for once. Tell us what you learned of the Guardians. We're told you found the place where they have been hiding, protected by some barrier, but somehow *you* were able to cross it. How?"

I try to remain stoic, but inside my heart is a ruckus. They already know far more than I want them to know, and I can only assume I can thank Nerul for that. If he's already been updating them regularly on my whereabouts, then they already know exactly where the camp is, and Acari, Gem, and everyone else there is already doomed. Regardless of whether or if I withhold telling the Council how to cross the boundary, it will only be a matter of time before they figure out a way through for themselves. They'll make it their priority, if they're as invested in locating the Guardians as I believe they are.

It's then that I realize how puzzling that is. As far as I can tell, the Guardians were tapped out. Acari asked them directly to heal his sister, and they said they were unable to do so. Why the Council would be interested in them is beyond me. Unless maybe they're the ones who created the boundary. I suppose that would make them useful to the Council.

"Well?" Nymane snaps, her lips tight.

"Yes, I found them. But I didn't learn much about them. They have no power to heal the princess, like the prince requested. They are worthless. They are no better than the other mortals."

A snickering ripples overhead from each of the Councilspirits.

"I assure you; they are of greater importance than you know," Leumas says, his smile fading.

The longer we hold each other's gazes, the more I sense something different about him. He is not his usual confident self, and neither is he showing me the pride he typically has in my work. Though my first thought is that he knows I am stalling and withholding information, as the laughter continues around him, and he declines to partake in it, staring only straight down upon me, digging into my eyes, I sense only his urgency. He is trying to communicate something with me, I am almost certain of it.

The laughter fades before I can decipher his code though. Leumas switches his smile back on.

"So, Reaper Sinisa, please respond to Councilspirit Nymane's question. How did you diffuse the magic to cross the barrier surrounding their stronghold?"

I swallow, buying half a second more that is still about an hour less than the time I need. I can't tell them what they want to hear, but I am not yet ready to face the Wraiths. I...I should have stayed at the healer's hut. I should have never left. The Council would have never been able to find me there, but now I am at their mercy. If I do not tell them willingly, they will surely have the Wraiths torture it from me.

A black glint flutters just outside my view, and I turn to find my crow flying up to the Councilspirits.

Caw, he squawks at me when he lands, his head jutting low and more forcefully than usual, like it's threatening me with the point of his beak.

Rage sparks through me like tinder catching flame. Hot and

mighty. The longer I stare up at him, the more hatred that seethes through me until I am pretty sure my body is one giant inferno.

I want to rip its head off. *His* head off. I want to stab him a dozen times over again, and I would if he was not so far out of reach.

"You will be rewarded for your efforts, Reaper Sinisa," Nymane purrs, clacking her lengthened fingernails together like claws. "Or should I call you, *Shade* Sinisa, hmm?"

The title draws my attention away from the crow for a moment, the coveted position of a Shade finally within my grasp. I had earned it; there was no doubting that. I had spent the past three years tirelessly collecting souls for Veltuur, abiding by every rule of the Reapers, worshipping the underrealm without fault, and now I was finally being recognized for my loyalties.

Or at least that is how it would have been, had everything been different. If I had killed Gem like I was supposed to and claimed my five thousandth soul right there in the palace, I would have accepted the role of Shade without hesitation and with immense pride.

But now the title repulses me. To carry it would be a constant reminder of the betrayal of the only mortal friend I have. To ascend to a role of power, and to work side-by-side with the Councilspirits, would make me complicit in the torture they put the Reapers through by making them work alongside the people they have slain.

The ruffling of the crow's feathers makes me clench my fists, and I snap my vicious gaze back toward him.

I feel Leumas' scowl as he assesses me. "Is everything all right? Is that not what you wanted? To become a Shade?"

Before I can answer, a cloud of smoke forms behind Leumas, and with a hollow pop of air, Nerul appears from within it.

The Shade bows deeply, his blond hair falling over the pale skin of his face. "Forgive my tardiness, Councilspirits. I was caught up recruiting another Reaper."

When we make eye contact, his lips curve, resembling the shriveling of rotten fruit. The expression leaves me just as sick as if I'd eaten some.

Although at first, his appearance surprises me, when I catch the warm greeting Nymane casts him, I realize he has likely just been summoned to provide the information that I have been hesitant to give.

"Well done," Nymane purrs. "We can always use another Reaper, especially one who's already lost so many. He'll have fewer...limitations."

"He'll have *none* once he kills his father," Nerul corrects. "Now, what did I miss? Have you passed the verdict yet on what to do with this *Reaper*?"

Though Nymane answers him, her words are drowned out as the weight of their conversation about recruitment hits me in the chest.

"Who?" I blurt, my skin cold and clammy. "Who did you recruit, Nerul?"

His smile widens. "The prince, of course. Easiest recruit I've ever nabbed. He was raring for a kill. All in the name of justice too. It's always a perfect motive. I figured his sister will likely be out of our reach now—no thanks to you—but the time we spent with that family didn't have to be a complete waste."

"No," I breath, but I make sure that no one above can hear me.

As Nerul continues, giving the Council a play-by-play of the last couple of days he spent tailing me, I find myself spiraling into my own thoughts. Acari is going to murder the king—his own father. In order to save his sister, he is going to condemn himself to the life of a Reaper, *and* once he reaches Veltuur, he will have no knowledge of it. The second he is initiated, he will lose all memory of it. He will forget who he killed and why; he will forget his sister, and his late brother and mother. Everything. The person he is will be erased from existence entirely, and he will never come back.

It is a fate I can't imagine. Not for him. Not for sweet, naive, compassionate Acari.

There has got to be another way.

Just then, the crow flies down into the pit, landing on the ground in front of me. He swivels his head, like he is waiting for me to do the thing I am not even sure I can do. Like he has been waiting for years for this moment.

It does not have to end like this for Acari. There *is* another way. Aulow had said as much.

The conversation continues above, the Councilspirits paying little to no attention to the crow and I below them.

I suck in a deep breath and whisper. "I... am..."

The words stick to my tongue like the slime of a snail. All it will take is one simple word, one tiny, little apology, and Acari and Gem can keep their lives. My contract on Gem's life will be broken, and I will cease being a Reaper. I am not sure what that will entail exactly, but I imagine as I am already before the Council, it won't much matter. They will send me to the Wraiths regardless.

But that is hardly the point. The point is: Acari won't have to make the mistake he is about to make. All I have to do is utter three simple words, a quick apology, and forgive the man that my crow once was.

But it is *not* a simple apology. It is the exact opposite of simple. I can't say I am sorry to the man that stole my innocence, to the man who violated more than just my body, and is the very reason I became a Reaper. He should be the one apologizing to *me*!

The crow ruffles his feathers with a hop, and it is almost like he is urging me on.

I am so conflicted that I bite my lip. This man does not deserve my apology, but Acari also does not deserve to become a Reaper and lose everything he has been fighting so hard for.

"I...I am sorry," I grit out, pained and sullied, like my own tongue has just betrayed me.

The crow blinks at me and I blink back. Time seems to stand still as I wait for something to happen. But the longer we stand there, the less I'm sure of what I am waiting for. A transformation? A flash of light? A vision of Aulow to appear in the air to tell me, "*Congratulations! Gem has been spared!*"?

But none of those things happen. Instead, nothing happens. I reach my hand up to my forehead and find that my runes are still gone.

My stomach churns. Aulow was wrong. It didn't work, and now all I can think about is how I have just apologized to the one person in the entire world who didn't deserve it, the person who laughed at me every time he stole me away and has likely been laughing at me every day since.

"No," I snarl, realizing only seconds too late that I have finally drawn the attention of the Councilspirits.

"Beg pardon?" Leumas asks, but I ignore him, my focus saved solely for the crow.

"No! I'm not sorry. You deserved to die." My voice rises with my fury. "You were cruel and vile, and because of me, you were stopped. Because of me, you never hurt anyone else."

Distantly, I hear the Councilspirits shift closer, inching to the edges of their pedestals to watch everything unfold. A wave of hushed, uncertain whispers carries through the chamber again, but it is Leumas that addresses me.

"You finally know."

If I had not devoted so much of my wrathful attention to the crow, I might have noticed the pride returning in his tone. Instead, I get swept up in my fury.

"We were just children! We were your wards! You had no right to take any of us, and I would kill you again and again if ever given the chance! I am not sorry, and I will never be sorry!"

From above, I hear Nymane delight at our spectacle. It serves only as fuel to my billowing fire.

I snap my attention up to the Council. "And you knew! All of you knew and you just let it happen. You stole my memories and made me work alongside *him*. After everything he did to me!"

The tears run freely now, tears that I didn't even know I was capable of shedding.

My chest heaves up and down, but there is too much going on in my mind for me to say it all. I trusted them! I looked up to them; I wanted to be just like them.

"Reaper Sinisa," Leumas says.

"*Shade*," Nymane corrects. "If she ends this drama and tells us how to infiltrate the Guardians' camp."

"I will not," I say through gritted teeth, my fists clenched at my sides.

I almost shirk from the words as they spill out, but once they are alive, I realize how much I really mean them. The Council, Veltuur, they have never served me. I have been loyal, and I have been diligent, and yet they let my rapist live out his days at my side and never once bothered to tell me. They are malicious, vile creatures, and I have no interest in serving by their sides. Not anymore. Not when a mortal boy whose sister I had been sent to kill showed me more kindness and warmth than the people I thought were my mentors.

"Reaper Sinisa," Leumas says slowly, taking me in with wide eyes. "Surely, you know what's at stake if you do not cooperate. The minimum sentence for failing to complete a contract is thirty years with the Wraiths. There would likely be further sentencing for disobeying additional orders. You could be looking at a lifetime sentence of torture. Are you sure your priorities are ordered correctly?"

Although he says the words like they are a warning to be heeded, I get the sneaking suspicion that the question has two meanings: one meant to appease the Council, and the other...dare I say that the other seems to be prompting me to reflect deeper.

Like I always have when it comes to Leumas' advice, I listen to his subtle encouragement. The simple answer I find is that I don't have a simple answer. My priorities seem to be changing, but for what purpose? I am powerless in making any real change. I can't disobey the order without consequence and therefore I have no chance at saving Acari or his sister. The best option I seem to have is cooperating in hopes of at least getting to befriend Acari again once he is initiated, but that still leaves me stuck working alongside the crow.

A new, heart-wrenching epiphany crosses my mind: if Acari completes his plan and murders his father, then he too would fall into the Council's clutches and be forced to work with his father forever, never knowing the betrayal either of them committed.

Acari deserves better. I deserved better too, but I can hardly change that now.

And that's when the anger slips away. With a flash of clarity, the realization sinks deeper: I can't change my past. It was unfair and I didn't deserve it, but it happened. Acari didn't deserve to lose his mother and brother, and Gem didn't deserve to be hunted, but we can't change any of that. All that matters now, all that we *can* change now, is what awaits Acari in his future.

With an ever-growing sense of understanding, my eyes draw back down to the crow still standing on the pit floor. Aulow had said that I needed to make peace with my past, not apologize to it. I never have to forgive him for what he did to me, but I also don't have to let it control me. I don't have to let it define me. I am more than just a Reaper with a crow. I am Sinisa Strigidae. I had a life before my initiation, and I can have another one, if I want it.

I fix the crow in my gaze, an invisible weight lifting from my shoulders.

"It doesn't matter what you did any longer. What's done is done. You paid for your crimes, and I have paid for mine." When I feel the faintest smile creeping up my cheeks, my hand floats to my face unsure that it is real. "You can't hurt me anymore."

Nymane pushes off from her throne. "What is she doing?"

Leumas can no longer maintain the charade. As I blink up at him, his proud smile is radiant and peaceful. "She is breaking her chains."

"Someone stop her!" Nymane shrieks.

The rest of the Councilspirits rise from their thrones like the blackened trees of Veltuur, their limbs writhing and frantic. They shout commands at each other and the shadows that lurk in the room, calling on them to recapture me before I can slip away from Veltuur.

But they are too late. I can already feel it. The shackles that have kept me bound to the underrealm have been broken. The crow at my feet dissipates like smoke with a soft, peaceful sigh.

As I lift my chin to the Council above, Veltuur shatters out of view and I am sucked back into the realm of the living.

24

HOME NO MORE

ACARI

"I can't do this," I say to no one but myself and the horse I'm riding, the one I found just outside the bandit—I mean, the Guardian camp. Its body jerks beneath me, but I do my best to hold on tight.

Yes, you can do this.

"No, I can't."

Yeah, you're probably right. You can't.

"See? Even my own mind agrees with me. I wasn't made for this." I groan before adding, "The Divine Lorik must be laughing down at me."

Though the Reaper I met in the woods never gave me an exact deadline, I get the feeling like I don't have long to end this before they send someone to take Gem. Besides, the longer I wait, the more I'll think about the repercussions and the greater risk there is that I'll talk myself out of doing this. I can't let that happen. I have to do this, for Gem. She is better off alive and without me than she is dead.

I dig my heels into the mare's flanks, and she whinnies, her hooves galloping harder, faster.

As we approach the kingdom, we settle into a calm gait, but being on a horse draws more attention than I need. I can't let word reach my father that I've returned. He can't expect me.

I tie the horse off at the first tavern we come across.

After being knocked unconscious on the forest floor, an encounter with wolves, and riding a horse for far longer than I ever want to again, I realize I must look awful, but I play that to my advantage. No one recognizes me as their former future king. Instead, in my rags, in the bloodstained tunic that has thankfully dried to a dirt brown, I manage to blend in quite well. It is, however, the first time I actually pay attention to the grime caked on my skin and under my fingernails. With a grimace, I wipe my hands on my legs, even though they too are covered in dirt.

Maybe once I'm a Reaper, being dirty won't bother me anymore. Not dirt, not spiders, not my own shadow. It might be the only thing I have left to look forward to: I will no longer be the awkward coward that I am. I'll be...

Well, I imagine I'll be more like Sinisa: fearless and brave and powerful and—oh, Divine Altúyur I can*not* think about this right now.

Unseen, I make my way to the palace amid the crowd of peasants and merchants. Instead of risking going through the main gates, I take one of the secret entrances, the same one Gem and I raced out of not two days ago.

I close the hidden door behind me, turning around to abruptly run into a servant with a heaping tray. As I stumble to the ground, she manages to pivot and spin, catching the weight of every glass on her platter without a single one of them falling.

"Sorry. I didn't see—"

"Acari?" Hayliel whispers, and my gaze snaps up to meet hers.

I never thought I'd see her again. My mouth is agape, ready to launch into the hundreds of things I'd like to say to her, but instead they clog my throat and I just sit there, staring, taking every inch of her in like I am seeing a spirit.

Tears fill her green eyes, and she's on the floor beside me before I can even stand.

"What are you doing here?" she asks slowly, setting the tray down on the marble floor. "Did you save your sister?"

"Not yet," I admit, steeling myself against what needs to be done. "But I will. It's why I'm here."

She draws back. "What do you mean?" The distance gives her a better view of the state of my dirty clothes. She peers behind me. "Where is she?"

"She's safe, for now. But I don't think she has much time." I pause when more servants walk by, their arms overflowing with yarrow, jugs of wine, and trays of decadent figs, chutneys, and other treats.

When they're out of earshot, Hayliel helps me to my feet. We both stare at where our hands have entwined themselves together, and she is the first to break away, her head lowered.

"Your father, he...he won't be pleased to see you have returned. Especially not on the first day of the Festival of Wings."

A dark chuckle escapes me. "No, he *really* won't be."

"What do you mean?

I shake my head. "It's nothing. I just—I have to do something, and he isn't going to like it. But I don't think I'll be able to move around the palace like this," I say, looking down at the dirt and blood caked on my chest and legs.

"No, you won't," she says, before jerking her head. "Come. Follow me."

Hayliel guides me down the open-air corridors, past curious and worried onlookers, and into the palace's launder. I don't normally have use for this place, so I had honestly forgotten it even existed. She grabs me a fresh pair of servant's garb from a nearby hanging line, and I dress in the far corner of the room, all too aware of my bare skin occupying the same room as hers—*not* that her skin is bare too or anything, just that—

She clears her throat. "Have you finished dressing," she asks the ground, her back to me.

I'm still finishing securing the final three of the jade buttons of the simple doublet, when I turn around to face her. She must sense my readied presence because she turns around to meet me.

Hayliel tilts her head. "I know it's not your usual—"

"Exactly, and that's what makes it perfect. No one can know I'm here, Hayliel. You have to promise me, you won't tell anyone."

"Of course, but...why not? What is it you plan to do?" Her hands, clasped in her lap, begin to work over themselves. Taking a moment to bite her inner lip, Hayliel crosses the space between us in shy, slow steps, the pink fabric of her petticoat ruffling in the quiet of the launder. There's a dim glow from the window that has been carved from the stone, and there's just enough light to make her runes—the ones that match her waistcoat—dazzle like unearthed rhodonites.

When she stops so close to me that I can smell the sweet warmth of her breath, my knees almost buckle.

From under her thick lashes, Hayliel looks up at me. "What are you going to do, Acari? I worry that, whatever knowledge you found out there, it is going to bring your demise."

I don't realize I'm doing it, but I'm nodding. I've never wanted to lie to her, and I guess part of me thinks that, since once all of this is done I'm going to forget everything, at least one person should remember, should know the sacrifice I made.

"I... The only way to save my sister..." My mouth freezes in motion, unable to voice what should be the unthinkable. Honestly though, that's not why I stop. The truth is, I *have* thought about it. I made up my mind and there is no changing it. But I know what I'm about to say will change things forever between me and Hayliel. I know it'll change the way she's gazing up at me right this very moment, and the truth is, changing that scares me more than anything else. But today isn't the day for being a coward. Today I am guided by the Divine Lorik. So, I take a deep breath and finish. "I am here to kill my father."

Her dazzling eyes ripple with tears. "Acari, you can't mean that," she says, bringing a delicate hand to her lips.

"I found the Guardians. They told me they couldn't save her, but that there are two other ways to save Gem from a Reaper's grasp. The first is to get the Reaper to end their contract, but the Reaper that took Gem, well..."

With a heavy sigh, I shake my head and avert my gaze to the window for a moment. After everything Sinisa has been through, I know it's not fair of me to be mad at her for running away. Perhaps that was the only thing she could think to do to try to save Gem. Who knows? At least, that's the version of the story I keep telling myself, not that she abandoned us when we needed her the most.

"She couldn't do it," I say finally, returning my eyes to Hayliel's. Her hand has fallen now, if only slightly, to rest on her collarbone. "And the second way is to kill the person who sent the Reaper."

I step past her, hoping to make it to the door in huge, leaping steps before she can summon the words to speak, but she grabs my arm, stopping me in place.

At her beckoning, I turn to face her, finding her just as close as before.

"Please, don't do this," she begs, a single tear falling down her cheek. "You'll be—I can't—"

As her lip starts to tremble, I remind myself that today I am guided by bravery. Before I can think myself out of it, I take her chin into my fingers, dip her head back, and kiss the sea salt tears from her lips.

They're soft, softer than the petals of a rose, and they press into mine. Every so often, they quiver again, as do mine, savoring and agonizing the moment for what it is: our first and only kiss.

When I break away, emotion escapes her like the waves crashing on the shore. "Please."

"I have to save my sister," I say, my own eyes tear-stained.

As I take my steps backward, making my way to the door, my heart breaks when Hayliel melts to the floor like water. I want to run back to her side, to kiss her again, to wipe her face clean of any ounce of pain that I have caused her, but as I pull the door open, I see that it can never be done. For as Hayliel peers up at me one last time, I see a new rune is glowing in her skin, freshly branded: the rune of grief and heartbreak.

25

THE WEAPON
ACARI

A few halls away from where I left Hayliel, I finally start to realize that I have no idea where I'm going. Though I spent hours on a horse deep in thought as I rode back to the palace, not once had I considered *how* I was going to do what needed to be done. I—I've never killed anyone before. I'm not really sure how I'm supposed to do it.

I suppose the obvious answer is with a knife. There are a dozen in the kitchen that I could choose from, but I can't help but laugh at the thought of feeble me wielding a blade against my boulder-esque father. If it came down to a battle of strength between me and him, he'd have me subdued in a matter of seconds.

Which means knives, and any real weapons of force, are out of the question. Not to mention, that sounds way bloodier than I can stomach...

Then, there's the option of poison. It seems a respectable enough way to die, albeit a less than respectable way to kill someone. Sure, it would be cowardly, I guess, but there would be no strength involved, no bloodshed; I wouldn't even have to be in the same room with him when it happened. I could slip something into the food prepared for him for the banquet tonight, let the servers take him his meal, and then wait for the deed to be completed.

However, who knows how long it would take for it to work. Oftentimes at large gatherings, my father spends far more time socializing than feasting, not to mention his meals are typically served from the same duck and boar as everyone else's. I know I'm going to be killing a lot of people in the near future, but I kind of don't want to add an entire kingdom to my death toll just yet.

Come to think of it, I don't even know where I'd get poison.

As I shuffle through the familiar halls of my home, racking my brain for the options at my disposal, I am lured by the fresh scent of foliage. You'd think that after spending the last day or more in the woods that I would be done with nature, but the Forbidden Garden will always have a special place in my heart. And after rushing out of the bandit—I mean, *Guardian* encampment without gathering my belongings first, I realize I don't have any more memory leaves.

It might be nice to see my brother and mother one more time before I...go.

Before I forget they ever even existed...

I nod at the servant walking by me, keeping my head down while they clear the hall. Once they're gone though, I dart through the remaining hallways until I find my way to the Forbidden Garden.

"Acari!" Borgravid gapes at me, losing focus long enough for his rigid posture to ease, but not enough to leave the doors unguarded. "Where have you been? The king has been searching for you. No one knew where you'd gone."

"I—I know. Listen, it's a long story, but—"

"Is it true then?" he asks, voice quiet. A dark shadow creeps over his face, making him appear at least a decade older than I remember. "About the king requesting a Reaper for your sister?"

My eyebrows arch. "You know about Gem?"

His head looks heavy when he shakes it. "Not until the day you left. I met the Reaper when she arrived, and when she told me who she was here for, I tried finding you."

"Yeah, sorry about that," I say, wincing. "I didn't know what you were going to do once you found me. I thought Father sent you."

He frowns, piecing things together, but there's a hint of a smile twitching the edges of his lips when he asks, "The handmaiden? She lied for you?"

"Yeah," I say, breathless and guileless. My hand finds the crook of my neck again.

Borgravid eyes me, his smile growing more absolute. "Never mind the girl. What does it mean that you have returned?"

Unable to look him in the eyes, I cast my gaze down the hall and pretend to be keeping a lookout.

"What of your sister?" he asks further. "Were you able to save her?"

"Not yet," I admit. "But that's why I'm here."

Bogravid reaches for my shoulder, forcing me to return my attention to him. When I do, he unclasps the talisman at his shoulder with his free hand, the one that represents his allegiance to my father. It falls to the floor with a metallic chime that echoes up the arched ceiling and down either side of the hallway.

"Whoa. Borgravid, you can't—"

"I swore an oath to protect the people of Oakfall, and I will do whatever I am able to protect your sister. Whatever you need, my prince."

I bury my face into my hands, lest he see the guilt behind my eyes. I can't ask him to do this. I can't make him an accomplice to what I have to do.

Bending my knees, I squat down to the marble to retrieve the golden emblem. When I rise, I hand it to Borgravid, but he doesn't take it. With a roll of my eyes, I finally fasten it back into the shoulder of his armor.

"I appreciate it, I really, *really* do, but I don't need anything from anyone. All I need is one last visit in the garden."

With a bob of my head, I signal to the doors behind him, and on cue, we both look through the crystal-clear glass, to the greenery just beyond.

He sighs heavily before turning back toward me. "If that is all you need, then of course, I will oblige."

Borgravid pounds his fist against his chest once before stepping aside.

I want to thank him for everything he's ever done for me, to say goodbye because I know we will never see each other again, but I can't bring myself to do either. With my head bowed low, I enter the Forbidden Garden one final time.

The serene beauty of the place instantly puts me at ease. Though I'd like to take a slow stroll along the pebble paths that have recently brought me so much comfort, it's a luxury I can't afford.

Hunched and keeping to the shadows, I make my way to the memory tree. I use its drooping branches to conceal myself as I gaze up along its trunk. Once I'm gone, I wonder if anyone else will visit this place and use its resources.

I tug a single leaf free from the branch and open wide. Though making a tea would help it taste better, I'm pretty sure that grinding them in my teeth will also release the oils, even if it means it'll be a potent experience.

But before I can place the leaf onto my tongue, I spy the greenhouse through the dangling branches and my arm freezes, the leaf so close that I can practically taste it. Though the Forbidden Garden is silent, hidden away from the commotion of the preparations for the Festival of Wings outside, it's like the aacsi are calling to me.

I can't believe the thought hadn't crossed my mind sooner.

Forgetting about the memory tree entirely, I maneuver through the hanging branches to the glass door and let myself inside.

At the back of the greenhouse, I face the wall of glass boxes.

It's only fitting, really. My brother and mother lost their lives to the aacsi, and because of their deaths, my father has finally decided it's time to end my sister. What better way to end all of this than in the same way it began?

I reach up to retrieve one of the boxes, jumping and nearly dropping the thing when the creature inside attacks the glass case with a hiss. It hardly looks more than a simple rock with sharp edges, but when it keeps throwing itself at my hands, where the beds of my fingers are pressed into the glass, I see the tentacles splay out from its maw as it prepares to launch its parasites at the first contact with skin it can make.

It hits me all too hard that I am holding a box with a deadly creature inside it, and I find myself feeling even more antsy to find my father. Before the first banquet of the Festival of Wings, the king always treats himself to a nice, warm soak in the baths.

Tucking the box against my chest, I exit the way I came, waving briefly back at Borgravid without another word.

I tense when I walk past the secret passage. It's not that Borgravid would know it's there, but I worry he does and that any second now he'll yell after me and ask what I'm doing. Although he just proclaimed his allegiance to me and doing whatever I need, I really don't think killing the king was on the list of things he considered I'd be planning.

I walk as fast as I can through Sungem Courtyard, trying desperately not to draw any more attention to myself than I can help. It's mostly a futile attempt, since now that I'm cleaned, many people recognize me, and stare perplexed at the clear box in my hands. Thankfully, not too many people in the palace know what is kept inside the Forbidden Garden though, so although they are clearly interested in my presence, none of them are alarmed. Still, when I pass a table of sheer cloths and embroidered fabrics meant to decorate the banquet hall, I grab one and drape it over the box.

The aacsi has finally stopped thrashing inside by the time I reach the door to the bathing house. Steam leaks from the crack below the doorway. I feel it lick my face like the hot breath of a wolf, just seconds before it bit into me.

Somehow, I manage to suppress a moan before I step inside.

The door's silence as I open and close it acts as my accomplice as I sneak into the nearly empty sauna. The darkness, too, conceals me in the large room, and I walk on silent toes down the rows of steaming baths. Each one I pass is empty. Dozens of baths, ready for the festivities to begin, but not until my father has this moment of solitude.

I finally spy him in the farthest corner of the expansive room, as far away from the commotion as he can be. I creep behind a pillar even though with his head resting back along the edge of the bath and a mask of papaya covering his eyes, I know he has no awareness of my presence.

Each step I take forward is more hesitant than the last, as the severity and finality of it all hits me.

But I have no time for second guesses. I am here to save Gem, and I'm the only one that can now.

My toes reach the edge of his overflowing tub. The small puddle that's spilt over onto the stone floor seeps into my shoes, wetting my toes in warmth as if I am already standing in my father's blood. I guess, in a way, I already am.

With one hand on the lid, the other clutching the bottom of the container, I bend down, placing the glass box beside my father's head. I take a final, deep breath and open the lid.

26

AACSI, SHADOW, DEATH

SINISA

T he musty scent of dusty linens sends me into a fit of coughing. But as Veltuur's smoke dissipates around me, and I am able to control the choking of my throat, I recognize the room immediately.

Eight beds line the walls askew on rickety, rotting frames. Most of them are bare, but a few are covered in sheets that hang over the edges like disheveled drapes and frayed cloth. The room is so empty and desolate that I shiver. At least, I tell myself that's why, until my gaze falls to the creaking floorboard beneath my feet and to the rust-colored stain that blooms like poison in the wood.

My old room, the place where I grew up before I was swept away to Veltuur, is just as I remember it, and yet horribly different. Tainted. Marred.

Forsaken.

My boot thuds on the panel flooring as I toe my way outside of the ring of dried blood. I flinch at the sound as it echoes down the empty halls. Suddenly, I'm that little girl all over again, afraid to make a noise, afraid of being noticed.

That's when I remember. More than just the night I killed him, but all of it.

The past three years are like a cyclone in my mind. The murder, my servitude, the Crow. But the spiral deepens, taking me further into my past than I have been in years. The orphanage I grew up in, the friends I loved, the family I lost, my favorite color, my favorite dish, the first time I had a bloody nose, the first time I lost a tooth, my dreams, my fears. All of it.

When the images returning to me finally cease, my hands find their way to my body like it is foreign to me now. I don't know what I'm searching for as they rove: to see if I'm still alive? To see if this is just a dream? But I appear to be solid, and the faint sounds of the busy streets outside lead me to believe that I am once again in the realm of the living, the realm where—I realize—I will be spending the rest of my days.

There is a speck of hope that threatens to burst inside me, but I keep it at bay and run to the nearest shattered mirror. My eyes are closed at first, too afraid to be proven wrong. After all, perhaps the Council just sent me back to complete my original contract? Or maybe this is the place the Wraiths take you to do their torture, a twisted version of my greatest nightmares.

But that can't be it. I have no crow, and I feel different here. The energy inside me is…lighter.

Finally, I bring myself to open my eyes, and they stare back at my older, but still young face. I don't think I have looked at myself in three years. My once round and childlike features have sharpened, becoming the defining marks of young womanhood. There is something in my eyes that seems heavier, and my hair has darkened.

But it is my forehead that I am drawn to and I nearly gasp at the sight.

Runes, a shade between lilac and thistle, are prominent in the space below my hairline. I blink, expecting them to be a dream, but each time I reopen my eyes, they remain. Still unconvinced, I reach up to touch them, just in case, but that is when I really gasp.

At first glance, my hands are so thoroughly covered that they appear to be dipped in purple ink from fingertip to wrist. I flip them around in front of my widening eyes to find they're not solid purple, but adorned in intricate lace, spirals, and feathers, just like Rhet, just like the healer, and just like Aulow.

My thoughts ache to figure out why we would all share markings that I have never seen before. Since Rhet and Aulow were Guardians, I had just assumed that that's how they had earned the runes on their hands. But if I have them too...

It does not take me long to venture a guess.

These runes can only mean one thing because only one thing has happened to me since I became a Reaper: I un-became a Reaper. The runes on Rhet's hands, the runes on the healer's and Aulow's hands, they are the marking of someone who is no longer a Reaper.

The waterfall of questions pours through my thoughts and makes me regret ever leaving the encampment, but so does something else. Acari. I trace a finger over one of my hands and realize that this is the sign I was looking for earlier, the verification that I have saved Gem.

And Acari does not know.

A lump forms in my throat. If I don't find him soon, he is going to make the biggest mistake of his life. But without knowing where he is, running all over the kingdom in search of him would take more time than I have. I have to meet him where he is going. I need to find his father before he does.

Without another thought, I race down the dilapidated staircase and out of the vacant orphanage, rushing toward the palace to find the king. I remember these streets like I used to, back when I was a child who would play in them every day. The palace is far, but I know the shortcuts.

By the time I am at the fortified walls, my lungs are burning. I hunch over my knees, catching my breath while I try to figure out how I am going to get inside without a confrontation.

"Welcome, lords and ladies," one of the guards shouts in greeting, drawing me up from my stoop, just in time to watch the large ensemble of people step through the gates. They're covered in feathers and flowers, carrying baskets and chalices of all types of offerings, from berries to gold to handwoven bracelets.

Though I was never given a royal invitation to the festivities that occur at the palace during the Festival of Wings, I recognize the outfits and offerings nonetheless. As a girl, the other orphans and I would leave the parade early to climb to the highest rooftops in the city to be able to glimpse inside the palace walls. Of course, we were never able to see a thing.

"Right this way," the guard says with a friendly nod. "We are honored by your presence. The king will be with you all shortly. Please, make your way through Dove Plaza and to Quetzal Wing where you'll find the great hall. Welcome, lords and ladies..."

While the guard repeats his instructions for the next batch of nobles he encounters, I slip in among the traveling party. Only the person beside me seems to notice, and though she stares at me with apprehension, eyeing my red tunic, I quickly pacify her with a giddy smile—something I forgot I even knew how to do. But to be honest, what surprises me more is that she actually smiles back. I was never shown such warmth from a mortal as a Reaper, and I suppose it will just take time to adjust to people who don't flinch in my presence.

Once inside, I tear myself away from the wandering crowd and start my search. Surely, there is a clue somewhere as to the whereabouts of the king. I suppose I really could have just followed the lords and ladies, as the guard *did* say the king would be with them shortly, however, something tells me that Acari will try to kill his father when they are alone, not in front of an audience.

As I amble through the halls, my stomach guides me toward the aroma of food. The banquet hall table is loaded with steaming plates of grilled boar, baked pears, pitted figs, different versions of mashed starches and legumes, and so much more, but my eyes narrow in on the pears. Saliva pools against my tongue at the memory of what pears taste like.

Just as I reach a hand out to snag a piece, a cluster of servants enter in with more trays.

Startled, I snap my hand back and push myself against the wall as if I can just melt away.

"Who are you?" one of them barks, the oldest of the four of them.

She sets her platter down on the table and the chalices clank into one another. "What are you doing in here?"

"I—"

"Sh-she's with me."

My gaze flits to the young woman behind her. Her eyes are puffy and red, though I see not a single tear. I search her for any signs that I should know who she is, but I find none.

The older woman scoffs, regathering her tray. "See to it that she leaves. We cannot afford to let anything go awry tonight."

When she and the others leave, the young woman approaches me. Up so close, I realize her facial runes match the fabric of her garb. It reminds me of how I used to do the same, although I rarely had the right items of clothing to choose from. But every so often, I would get a new lavender ribbon for my hair, or the matron would purchase new chemises or—on rare occasions still—new dresses, and I would always try to select one that matched my runes, as did the other girls.

"What are *you* doing here?"

I blink at her in surprise. Though disdain is not unknown to me, I'm not used to it being so personal.

"Do I know you?" I ask.

She lowers her head, glowering at me from under her brow. "You're the Reaper. The one sent to kill Gem." She restores some of her gumption then, and I start to remember her a little more clearly, the other girl who was with Acari when I chased him out of the palace. "Well, I hate to inform you, but you won't find her here."

"I-I'm not a Reaper anymore—" seeing the look of mockery and disbelief arch her brow, I add hastily before she can argue—"And I'm not here for her. I'm here for the prince."

A cry breaks from her lips, despite her hands trying to conceal it. When they fall though, revealing her quavering lip, she speaks. "I guess he's really done it then. He actually killed his own father. Are you here to take him away?"

The same time the question leaves her lips, I see her eyes flit to the runes on my forehead. Her confusion is as plain as day.

"What? No! I told you, I'm not a Reaper. I have come to stop him."
I point to the runes that mark me as mortal once more. "I did what
needed to be done to end my service to the underrealm and save his
sister. But he does not yet know. I have to find him before...before he
does something terrible. Do you know where he is?"

Her head jerks in quick, small motions, but when the servants
return with new platters of figs and pistachios and wine to set the
tables with, she addresses them. "Do any of you know what the king
does before the banquet?"

The oldest woman frowns. "I suppose before he dresses, he's
likely to soak in a bath. Why?"

Neither of us answer her. The pressure of time weighs in on us,
and it's like no one else is in the room.

"Do you know where I can find the baths?" I ask.

The young woman nods. "Follow me."

"Hayliel!" the old woman yells as the presumed Hayliel takes me
by the hand and tears out of the room with me in tow.

The pristine, golden details of the inside of the palace blur past
me as I race to keep up with Hayliel. She twists and turns down each
corridor, none of them seeming familiar to me, even though I was
just here a few days ago.

When I am hit in the face with a few wet droplets of water, I
realize she is crying again. It dawns on me that she knew the king was
in trouble before I even said anything. She even recognized me, even
though I barely remember seeing her the day I came here for Gem.

"We're almost there," she calls over her shoulder, breathless. "It's
just up ahead."

I peer past her and find a single door at the end of this hallway.
Before she can barrel inside, I scramble my feet to a stop, tugging her
back with me.

"What? Why did you stop? It's just there—"

"I see it. Thank you. But you can't come with."

"I must! You don't understand," she says, lip quivering again.

"No," I say softly, sensing the desperation inside her. I suppose if I
were better at expressing myself, I might look a lot like her right now,

trembling and frantic. I feel it inside me, even if on the outside I am poised. I guess years as a Reaper will do that to a person. "*You* are the one who does not know what lies beyond that door. If Acari has already done what he intended to do... You don't want to be there when the Wraiths come. You don't want to see the damage a person can cause another when they have no other choice but to kill."

Hayliel breaks into a sob, but she nods before managing a request. "Call for me as soon as it is safe for me to enter. Please?"

"Of course," I say, before barreling through the door and into the steam of the bathing room.

The force sends the door into the wall before it swings back and crashes shut, plunging me into darkness. But my eyes know the dark. They know how to find movement and light, and they know how to make sense of obscurity and blackness.

I recognize Acari's figure at the far end of the bathhouse, and his name bursts from me like it has a life of its own.

"Acari!"

The king jerks, and for a moment, I feel relief surge through me when I realize I have just thwarted whatever attempts on the king's life that Acari was about to take. I have alerted the king, and now he and Acari both shall live.

My running feet slow to a stop though once I'm close enough to see how very wrong I am. In Acari's hands is an empty glass box. The king's thrashing continues, not the startled jerking of someone who has just been surprised, but the frantic and desperate flapping of limbs of someone fighting for their life.

"No," I whimper. "You didn't. Please tell me, you did not just kill him..."

The king convulses once more, twice. As his body floats in the water near stillness, I see the mollusk-like creature attached to his neck, and I recognize the aacsi, the same creature that has now taken all but one of Acari's family members from him.

The king blinks up at the ceiling, before his final breath wheezes from his lungs.

My tear-filled eyes find Acari's. His gaze lingers on my forehead, then shifts to my hands.

"You—your hands are... What did you—How did you—"

If he has no words, then neither do I. Maybe if we had more time, but I already know we do not. The king's dying breath is like a beacon. It won't be long now before—

The shadows in the room waver, inky blackness creeping along the walls and ceiling. They reach across the floor, clawing for Acari. He scrambles backward, trying to get away, only to stumble into a waiting claw. Another emerges. Then another.

"Help!" he yells, reaching toward me.

If I was anyone else, I would likely charge toward him. I would grab his hands, and I would yank and pull, I would strain my muscles to try to pry him free. But I am not someone else. I am a former Reaper. I was claimed by the Wraiths and taken to my own initiation in Veltuur, and I know that now that it has begun, there is nothing that can be done.

I shake my head, trying to convey my sorrow.

His hand drops, slowly to his side, understanding settling, though it does nothing to tamper the rampant rise and fall of his chest.

Once the Wraiths have hold of his ankles, I hear the feathers.

I duck as birds soar through the room, diving at me and diving for him. They circle him, closing in tighter and tighter until I can barely see him.

As I watch Acari disappear behind smoke and feathers, I yell the only thing I can think might bring him comfort. "I will protect her! I will protect Gem!"

But he does not respond. Instead, the shadows blink, and the room goes back to normal, and I am left entirely alone, with nothing but a corpse and a satiated aacsi for company.

27

A REAPER BORN

ACARI

Stagnant air fills my lungs and fogs my mind. I blink rapidly, eagerly, trying to remember...something. I rub my hands together to help me focus and notice they're clammy to the touch, but I can't remember why.

"Acari."

The name is familiar and sweet, and I long to respond to it, like it is a summons that I can't deny.

I turn to face the person using it and find a gaunt man in red robes. I—I should feel something, but I don't. I am just simply *here*.

"Welcome," the gaunt man says, his smile thin and taut. "You know what is to come?"

I think for a second, considering the question. When an answer comes to mind, I wonder if maybe that's what I was trying to remember earlier. "Yes, Councilspirit."

The other Councilspirits emerge around him, and I nod at each of them with respect. I don't know why, but it feels like the right thing to do.

"Then go, walk among the trees and select your crow."

To be continued in...
Heart of the Sungem
Read now!

Thank you for reading *Soul of the Crow*!

Leave a Review
Help other readers find this epic, dark fantasy saga by leaving a review on Amazon, Goodreads, Bookbub, or any other reading website. Even simple ones like "I loved it" really help with a book's success!

Free eBook
Obsessed with this world of Reapers & Guardians? Check out the short story prequel, Assassin Reaper for FREE by signing up for my newsletter!

Social Media
And last but not least, if you'd like to stay connected, you can find my social media links here: https://linktr.ee/jessaca_with_an_a

PRIMORDIALS OF SHADOWTHORN
Epic Dark Fantasy Romance

Ruled by tyrants. Hunted by demons.
This vengeful huntress is ready to fight back.

When Halira's parents are slaughtered by the horrifying demons that plague her lands, she joins the Shadow Crusade, a legion of warriors determined to slay the last living Primordial, end its reign of darkness, and destroy demon-kind once and for all.

But as her training begins, Halira soon discovers a secret about the forgotten magic that once thrived throughout the lands, one that could threaten her very survival.

Will Halira be the savior her country needs, or will her own dark secret force her to hide in the shadows?

~Check out the Primordials of Shadowthorn series on Amazon~

A DELICATE BETRAYAL
Epic Fantasy Romance

A marriage to save the kingdom. A knight to steal her heart. A dragon to be slain.

When Aenwyn's magic unleashes a reign of dragons upon the land, she agrees to marry King Everard to atone for the devastation she's caused.

Queendom proves to be almost as dissatisfying as their loveless marriage. But soon fate answers her pleas for adventure with a vision of dragon's fire and an aggravatingly handsome knight intent on blocking her path.

Sir Dedric Graeme can't let her flee the castle. But nothing will stop Aenwyn from claiming the dragon's heart—and maybe even the knight's as well.

~Check out A Delicate Betrayal on Amazon~

Can Sean and three strangers unite the remnants of mankind when everything else has fallen apart? Can they face the darkest horror this new world has yet to offer?

~Check out The Awakened Quadrilogy on Amazon~

ACKNOWLEDGMENTS

Special thanks to my brother Michael and my mom Julie for letting me brainstorm this series extensively with them.

As always, I also have to thank my editor, Sandra Ogle, who continues to amaze me with her fine attention to detail. Any typos still existing in this text are most certainly my fault for making last-minute tweaks.

My cover designer, Clair Holt of Luminescence Covers deserves a *tremendous* round of applause as well. Not only did she rally behind me when I told her I wanted to get this book on a bestselling list, but she went above and beyond to do everything she could to help me do so. At the time of writing this, the book was still on pre-order, so I'm not sure if it made it, but regardless, I will always be grateful to her for sprucing up the original premade cover I had purchased from her a year prior.

And last, but certainly not least, a HUGE shout-out has to go to the alpha readers for this one: Elina V., Geetha K., Tony D., Eryn R., and of course my Ink & Insights judges: Amy, Brittany, Esther, and Jennifer. Your feedback *changed* this story, and for the better! It helped me get a better understanding of my characters and the world I created and thought I knew. Thank you so much for taking the time to read the first draft and write-up your feedback.

ABOUT THE AUTHOR

Jessaca is a fantasy writer with an inclination toward the dark, epic, and adventure sub-genres. She draws inspiration from books like Nevernight & ACOTAR, videogames like Dark Souls, and television shows like Game of Thrones and The Chilling Adventures of Sabrina. She is a self-proclaimed nerd who loves video games & comics, and if you live in the PNW, you might see her at some of the local comic conventions in cosplay!

Made in the USA
Monee, IL
01 January 2023

24216037R00129